DON'T
TURN
BACK

ALSO BY
D. S. BUTLER

Lost Child
Her Missing Daughter

DS Karen Hart Series:

Bring Them Home
Where Secrets Lie

DS Jack Mackinnon Crime Series:

Deadly Obsession
Deadly Motive
Deadly Revenge
Deadly Justice
Deadly Ritual
Deadly Payback
Deadly Game
Deadly Intent

East End Series:

East End Trouble
East End Diamond
East End Retribution

Harper Grant Mystery Series:

DON'T TURN BACK

DETECTIVE KAREN HART SERIES

D.S. BUTLER

THOMAS & MERCER

Text copyright © 2020 by D. S. Butler
All rights reserved.

Published by Thomas & Mercer, Seattle

www.apub.com

Amazon, the Amazon logo, and Thomas & Mercer are trademarks of Amazon.com, Inc., or its affiliates.

ISBN-13: 9781542017565
ISBN-10: 1542017564

Cover design by @blacksheep-uk.com

Printed in the United States of America

DON'T TURN BACK

PROLOGUE

He was going to die tonight.

But that didn't slow him down. His death might have been inevitable, but a primitive urge to flee kept his legs moving as he stumbled up the mist-cloaked escarpment.

Adrenaline flooded his system. Fight or flight. And there was no way he could fight, not against them, not now they'd realised what he had done. What he had taken from them. What a fool he'd been to think he could bring them down.

He clutched the blue leather notebook to his sweaty chest. Where could he hide it? He couldn't keep running forever. His legs were tiring, and the ache in his chest was getting worse.

They would catch up with him eventually anyway, and it would all be for nothing if they found the book.

He slipped and skidded as he desperately tried to climb the dew-soaked grass slope. Though lactic acid made his legs burn and a demand for oxygen made his chest tight, his muscles continued contracting and pushing forward as he climbed the hill.

He'd been running along the road first, his dirty trainers hitting the tarmac hard as he tried to escape the inevitable. Though his brain was a mass of jumbled panicked thoughts, his instincts had taken over. On the road, he was easy to spot, easy to catch. Before he reached the petrol station, closed and dark at this hour, he had turned and run into the open field.

A faint glow on the grey horizon told him dawn was approaching. It was still dark, but as the light improved, his chances of evading his pursuers fell even further. A sound made him pause.

He stiffened, his harsh breath sounding ridiculously loud in the early-morning silence. Then he heard it again – a dog barking. One of theirs, probably. Was it following his scent?

He was halfway up the hill when he realised another mistake: he was exposed in the middle of misty grassland. He needed cover of some sort. Camouflage.

There were plenty of trees and shrubs in the vicinity, but panic had made him stupid. He pivoted quickly. Too quickly. His knee gave out from under him and he crashed to the ground, dropping the book.

With a groan of pain, he snatched it back up and, muddied and bruised, headed for a copse of trees.

He hadn't had time to formulate a plan. Instinctively he'd been heading for the towering spire on top of Canwick Hill. A landmark that could be seen from all around. A monument to the lives and deaths of those who had served their country. But no one would mourn his passing.

He thought of his daughter then, regret hitting him even harder than his fear. A rasping sob tore from his throat. But still he pushed on, until beneath the trees, he paused. The dawn light gave the copse an unworldly, fairy-tale appearance. He could almost believe he'd be safe under the protection of the boughs of the old oak that towered above him. Almost.

But the sharp, eager bark of a dog, closer now, made him catch his breath. Dropping to his knees, he set the book down on a tuft of grass and began to scrape away at the earth with his hands. The smell of musty, damp, decaying plant matter reminded him of what was to come. What we all become in the end.

His fingernails broke as they scratched the ground, and the raw skin beneath began to bleed, but he didn't stop, clawing at the dirt over and over until the hole was large enough to hide the book in.

The next bark made him whimper. They were closing in. Almost there. He had only minutes left. Maybe only seconds. He shoved the notebook in the hole, bending the cover, not caring that dirt wedged itself between the pages. Then, hastily, he replaced the dark soil, frantically patting it down before covering it with bracken.

Pushing up, he staggered away. They couldn't discover him here, near the book. He couldn't let them find it.

Leaning against the rough bark of a beech tree, he panted as he tried to sort through his options. Fear had turned his brain to mush. But if he could just lure them far enough away from the buried notebook . . .

He moved, forcing his tired limbs to work as he darted out into the open again, crossing the grass and heading for the next group of trees, which were further down the hill. If he could get past them . . . then the road would be in view again . . . the B1188 out of Lincoln. If he was lucky, someone would be driving along, even at this time of the morning.

He might get away after all. He could flag down a car, ask the driver to call the police . . . Or he might even get as far as Canwick village and rouse some sleeping resident.

Hope gave him another burst of speed.

He ran at full pelt into the next cluster of trees, as young branches whipped and scratched at his face and chest. He stumbled over dips and roots, but still kept moving. The road was almost in view – safety was so close.

A larger branch slammed against his temple, making him cry out and stagger. Then the barking was right behind him. Snarling. A man's voice. The bouncing beams from a torch hit the trunk on a tree directly in front of him.

Terrified, he turned to face the snapping jaws and heard the cold laugh of victory – the sound of a man who'd caught his prey.

CHAPTER ONE

Marissa Clerkwell shaded her eyes against the bright sunlight of the May afternoon. She'd headed out for her regular walk along the South Common later than usual, after waking up with a terrible hangover. She'd consumed half her body weight in coffee but still the nagging headache remained. All self-inflicted, she thought glumly as she trudged up the hill, watching her black dog, Toots, frolic happily, chasing a butterfly. If only she had the dog's energy, Marissa thought with a sigh.

Marissa had adopted Toots from a rescue centre three years ago. Her pedigree was uncertain, but Marissa suspected she was a German Shepherd and black Lab mix. Thanks to a deformed front paw, she'd been in the centre for months and had been overlooked by most people wanting to adopt a dog, but Marissa had fallen in love the moment she'd walked into the kennels. Toots's paw still caused issues from time to time. But today she was content racing up the hill. Marissa smiled. It certainly didn't hold her back.

Marissa managed to raise a polite smile for the couple walking down the hill towards her. They had a gorgeous grey Weimaraner on a leash. The alert dog strained and jumped enthusiastically as they approached.

'What a beautiful dog!' Marissa said as they passed.

'She is. Still a puppy at heart, though. If she decides to chase a rabbit, she'll be halfway across Lincoln before we catch up with her. That's why she's on the lead.' The man chuckled and leaned down to scratch the dog behind the ears.

Marissa paused and watched as the couple walked down the hill arm in arm, then turned her attention back to her own dog.

'Toots!'

The black dog halted immediately and turned in a tight circle before running back to Marissa's side.

'Good girl!'

Marissa leaned down to stroke Toots's black fur and looked into the dog's adoring brown eyes. Toots was the most loyal, loving dog, and despite her boundless energy was usually quick to follow instructions.

She straightened and clapped her hands, signalling Toots could continue to play. The dog dashed off up the hill.

The South Common was a pleasant place for a walk. There were always people around, so Marissa felt comfortable walking Toots on her own. Today, there were even more people than usual, owing to the fine weather. The early-morning mist had given way to a sunny afternoon, though the breeze was bracing. The fresh air was slowly helping Marissa feel more human again.

She probably shouldn't have anything to drink today, not after last night, but a Sunday roast really wasn't complete without a glass of red wine, in her opinion. Toots was still running ahead so she quickened her pace. Already breathless from walking up the hill on slightly uneven ground, she called out, 'Toots! Here, girl!'

Obediently, Toots returned to Marissa's side and was rewarded with pats and whispered endearments. But Toots's body was tense, her muscles longing to run and expend some of that seemingly inexhaustible energy. After Marissa's clap, Toots took off again, bounding up the grassy slope.

There was a man off to their right walking a Jack Russell, but apart from them, it was just her and Toots on the hill now, surrounded by grass, trees and a big, open blue sky.

Partway up the hill, Marissa paused and turned to look down at the city of Lincoln. The cathedral dominated the landscape, and the sun's rays caught it in a way that made the stonework appear to glow.

She took a deep breath and then turned back, continuing her walk up the hill towards the memorial spire and the International Bomber Command Centre.

Though she walked Toots on the common every weekend, she hadn't yet visited the centre. She kept meaning to go – it was one of those things on her to-do list that she never seemed to get around to. It must have been open for nearly a year now. She decided to take a look next weekend, when hopefully she wouldn't feel quite so queasy.

A sharp wind blew from the east, and she shivered.

Tugging her lightweight jacket tighter around her body, she quickened her pace after Toots. Telling herself she didn't really need to get right to the top of the hill today, she picked a spot near a cluster of trees where she'd turn around and make her way back down. That would be quite enough exercise for a Sunday. She was looking forward to relaxing with a glass of wine and her oven-ready roast.

'Toots!' she called out, noticing the dog was roaming a little too far, but the wind whipped away her words and Toots kept galloping determinedly towards a group of trees.

Marissa sighed. Had Toots heard and purposely ignored her? Usually well-behaved, the dog had a stubborn streak at times, and perhaps having sensed Marissa was planning a shorter version of their usual walk, was determined that wasn't going to happen. Sometimes she was convinced Toots thought she was the boss in their relationship.

Muttering under her breath, Marissa followed the dog and looked up just in time to see her black tail disappear into the trees.

She frowned. That certainly wasn't on their usual route. They didn't go into the woods. Well, they weren't woods really, just a few trees, but as a woman walking a dog on her own, Marissa tended to keep to open areas, those popular with other dog walkers. It was a sad state of affairs that she had to worry about such things, but in this day and age it paid to be careful.

Feeling slightly irritated with Toots, she entered the copse. Now that she was out of the sunshine, the chill of the afternoon crept over her. A shiver ran down her spine.

'Toots!' she shouted in a tone that meant she was not messing about.

Despite having a mischievous side, Toots was on the whole obedient and usually returned when Marissa called her, but this time there was no sign of the dog happily trotting towards her.

She turned, nervously scanning the trees. She was alone. There was no sign of Toots.

Tentatively, she took a few more steps into the woods. 'Toots! If you don't come here, there will be no doggy treats for you this afternoon,' she grumbled, as she walked into the dappled sunlight shining between the leaves of a huge beech tree.

She called for the dog again, and this time heard a bark in response. She turned to face the direction of the bark, and in the dim woodland light, among a cluster of fading bluebells, she could just about make out the familiar sight of Toots wagging her tail.

'There you are!' Marissa said with exasperation. 'Come here now, otherwise I'll put you back on the lead.' She waggled it in warning, but Toots ignored her, focusing on a spot of ground, scratching it with her front paws.

Melissa felt her stomach drop. Oh no. Not again. Toots had probably discovered some poor dead or injured animal. Last time it had been a dead baby squirrel, and the time before that, an injured crow.

She stomped through the wooded area, ordering Toots to leave whatever it was alone. She stopped abruptly when she got a better look at what was lying on the ground in front of the dog.

It wasn't an animal.

Melissa clamped a hand to her mouth and used her other hand to pat down her jacket, trying to locate her mobile phone.

There was a man lying on the ground in front of Toots. He must have collapsed here, maybe he'd had a heart attack . . . She'd taken a first-aid course, years ago, but her knowledge was hazy now. Was she supposed to put him in the recovery position? No, she had to check his airway was clear first . . .

Marissa had pulled out her phone and pressed 999 on the touchscreen before she realised that the man was beyond help. She stopped a couple of feet away from Toots, looking down in horror at the man's twisted body. Blood, cracked and dried now, coated his forehead and had soaked into the earth, making it look black. His skin had a deathly grey tinge.

She didn't need a medical degree to know he most certainly hadn't died of a heart attack.

She grabbed Toots by her collar, dragging the dog away. Whoever this poor man was, he'd been viciously killed. With a shaking hand, she lifted the mobile to her ear and waited for the call to connect, unable to tear her eyes away from the terrible sight. When a female voice answered, Marissa calmly reported what she'd found.

Only when she'd finished talking did she feel the weight of vomit in her throat. Dropping her phone, she fell to her knees and retched.

CHAPTER TWO

Karen Hart wafted away an annoying fly as she stepped out of the conservatory into her garden. Today was going well. It was the first time since her husband and daughter had died that she'd hosted a barbecue. In the past she'd found it too hard, a harsh reminder of the two people who were missing from her life. But this afternoon had been a happy occasion, and she was pleased with how she'd coped. Not that they were banished from her mind. No, she could picture them clearly. Josh wearing his ridiculous chef's apron, insisting on making a special spice blend for his homemade burgers. Tilly eating a sausage in a bun, up and down like a yo-yo, unable to sit still for a second. Memories were everywhere.

Her brother-in-law, Mike, had offered to grill the meat, and Karen had gratefully accepted. She'd made a couple of salads, some spicy rice and garlic bread, and they'd all eaten until they were fit to burst.

Everyone was trying to make the afternoon as easy as possible for her.

Her niece, Mallory, shrieked with pleasure as she chased her grandad down the garden, squirting him with a water pistol. It was impossible not to notice the similarities between Tilly and Mallory. The curve of Mallory's cheek, the stubborn way she set her jaw when she didn't get her own way, the sun-kissed hair. She was so like Tilly that in unguarded moments it stole Karen's breath away.

She blamed the bright sunlight for the tears that threatened to spill.

'Silly old fool,' Karen's mother muttered, leaning back in the garden chair and loosening her floral chiffon scarf. 'He'll do himself an injury running around like that.' But she smiled fondly as she spoke.

'I don't know,' Karen said. 'It looks to me like he's having just as much fun as Mallory.'

She handed her mother a gin and tonic and then sat down beside her old boss, ex-DCI Anthony Shaw. His legs were stretched out in front of him and his head dropped forward as he dozed in the sun.

'I suppose we should consider ourselves lucky it's just the water pistol today,' her mother continued. 'It won't be long before Mallory is asking for the paddling pool again.'

Mallory loved the water. It didn't matter what time of year it was, she always wanted to go swimming, and absolutely adored splashing around in the water. Another thing she had in common with Tilly.

'I'm just thankful she's forgotten about the camera.' The motion-sensing security camera beside the front door had been installed a few months ago, and Mallory thought it was great fun to set it off and pull faces at the camera and watch them appear on the app on Karen's phone.

Karen had found it funny the first few times. The tenth time hadn't been quite so amusing.

The camera had been recommended by Anthony. He'd installed it and got it up and running for her, telling her it was a wonderful gadget and regaling her with a recent incident where he'd spoken to a delivery man using the security camera at his front door while he was in the supermarket. She suspected the real reason for the recommendation was because he worried about her living alone. Karen usually slept through the alerts at night. Not that that was a bad thing. It was sensitive, and typically the alerts were down to the neighbour's cat, and when it went off during the day, it was usually triggered by the postman or someone delivering leaflets.

There were raised voices from the other side of the garden. Karen's sister, Emma, was hovering beside her husband, issuing instructions as he finished grilling the remaining sausages and burgers.

'That one's burning. You need to flip it over.'

'If you think you can do a better job, you're welcome to take over, Emma,' he snapped.

Emma put her hands on her hips. 'Don't say I didn't warn you. Look! It's turning black!'

Karen caught her mother's eye and grinned. Karen had given Emma the nickname 'Little Miss Bossy Pants' when they were children, something her sister had never quite forgiven, but the name still suited her.

Emma was goodhearted and kind, but she had her faults. Namely, she thought she knew best about everyone and everything, and that could get a little annoying at times.

Karen said, 'I think I'll go and get Mike another beer. He probably needs it.'

Her mother chuckled. 'That's a good idea.'

She went into the kitchen and opened the fridge. She'd bought far too much food and drink for the barbecue. A large fruit-covered meringue took up a whole shelf. She'd give it another ten minutes before offering everyone dessert. She was stuffed, and Mike was still cooking even though no one could eat another bite at the moment.

They'd all have to take home some of the food to snack on later. There was no way she'd get through it all on her own.

She looked up as her sister walked into the kitchen. 'Another drink, Em?'

Emma nodded. 'Yes, I'll have another fizzy water. Thanks. I don't know what's wrong with Mike today. He's ever so touchy.'

Karen tried to hide her smile and pointed at the window, where they could see Mallory shrieking and laughing as she ran towards the house. It seemed Grandad had grown tired of being the victim and decided it was his turn to use the water pistol.

'She's certainly enjoying herself. But I hope she realises she can't use the water pistol in the car on the way home.'

Karen handed her sister a bottle of fizzy water from the fridge. 'I'm sure she does. Besides, at this rate she'll be too tired to put up any arguments. I bet she falls asleep in the car.'

Emma smiled as Karen rummaged through a drawer, searching for the bottle opener. 'I expect you're right.'

'I'll just give this to Mike. He did a great job on the barbecue today.' Karen prised the lid from a bottle of beer.

'Wait,' Emma said, reaching out and putting a hand on Karen's forearm as she moved past. 'You know Mum is worried about you, don't you?'

Karen felt her good mood begin to evaporate. She bristled. 'Why? I'm fine.'

Emma rolled her eyes. 'You know why.'

'Emma, don't ruin today. It's been really nice.'

'I don't want to ruin anything. I just thought you should know Mum and Dad are worried.'

'There's no need. I'm fine, Em.'

'Are you, though? All you do is work, sleep, work, sleep.'

'There's nothing wrong with that.'

'Do you even have any friends outside work these days?'

'Yes, Christine. We go to the pub quiz every single week.'

Emma gave an exasperated sigh. 'Christine is in her sixties.'

'So?'

'Is there anyone on your pub quiz team under the age of sixty?'

'Scott goes sometimes.'

'Scott? Your boss?'

'Yes. What's wrong with that? Christine adores him. Apparently, his knowledge of British rivers is unparalleled.'

Emma gave a derisive snort.

'It's fun,' Karen insisted. 'I find it relaxing and they're a nice crowd. Who cares about their ages?'

'I'm just saying you need to enjoy life more. Get out and about.'

Karen tightened her grip on the neck of the beer bottle. 'I do.'

Emma raised an eyebrow. 'Visiting crime scenes doesn't count as getting out and about.'

'Look, I'd be perfectly happy if you stopped trying to shape my life into something I don't want. You know, maybe if you didn't nag as much, things would be better between you and Mike,' Karen snapped.

She regretted the words as soon as she'd spoken them.

Her sister paled, blinked rapidly and folded her arms over her chest.

'I'm sorry. I shouldn't have said that. It was a horrible thing to say.'

'I was just trying to help,' Emma said with a sniff.

Karen sighed and put the beer bottle down on the kitchen counter. 'I know. But you can't live my life for me, and I can't live yours for you. If I need your help, I'll ask.'

'That's just it. I can see you need help, but you never ask.'

Karen shook her head. There was no getting through to Emma sometimes. Karen was happy with her life the way it was. Yes, she worked long hours, but her job was rewarding and gave her little time alone to mope and think about the past. Everyone, including

Emma, thought a new relationship would be just the ticket to fix her problems. But that was the last thing Karen wanted.

Surely she knew what was best for herself? She didn't want to be patched up and shoved back on the dating conveyor belt. The very thought made her skin crawl. Taking each day as it came, plodding onwards, one foot in front of the other, suited her just fine.

Emma's eyes filled with tears. Karen sighed again. No one could hold a grudge like her sister. She'd be upset and hurt for weeks.

Karen felt like the meanest person in the world. Snapping at Emma was like telling off a puppy. Emma didn't understand why her behaviour grated, and really was only saying these things because she cared. Karen was lucky to have her sister rooting for her, and her mum and dad in her corner. They were all concerned because they loved her, though at times they watched her so closely she felt like she was suffocating.

She picked up the beer again and held it out to her sister. 'Why don't you go and give this to Mike and tell him what a fab job he's done with the sausages?' Karen suggested with a wink.

Emma tried not to grin, but the edges of her mouth quirked upwards. 'I'll give him the beer, but I'm not giving him any compliments!'

'I think I'd better head home,' Anthony said, stifling a yawn as he entered the kitchen. 'I've eaten myself into a stupor. Fell asleep out there. Next thing you know, I'll be snoring. Oh . . .' He broke off and lifted his bushy eyebrows. 'Sorry, I'm not interrupting, am I?'

'Not at all,' Emma said briskly, sweeping past him and heading back to the garden.

'My timing is impeccable, as usual.' Anthony put his glass on the counter.

'It's not you. Emma would just prefer me to live my life differently.'

'Ah, I see. I'm sure that's just because she cares.'

'I'm sure it is too, but sometimes I wish she wouldn't care quite so much.'

'It's hard for normal folk to understand the job, Karen.'

She started to load glasses into the top rack of the dishwasher, and looked over her shoulder at Anthony. 'Is it bad that I'm hoping for a work call to get me away from Emma and her plans for my perfect life?'

He laughed. 'Yes, Karen, it is. Very bad. Now enjoy the rest of the day with your family.' He wagged a finger. 'That's an order.'

After Anthony had gone, Karen poured herself a glass of orange juice and carried it out to the garden. She was about to sit beside her mum when her mobile rang. She fished the phone out of the back pocket of her jeans and glanced at the display. It was DI Scott Morgan.

'DS Hart,' she answered as her mother shot her a sympathetic glance.

'Karen, it's Scott. A dead IC1 male has been found in woodland in Canwick, at the top of the South Common. He's been bludgeoned to death. I don't have any more information at this stage, but can you meet me at the scene?'

That was typical of DI Morgan. He wasn't one for small talk.

'Absolutely. I can be there in fifteen minutes.'

After she hung up, she saw the disappointed look on her mother's face and tried to match it.

'I'm sorry, Mum. It's work. You've got the spare key with you, haven't you? You can lock up?'

Her mother stood and gave Karen a peck on the cheek. 'Of course, darling. Just take care of yourself.'

'I will. Tell everyone I'm sorry I had to dash off. Enjoy the rest of the barbecue. Don't forget the meringue in the fridge!' Karen called over her shoulder as she headed inside to grab her car keys.

CHAPTER THREE

When Karen arrived at the scene, DI Morgan was already present – along with Raj, the pathologist, and the crime scene crew. Karen donned a white protective bodysuit and blue overshoes before following the carefully marked path under the trees.

She tried to force herself to relax and make her muscles unknot, but her stomach continued to churn violently and her body felt rigid and awkward as she walked to the scene. She always had the same reaction when attending the aftermath of a violent crime. As a rookie PC on the beat seeing her first dead body, she'd assumed her strong physical reaction to such sights would fade eventually. But it hadn't. The tension, the dread, it was there every time she visited a scene like this one. Maybe it was even worse now that her head was filled with images of previous victims.

She muttered a hello as she passed two crime scene officers who were taking photographs of what looked like a fresh shoe print in the dark soil. Under the trees, the limited light meant bare patches of earth existed between clumps of long, tough grass and bluebells gone to seed. That could help them when it came to footprints, though this area was popular with dog walkers and eliminating prints from innocent walkers wouldn't be easy.

DI Morgan was standing back some distance from the body, talking to the pathologist. He nodded when he saw Karen. Rather than head over to her boss straightaway, Karen felt her eyes drawn to the body at the foot of a tall beech tree. He was white, medium height and build, shabbily dressed in dirty jeans and an old, frayed, checked shirt and scuffed trainers. The arms of the shirt had been rolled up to reveal tanned forearms. On his left arm, he had a small infinity tattoo midway between his wrist and elbow. Karen stared at the mark, then the rest of his body, taking her time, noticing the details and filing them away. She had a strange urge to pull him away from the tree roots that looked like they were digging into his hips and ribs, so he'd be more comfortable, but of course, that was stupid. He was beyond pain. He couldn't feel anything now. Someone had made certain of that.

She took a step to her right and crouched down, not getting too close but near enough to see the tiny blond hairs covering his tanned arms. His hands were dirty – filthy, really. Were those bite marks? Had they occurred before he'd died or after? From a scavenging fox perhaps?

She wondered how long he'd been outdoors. Was he homeless? An addict? Was this violent crime some kind of retribution from an angry dealer? Or perhaps he was a small-time dealer himself.

They couldn't jump to conclusions at this stage. She allowed her gaze to slowly travel up the body towards the head, preparing herself for a grisly sight. Her stomach protested, still full from the barbecued food she'd eaten earlier, but she kept her gaze steady, assessing his injuries, processing them, making a mental list of the details that could be pertinent later. His face had been destroyed. The delicate bones near his eyes were smashed, and the nasal cartilage was dislodged so his nose was squashed into his face. Even the stronger bones protecting his brain hadn't stood up to the assault. An area just above his ear was caved inward.

Thick, dark blood coated most of his scalp and face, obscuring any identifying features. He'd worn his hair in a buzz cut.

Bristle-like fuzz protruded from his scalp. Most of his hair was tinged dark red from his head wounds, but the few remaining areas not coated with blood revealed the colour to be a mix of light blond and grey. His face was so badly damaged it was hard to judge his age. Perhaps early to late forties?

'Karen?'

Karen turned to see DI Morgan and Raj behind her. She straightened. 'It's a nasty one.'

Morgan nodded, his mouth set in a grim line. 'Whoever did this was very angry. It looks personal to me. They've completely obliterated his face.'

'It certainly makes him harder to identify,' Raj said.

'Did you find any ID?' Karen asked, turning to Raj.

The pathologist shook his head. 'We haven't found his wallet and there was nothing on him to give us a clue to who this poor bloke was. No house or car keys, and no mobile. We'll check DNA and see if he's in our database, otherwise we'll have to look at other ways to identify him – dental records and so on.'

'Any idea on the weapon used yet?' Karen asked. It must have been something heavy to inflict that much damage to his face. The extensive injuries couldn't have been caused by a fist fight, so the person who attacked him must have used something. Maybe they'd get lucky and find that the killer panicked, dumping a weapon loaded with fingerprints nearby.

'We've found nothing so far,' Morgan said. 'But we'll be expanding the search perimeter soon.'

'It was some kind of blunt instrument, something heavy,' Raj said.

'A branch?' Karen suggested, looking around at some fallen branches and twigs scattered on the floor around them. 'I suppose it would have to be a large one.'

'Unlikely. A big branch could have been heavy enough, but I would have expected to see fragments of bark or wood embedded in the head wounds when I examined him if that was the case, and I didn't.'

'So you don't think the weapon was made of wood?' Morgan asked.

'I'm not saying that,' Raj clarified. His eyes twinkled and he tottered around in a circle, reminding Karen more than ever of Hercule Poirot. 'It could have been some kind of processed wood, a cricket bat or something similar in weight, or the murder weapon could be made of metal or coated with plastic. I'll know more after the swabs I've taken are analysed at the lab.'

'I noticed the bite marks on his arms,' Karen said. 'What do you think? A scavenger?'

'No, he was bitten multiple times, likely by a dog. A large one. Either before or immediately after death. There was bleeding from the wounds.'

'Just the one dog?' Morgan asked.

'Hard to say at this stage.'

'How long has he been here?' Karen glanced back at the body.

'A good few hours. At least ten, I'd say.'

'And was he killed in situ?'

'In my opinion, yes.' Raj pursed his lips, causing his black moustache to twitch. 'There was one thing I noticed that may or may not be relevant – he's not very clean.'

'I noticed the dirt on his hands and under his nails,' Karen said.

'Well, yes,' Raj said. 'But I was actually referring to other areas. He has grime behind his ears and there's a boil on the back of his neck. Not that boils can't affect people who keep themselves clean, but his skin is coated with grease and embedded with dirt. He's probably been neglecting personal hygiene for some time.'

'So he hasn't had access to washing facilities,' Morgan mused. 'Perhaps he was homeless.'

'Perhaps.' Raj glanced down at the body.

A memory of Josh hit Karen out of the blue. He'd been working in the garden, digging holes for a rose bush they'd bought, and had discarded his gloves after he'd ripped one of them. He'd used his bare hands to finish scraping out the hole, creating enough space to plant the rose. Tilly had loved it, joining in by using the hose pipe and making mud pies. The pair of them had come back inside the house, and Tilly had been caked with mud. Karen had argued with Josh. A stupid thing to row about now she looked back on it, but she'd been paranoid Tilly was going to catch an infection from the soil bacteria . . . Tetanus – or something equally nasty. Josh had just laughed it off, saying kids needed to be kids. She'd snapped back, asking him what was his excuse?

Karen shook her head. It wasn't time to indulge in her past. But the murder victim's hands reminded her of Josh's hands coated with dirt after he'd been digging the hole for the rose.

'Even without washing facilities, I wouldn't expect fresh earth to be coating his fingernails like that,' Karen said. 'Would you? I think he's been digging for something.'

DI Morgan frowned and then looked at the victim's hands again. 'You could be right. I'll check with the crime scene manager and the officer in charge of the search to see if they've spotted anything.'

Karen turned away from the victim. 'It's going to be a struggle to ID this chap if we don't get a hit on the database. Did he have nothing on him at all, Raj?'

'Actually, he did have *something*,' Raj said with a shrug. 'Though I'm not sure how helpful it will be. We found a beer mat in the back pocket of his jeans.'

'Can we see it?' Morgan asked.

Raj led them over to the crime scene manager, who was in charge of filing the evidence collected from the scene. He exchanged a few words with Raj and then held out a clear plastic bag containing the beer mat.

DI Morgan took it and thanked him, turning it over in his hands. Raj excused himself to go and finish up.

When Karen saw the name of the pub printed on the red cardboard square, she bit down hard on the inside of her mouth.

'The Red Lion, in Canwick,' Morgan said thoughtfully. 'Do you know it?'

Karen swallowed hard. 'I do. I've had a few run-ins with the owners. There were no charges filed against them. But they're a bad lot.'

'How so?'

Karen wrapped her arms around her midsection and shivered, wishing she was out from under the trees and standing in the sunshine. 'Nothing I can prove, but I have my suspicions. I haven't spoken to the owners for over five years, though, so it's possible the pub has changed hands. At the time, I thought they were exploiting workers. We had reports they were paying less than the minimum wage, keeping things off the books and a high turnover of staff. I paid them a few visits. We got a warrant to search the premises once, but someone must've tipped them off because everyone was legal and on the books when we went to serve the warrant. Surprisingly they'd all been officially employed the previous week. Very convenient, wouldn't you say?'

Morgan frowned. 'And this was five years ago?'

'Yes.'

'And it was never followed up?'

'Not to my knowledge.'

Morgan turned his attention back to the beer mat, squinting at it. 'I think there's something written on here.'

Karen peered over his shoulder. He was right. In tiny printed lettering someone had written a date and time.

22 May, 15.00.

'What do you think that means?' Morgan asked.

Karen shook her head. 'I've absolutely no idea.'

'Maybe the owners of The Red Lion will be able to point us in the right direction. I think we should pay them a visit. Maybe he worked there, or was a regular.'

Karen suppressed another shiver. 'I suppose he had to get the beer mat from there, so a visit makes sense.'

'Perhaps he had a late-night disagreement with someone at the pub. You never know, we might have this case solved in a couple of hours.'

'Why would he come here though?' Karen looked around. The place was peaceful now, despite the bustling police officers and crime scene team still busy in the area. Birds were singing in the trees and the sun was trying to stream through gaps in the branches. At night it would be a very different story – dark, creepy. The type of place you could arrange a clandestine meet-up away from prying eyes.

As though he could read Karen's thoughts, Morgan said, 'Maybe he met someone up here. It's a good place for a meeting if you don't want to be seen.'

'He could have been selling or buying dodgy gear, or drugs.'

Morgan rubbed his chin. 'Maybe. Let's take my car and go and talk to the staff of The Red Lion.'

'Sounds like a plan,' Karen said, forcing a smile and falling into step behind her boss.

They followed the marked trail out of the trees and on to the open grassland of the common. Below them, the city of Lincoln was spread out in a sprawling circle. Karen studied the grand, gothic cathedral perched on top of the opposite hill, and morbidly wondered how many murders had occurred within sight of the spectacular building over the years.

As they made their way to Morgan's car, Karen tried to shake the sense of unease that prickled at her skin.

It wasn't like her to shy away from a case. But she couldn't ignore the fact she found the link to The Red Lion very disturbing indeed.

CHAPTER FOUR

Once they were in the car, DI Morgan said, 'Tell me about the owners of The Red Lion.'

Karen fastened her seatbelt. 'It's owned and run by Rod and Patricia Perry. The pub is freehold.'

If it had changed hands, she would have known. She was sure the couple were still there. Karen lived only a mile away, in Branston, and despite her best efforts to exist like a hermit for the past five years, her next-door neighbour, Christine, simply wouldn't allow it. A gentle, motherly woman, Christine had supported Karen through the darkest days of her life and continued to do so even now. She kept Karen up to date on all the local gossip. If The Red Lion had changed hands, Christine would know, and she would have told Karen.

'They're in their late fifties,' Karen said. 'They have a son, but I can't recall his name. He'd be in his teens now, I think. They're a bolshy pair and don't get on well with the police, as you might have guessed.'

'No convictions?'

Karen shook her head. 'Not unless they've been charged with anything new in the last few years. If you want, we could run a background check at the station before we pay them a visit.'

She saw the look of surprise on Morgan's face and looked away. Why was she trying to get out of this meeting with the Perrys? It wasn't like her to try to delay things. She was normally the one wanting to push the investigation forward, and it was DI Morgan who was the more cautious, 'let's play everything by the book' officer.

They'd been driving for less than two minutes when the large red-brick building came into view. 'The pub is just there,' Karen said.

Morgan slowed and indicated before turning into the car park. 'I think it's worth talking to them now. The first few hours after a murder are crucial. We need to speak to them before our leads grow cold.'

'Yes, of course, you're right.'

'I was wondering, don't take this the wrong way, but—'

'Whenever someone says, "Don't take this the wrong way", they're planning to say something the other person won't like,' Karen said.

Morgan smiled. 'I'm just curious. We've worked together for a while now, and you're not the type of officer to abruptly give up on a case for no reason. If you suspected the Perrys of criminal conduct, why did you drop it?'

Karen had known this was going to come up, but that didn't make answering the question any easier. She stared straight ahead, not wanting to look Morgan in the eye as she spoke. 'When we got the warrant to search the Perrys' property, it was just before Josh and Tilly died. After the accident, I wasn't at work for a while, and my cases were handed over to other officers. By the time I came back to work, the case had been closed due to lack of evidence, and my boss kept me busy with other things.'

'Sorry, I should have guessed that from the timeline.' Morgan exhaled a long breath. 'Five years.'

'Yes, five years,' she said quietly. 'I can hardly believe it's been that long.'

Karen stared at The Red Lion as Morgan pulled into a parking space. There were only two other cars parked on the cracked concrete.

Two overflowing large black bins sat next to the side entrance. The front of the pub had been coated in pebble-dash and painted terracotta. The dull paint was old and flaking away in sections. A large sign protruded from the side of the building. It displayed an image of a red lion with a curly mane on a gold background. It too had seen better days.

As they got out of the car, the wind picked up, blowing a discarded Coke can that rattled across the concrete. The sign creaked as it swung back and forth.

Karen shut the car door then paused, fighting the desire to get back in the car and drive away. Her chest tightened at the thought of going back inside that pub.

The small dark windows looked like eyes, watching her with malevolent intent.

Karen shivered.

The Red Lion. She had to swallow hard and turn away. Five years ago, when she'd last come to this pub, her life had been perfect – or as near to it as possible. She hadn't known that then. The morning they'd got the warrant, she'd snapped at Tilly for spilling her breakfast cereal and rushed off without talking to Josh. She wished—

Karen shook her head, trying to focus on the job.

Get it together.

'Are you okay?' Morgan asked, pressing the button on the key fob to lock the car. 'You seem shaken. What exactly went down between you and the Perrys?'

'We didn't really hit it off,' Karen said, reluctant to elaborate. 'You'll understand when you meet them.'

A suspicious thought wormed its way to the front of her mind before she could push it away. She'd visited the Perrys just before the accident. Had they been responsible? Involved somehow? No. That was very unlikely. Though Karen suspected something about the accident had been hushed up, the Perrys didn't have the clout or influence needed for such a cover-up.

She glanced back at the car. Would Morgan think less of her if she asked for someone else to take over her role on this case? Would he understand? She glanced at him, serious and unsmiling. An outsider might think he looked cold and uncompassionate, but Karen knew better. He'd be quick to reassure her, understanding if she explained. But she wasn't going to fall apart. She didn't need his compassion. It was just a pub, and the Perrys were just an obnoxious couple on the wrong side of the law.

Yes, the case brought back memories of the worst time of her life, but that was over. She'd moved forward. This was Karen's job and she was good at it. She was sick of sympathetic looks and people treading on eggshells when they were around her.

She wouldn't crumble when faced with the Perrys. She was stronger than that.

Karen marched towards the pub's main entrance. The doors were locked. It was only four thirty, and the pub didn't open until six.

She pressed the doorbell, and then used the large brass knocker for good measure.

When the door was finally unlocked, it was only opened wide enough for a dark-haired woman to stare out at them suspiciously. Karen could just make out the woman's round, pale face and dark eyes. Patricia Perry. Karen would recognise her anywhere.

It seemed the same was true for Patricia. Her eyes narrowed as she focused on Karen. 'Oh, it's *you*,' she said with distaste. 'I thought we'd seen the last of you.'

'Patricia Perry?' DI Morgan asked.

'Yes. Who are you? I recognise her,' she said, pointing a stubby finger in Karen's direction, 'but I've never seen you before.'

'I'm DI Scott Morgan. Can we come in and have a word with you and your husband?'

She hesitated, and Karen expected her to slam the door in their faces, but after a moment, she stepped back. 'Suit yourself.'

They followed Patricia into the dim entrance lobby, then into the main bar.

She waved them into the kitchens. Karen recognised the layout; not much had changed. The kitchen for the pub's clientele was kitted out in stainless steel and looked reasonably clean, but then Patricia led them into another room, the Perrys' private kitchen. It was much smaller, cluttered and certainly not as clean.

The air smelled of stale beer, strong coffee and cigarette smoke. In the centre of a round, pine table, a glass ashtray sat on top of a pile of magazines. A curl of smoke steadily twisted up from the cigarette burning away in the middle of the blue glass.

The small sink was overflowing with saucepans, a remnant of a roast dinner. Three plates had been left on the draining board, still smeared with gravy; one containing a leftover greasy potato and a squashed floret of broccoli.

'So, what do you want?' Patricia Perry asked without preamble as she picked up her cigarette. She was a barrel-shaped woman, with a beak-like nose and watchful eyes.

'Where's Rod?' Karen asked.

'Out the back, working on something in the garage.'

'Can you get him, please?' Morgan asked. 'We'd like to speak to both of you.'

'Tell me what you want first, and I'll decide whether or not to bother Rod with it. If this is you lot restarting your harassment campaign against us, I'm warning you – you'll regret it.'

'It's not always about you, Patricia,' Karen said. 'We're working on a murder enquiry.'

Her eyes sparkled with interest. There was no pity or shock in her expression, just curiosity. 'Murder, eh? Who?'

'We think there could be a connection to your pub, so we'd like to speak to you and your staff,' Morgan said.

'We don't have any staff,' Patricia said, tapping her cigarette on the side of the ashtray. 'We do all the work ourselves these days.'

'You run the kitchen and Rod works behind the bar, seven days a week, and you don't have any help?' Karen raised an eyebrow.

'That's right.' Patricia's face tightened. 'It's the economic down-turn. We had to tighten our belts like everyone else around here.'

'I find that hard to believe,' Karen said.

'I really don't care what you believe, duck. I don't have time for this. Either you tell me who was murdered or leave.'

Karen was about to respond but Morgan cut in first. 'Patricia, we just want to solve the murder. Was there any kind of disturbance at the pub last night?'

'Disturbance?' Patricia wrinkled her nose.

'Yes, a fight or disagreement between the staff or punters?'

'I told you, I don't have any staff.' She jabbed a finger in Morgan's direction. 'You're trying to catch me out, and I don't appreciate it.'

'Just answer the question, Patricia,' Karen said.

The woman looked at her and scowled. 'No, it was quiet last night. Quiet for a Saturday, anyway. We had a special on steaks, so we were busy until around eight or so, but nobody argued. Everything was fine. Happy now?'

'The victim was in his forties, we think,' Karen said. 'A white male, average height.'

Patricia snorted. 'Is that all you've got to go on? I think you need to go back to detective training school, DS Hart.'

Karen considered giving more details about the items of clothing the victim had been wearing, but she didn't see the point. It wasn't in Patricia Perry's nature to be helpful to the police.

'We'd like to speak to Rod now,' Morgan said.

Patricia stubbed her cigarette out in the ashtray and then folded her arms over her chest. 'I'm sure you would, duck. But he's busy.'

'It really won't take long, Mrs Perry,' Morgan said. 'And it's important.'

She shook her head stubbornly. 'No. I've had enough of all this. Knowing you lot, you're trying to find a way to pin the blame on Rod.' She picked up a mobile from the kitchen counter and began to tap the screen as she continued to talk. Was she messaging Rod? Sending him a warning? 'If you want to question us again, you'll have to do so in the presence of our solicitor. Got it? Now, I'm asking you nicely, please leave my pub.'

Morgan shook his head. 'We're not trying to pin the blame on anyone. If you think of anything that could be relevant, please get in touch.'

He held out his card, but Patricia made no move to take it from him. She stared at it distrustfully as though she thought it might burst into flames.

He put it on the table. 'All right. We'll leave now. Thank you for your time.'

'I'm sure we can always get a warrant to search the premises again,' Karen said as Morgan walked out of the kitchen.

Before she could follow Morgan out, Patricia suddenly leaned forward, putting her face right up to Karen's, and hissed, 'You should have learned your lesson last time.'

Karen stepped back. 'What do you mean?'

Patricia didn't answer. Her eyes gleamed maliciously, and she smirked when Karen stalked out of the kitchen, blood boiling.

◆ ◆ ◆

'That went well,' Morgan said dryly as they walked across the car park.

'She really is a piece of work. Did you hear what she just said to me—'

'Hang on a sec,' Morgan said, turning sharply to the right and cutting Karen off.

She looked at the spot where Morgan had focused his gaze. There was a large garage at the back of the pub, close to the single-storey extension. They could just about see it from where they stood.

'What is it?' Karen said.

'What's the extension for? Another bar?'

'Apparently the extension was added on so they could offer bed-and-breakfast facilities. I don't know if they still do. There's no sign advertising rooms,' Karen said, looking around. 'I doubt they get much business since they're right next to the Premier Inn.'

'Is that Rod?' Morgan asked as a man shuffled out from the back of the double garage.

'Yes, it is.'

Rod Perry was a short man, only an inch or so taller than his wife. He had a shiny bald head but incredibly bushy eyebrows, which gave his face a perpetually angry expression.

'What do you two want?' he asked, standing in front of the garage. 'The pub doesn't open till six.' He hitched up his jeans, which had been sagging down below his ample stomach.

As they walked towards him, he nervously licked his lips and looked over his shoulder. Why was he so nervous? Did he have something to do with the murder?

He rearranged his features into a scowl. 'DS Hart. To what do I owe the pleasure?' he asked sarcastically, recovering himself and regaining his usual mardy expression.

'We wanted to have a word, Rod. You're not too busy, are you?' Karen asked.

'As a matter of fact, I am.'

Morgan held out his ID and introduced himself. 'There's been a murder in Canwick,' he said, as Karen walked past Rod and headed towards the garage.

Rod craned his neck, watching Karen, ignoring Morgan. 'Oi, where do you think you're going?'

She wanted to get a better look at the garage. It was a large structure, detached from the pub, and had a battered white door. A long, thin window ran along the side wall, and Karen thought she'd seen a movement.

It could have been a shifting shadow from a cloud moving across the sun, but she wanted to make sure.

As she got closer to the garage, Rod began to panic and rushed after her. 'You can't go over there. Oi, if you don't have a warrant you can't just . . . Are you even listening to me?'

Karen ignored him and peered through the glass. Again a shadow shifted inside, and she wondered whether the Perrys were keeping animals. She wouldn't put it past them to have neglected animals locked up in their garage. They didn't treat humans well, so why would pets be any different?

She put a hand above her eyes and leaned right up to the glass to get a better look. Knowing the Perrys as she did, she prepared herself, expecting to see something horrible.

But as the object inside the garage moved again, Karen stepped back in shock. She hadn't been expecting that.

'You should come and take a look at this, sir,' she said to Morgan.

When she turned back to the window, a pair of brown eyes stared back at her.

CHAPTER FIVE

'I think you've got some explaining to do,' DI Morgan said.

Rod Perry's gaze darted around the car park, his body poised as though he might try to run.

Karen took a step to the right to block his exit. 'Things are only going to get worse if you try to leg it, Rod.'

Rod's face scrunched into a scowl, and he looked away. He rubbed a hand over his shiny scalp. 'It's not what it looks like. I was helping them. They're homeless, they had nowhere else to go.'

'So you're letting them stay in the garage out of the goodness of your heart? Is that what you're telling us?' Morgan asked.

Rod nodded, raising his chin and looking up at Morgan defiantly. 'Yeah, that's it.'

'Why don't you open up the garage for us, Rod?' Karen said, her tone cold. 'We're going to need to look inside.'

'You don't have any right . . .' Rod started to say, but then he trailed off when he saw Morgan's expression, and trudged around to the front of the garage.

He leaned down, grabbed the handle on the dented white door and lifted it with a grunt. 'You'll be sure to mention I cooperated in your report, detectives, won't you?' Rod asked as he heaved up the metal door.

There was a long, drawn-out creak as the door rose, and Karen took a step back as the stale air from inside the garage was suddenly freed. The smell hit her hard.

Her stomach churned. Unwashed bodies, urine and what smelled like rotting food was a pungent combination.

The garage floor was covered with six large mattresses, bunched up together on the concrete, all dirty and stained. Equally grubby sleeping bags lay in crumpled heaps on top.

Two buckets sat on either side of the garage, and Karen guessed from the stench they'd been using them as commodes.

'These are your *guests*?' Morgan asked, turning to Rod, not concealing the disgust in his voice. 'You don't even let them use the bathroom.'

Rod said nothing.

Despite the six mattresses, there were only three figures inside the garage, all of them male. They remained frozen. Two of them were hunched up together in the back corner, sitting on one of the mattresses. The other remained standing, staring warily outside.

'Do these men work in the pub, Rod?'

'No. They might lend a hand from time to time, just as a favour, but they're not employees. Like I said, I'm just letting them stay here until they get themselves sorted.'

Patricia Perry's voice carried across the car park. In a rasping screech, she demanded to know what was going on.

Rod took a few steps towards his wife. 'Call Norris. Tell him we're going to need his help, but *don't* call anyone else.'

Rod wasn't a particularly intelligent man, but he hadn't just fallen off the turnip truck either. He was savvy enough to know that the police would be looking at the couple's phone records after this incident. No matter what Rod said, Karen was convinced he was exploiting these men for either unpaid or very low-paid labour.

Keeping them in these conditions was shocking. The situation was far worse than Karen had believed possible.

She lived less than a mile away from the pub. How could this sort of thing go on under people's noses? How did it go unnoticed?

'Who is Norris?' Morgan asked Rod.

'Our solicitor.' Rod smirked. 'You'd better make sure you've got your ducks in a row, or he'll make mincemeat out of you. Once he's on the case, he'll make sure me and the missus are back home in our own beds tonight, laughing about this.'

Morgan ignored Rod's attempt to rile him, then stepped into the garage and asked the men to come out.

As far as Karen could see, there was no electricity or running water in there. And it certainly wasn't well insulated. It was May, but the nights could still be very cold.

All three men shuffled out into the sunshine, blinking and terrified.

Karen approached the first man and gave him a reassuring smile. He was short with a slight build, his skin dark. His brown eyes regarded her steadily. It was his face she'd seen from the window.

'I'm Detective Sergeant Hart. Karen. What's your name?' she asked.

He blinked a couple of times before replying in a trembling voice. 'Vishal Salike,' he said. 'I don't want any trouble.'

'Tell them I was just letting you stay here as a favour, Vishal. Tell her you don't work for me.' Rod Perry pushed his way forward.

'That's enough, Mr Perry,' Morgan said. 'Please go and wait over there facing the wall.'

'You what? You can't send me to stand in the corner like a naughty schoolboy.'

'It's either that or I handcuff you and put you in the back of my car. Your choice.'

Rod glowered at him, then hitched up his trousers and stomped over to stand by the wall. Over his shoulder, he shot daggers at the three men.

Morgan pulled out his mobile and addressed Karen. 'I'm going to give the superintendent a call. She'll want a heads-up on this. We'll need support, too.'

He was right. They would need to get all of these men checked out and interviewed, and if Karen's suspicions were correct, the men could be victims of modern slavery, which would result in a long, thorough investigation. The best source of information and evidence would be the three men in front of them.

'It's all right, Vishal,' Karen said as Morgan turned away to make the call. 'We'll get a doctor to take a look at you and then get you a proper bed for tonight, okay?'

Vishal nodded but kept his eyes fixed on the ground.

Karen moved on to the next man. 'And what's your name?'

He was muscular, light-skinned and fair-haired. Much taller than Vishal, he looked healthier and not as dirty. Karen wondered if he'd been a recent addition to the Perry staff. He looked strong enough to overpower Rod Perry easily, but things were never as simple as that. In these kinds of cases, the perpetrators often exerted a psychological control over their victims, perhaps by threatening loved ones or just treating them in such a way that they felt worthless and unable to fight back.

The big man stared at her before nervously looking around at the other two men.

'What's your name?' Karen asked again.

His gaze met hers and then shifted away. He glanced to the side, at Rod Perry, and shook his head.

Karen turned to Vishal. 'Do you know his name?'

Vishal looked horrified to be put on the spot. He opened his mouth, but before he could speak, the big man cut in. 'Aleksy. Aleksy Iskow.'

'Okay, Aleksy, we'll get you checked out by the doctor, too. Have you been working here?' Karen asked.

He regarded her stonily. A muscle twitched at his jaw, but he made no indication he'd understood her question.

Karen decided to come back to him and turned her attention to the third man. He had light brown hair, blotchy pale skin and a wild look in his eyes. His hair was fine and thin but stuck up at odd angles as though he'd been pulling at it.

'And what's your name?' Karen asked him.

His breathing was rapid, and he was trembling.

'It's okay, I only want to know your name.'

'It's Joe,' he said, and Karen was surprised to hear his Lincolnshire accent.

'You're a local boy, Joe?' Karen asked.

He swatted a hand around his head as though a fly or bee was buzzing near him, but Karen couldn't see one. 'Yeah, I'm a Lincolnite.'

He grinned at her, displaying yellow, decaying teeth. He wasn't old – Karen thought he was probably under thirty – but his dental hygiene had definitely been neglected for years.

'Where are you from, Vishal?' Karen went back to the small man, as although he seemed nervous, he was the least jumpy of the three.

'Originally, I'm from Nepal.' He spoke excellent English with only a faint trace of an accent.

'How long have you been in England?'

'Ten years,' he said.

She tried Aleksy again. 'Aleksy, where are you from? Europe?'

Aleksy stared at her stubbornly and wouldn't reply. Karen didn't know if he was non-responsive because he was scared, or if he didn't understand English well enough to answer her.

'Aleksy? Is that a Polish name? Russian?'

Still no answer.

Eventually, Joe piped up. 'Aleksy's from Poland.' He looked confused, a frown crumpled his forehead. 'But I don't understand—'

Joe fell silent and shook his head. Clutching his arms around his chest, he began to shuffle from foot to foot, clearly distressed.

'It's all right, Joe, we're going to take you somewhere safe and we'll have a chat. Everything will be explained to you.'

All the men would need medical attention, but Karen suspected Joe was suffering from mental health problems and would need specialist help. It made sense. Often, exploited workers were people who came from vulnerable backgrounds. Immigrants, individuals with psychological issues and addicts were commonly preyed upon.

The men were a strange mix. A Lincolnite, a Polish man, and a man from South Asia. She wondered what circumstances had brought them all here.

DI Morgan approached with an update. 'I'm going to bring the Perrys in. I think we have enough on them. We'll need a warrant to search the premises, and I've arranged for the men to be taken to Nettleham HQ to get checked out before questioning.'

'Right. I think we might need a translator, too. Aleksy is Polish. He's not responding to my questions, so I think arranging a translator now will help speed things along.'

Morgan nodded. 'I'll get the ball rolling.'

Karen attempted to keep the men calm as she kept one eye on Morgan's progress, ready to step up if he needed any help. But he looked like he had the arrests under control.

◆ ◆ ◆

The Perrys were sitting in the back of Morgan's car when backup arrived. The three men they'd found in the garage relaxed a little once Rod and Patricia were out of sight.

The team would have a lot of questions for them, but before they could make a start on the investigation, all three would have to be given appropriate medical attention and care. They'd been living in squalid conditions. Physically, Joe and Vishal did not look well, and Karen suspected that their mental health could be even worse.

Once the three men had been taken for processing back at Nettleham, and the Perrys were in the back of a marked police car, Morgan asked, 'Who is this solicitor – Norris? Do you know him?'

'Not really. I think he's been the Perrys' solicitor for some time, at least going back five years. He objected to our warrant the last time the pub was searched, but the objection was overruled.'

Morgan looked thoughtful. 'Perhaps we could look into his client list.'

They walked back to his car in silence. A great deal of work lay ahead of them on this case.

'Should we call in Rick and Sophie?' Karen asked.

Morgan thought for a moment and then shook his head. 'Not yet, it's Sunday evening. It's better if they're in bright and early tomorrow. We won't be able to get much out of those three men tonight. Let's focus for the next few hours on trying to get an ID for our murder victim.'

Karen wasn't sure they'd be able to get an ID within a few hours. 'Do you think all this has anything to do with the murder?'

Morgan frowned as he unlocked the car. 'I'm not sure, but I'm glad we paid the Perrys a visit today.' He opened the driver's-side door and got in.

As he started the engine, he said, 'It's awful, isn't it? To see human beings treated like that.'

Karen agreed. She found the whole situation very disturbing. The Perrys were a bad lot, but even she hadn't suspected them of that level of evil.

She should have been focused on the next steps in the investigation, but her mind kept returning to Patricia Perry's words: *You should have learned your lesson last time.*

CHAPTER SIX

When they got back to Nettleham police station, Karen organised medical care and temporary accommodation for the three men they'd found in the Perrys' garage. She ran the background checks while Morgan filed a warrant.

By the time the Perrys' solicitor, Andrew Norris, arrived, they'd managed to get through a lot of the paperwork.

Norris was a slippery character, and as Karen had expected, the interview didn't go well. They interviewed Patricia first. She sat beside her solicitor, looking incredibly smug.

Norris had red, watery eyes. 'Sorry. Hayfever.' He sniffed. 'My client is happy to help with your enquiry, but I'd like to make it clear she has done nothing illegal.'

'We suspect Aleksy Iskow, Vishal Salike and Joe Rowland were working for your client without payment, and were housed in squalid conditions,' Morgan said.

Patricia Perry's eyes narrowed and she pursed her lips. She leaned forward, about to say something, but Norris put his hand on her forearm.

'Mr and Mrs Perry are simply guilty of having too much community spirit. They were looking after those poor men when they had nowhere else to go,' he stated in a nasal voice.

'They were using a bucket as a toilet,' Karen said. 'I doubt many people would choose to live like that.'

'That's their lookout,' Patricia Perry snapped. 'If they can't be bothered to walk to the lavatory, it's up to them. And as for the men staying in the garage . . . I don't see why I should be expected to clean up after them.'

Norris delivered a stern look of warning to his client. 'The Perrys simply provided the accommodation they had to hand. Of course it wasn't ideal, but it was better than the poor men sleeping rough on the streets.'

'There are shelters in Lincoln that could have accommodated those three men in a lot more comfort,' Morgan said.

Norris pulled a white handkerchief from his suit jacket. 'Yes, but the men wanted to stay with Mr and Mrs Perry. It was their choice.'

'And why would they choose to do that?'

'You'd have to ask them,' he replied, dabbing his eyes with the handkerchief.

Keeping her writing small, Karen scrawled a note on the pad in front of her: *Money?*

Norris wasn't cheap. How could the Perrys afford to pay for his services? They hadn't hesitated to call the solicitor as soon as they knew they'd be questioned. Interesting. It made Karen wonder if Norris's bill was being paid by someone else. Someone with a lot of ready cash whose business interests were tied to the Perrys.

Patricia Perry cocked her head and squinted at the pad. Karen turned it face down on the desk, making the woman scowl.

'We'd like to ask you some questions about a murder that took place in the early hours of the morning,' Morgan said.

'I already told you I know nothing about that. Why do you assume we're involved?' Patricia snapped.

'We're not assuming anything, Mrs Perry. We just want to ask some questions because the murder occurred not far from The Red Lion.'

Norris put a hand on Patricia's arm again. 'My client knows nothing about the death of that poor man.'

'Just because it happened in Canwick doesn't mean we know anything about it,' Patricia insisted.

Karen and Morgan had decided not to mention the beer mat during the interviews. The time and date written on the mat could be important, and they didn't want to tip off the Perrys. Karen suspected the twenty-second of May at three p.m. referred to a drop-off or a meeting at the pub. If the Perrys thought they'd be caught out, they could cancel whatever was supposed to happen this Wednesday, but if it went ahead, they might be caught red-handed.

The interview continued, with DI Morgan leading the questions. Norris still insisted his clients were being Good Samaritans. Everyone was entitled to legal representation, but Norris had to know the Perrys had been exploiting these men, so how did he look himself in the mirror after working for them?

When Patricia Perry began to answer each question with a smirk and 'No comment', Karen knew they were wasting their time, but a case like this one was a waiting game. They'd need the evidence from the three men, along with information from regulars at the pub and any other staff they could track down. With some luck, a search of the premises would provide evidence that even Norris couldn't refute.

After the interview had ended, and Karen and Morgan were preparing to go and get Rod so they could sit through what would likely be the same ridiculous circus all over again, Patricia Perry called out, 'I'll have a cup of tea while I wait for my husband. And a couple of biscuits. Good ones. I'm partial to a chocolate digestive if you have any.'

Karen gave the woman a tight smile and replied through gritted teeth, 'I'll see what I can do.'

The arrogance of the woman was breathtaking. She really didn't think she was in any trouble at all. She'd escaped without charges last time, and probably assumed she'd get off scot-free this time, too.

'That was one of the most infuriating interviews I've ever sat through,' Karen said as they headed down the corridor towards the custody suite.

'Yes, and we're unlikely to charge them today. Hopefully we'll have more luck when we get the warrant.'

'We saw how those men were living. How can Norris possibly expect us to believe they were acting altruistically?'

'He doesn't. He has to know what the Perrys are like. He simply doesn't care. As long as he gets paid, I suspect he's perfectly content.'

Karen checked her watch. 'Before we make a start with Rod, I should go and check on our three victims.'

'Yes. We'd better get them something to eat.'

'I left them with some sandwiches earlier, but they probably could do with a hot meal. I've arranged for temporary accommodation at the rest centre in Lincoln.'

'Good. Did the background checks reveal anything troublesome?'

Karen's checks hadn't revealed any criminal records or outstanding County Court Judgements. She'd only run into one problem. 'Aleksy Iskow and Joe Rowland are registered and have a paper trail. But I can't track Vishal down. He's never been on the electoral roll. No National Insurance number and I can't trace him in any database. It's like he doesn't exist.'

Morgan nodded slowly. 'I suppose that can only mean he didn't enter the country legally.'

'He says he's been here for ten years, though,' Karen said. 'I need to do a bit more digging. Maybe I've missed something.'

Morgan shot her a look. He knew as well as she did that it was unlikely she'd missed anything. But if Vishal wasn't in the country legally, that certainly complicated things. They would need to inform border control, and unlike the other two men, Vishal wouldn't be free to come and go.

It was likely he'd end up in the Immigration Removal Centre at Swinderby.

'We need to question him, so if he's amenable, we could keep him here,' Karen suggested. 'Obviously we can't just let him go to the rest centre where he could walk out at any time, but I'd feel better if we knew more about his background before handing him over to border control.'

Morgan looked thoughtful. 'Perhaps. That could work, but we have an obligation to inform the relevant authority.'

'True, but he's an important witness in this case, and it's still possible we'll find he entered the country legally.'

Morgan raised a sceptical eyebrow. 'Perhaps,' he said again. 'I have a feeling this runs deeper than just these three men. From what you told me about the previous case, it looks like the Perrys have been exploiting people for a long time. And who is easier to exploit than someone who's in the country illegally? They have no one to turn to for help.'

Karen pushed open the door and they entered the stairwell. Morgan was right. It was likely Vishal was an illegal immigrant, which meant he would go from being treated terribly by the Perrys to living in the Immigration Removal Centre until he was sent back to Nepal.

◆ ◆ ◆

Rod's interview turned out to be even more frustrating than his wife's. Each time he said 'No comment', he gave a smug little chuckle that really got under Karen's skin.

Both interviews had been a mammoth waste of time. But the Perrys wouldn't be so smug once the warrant was granted.

Towards the end of the interview, as Morgan prepared to wrap things up, Karen suddenly said, 'What did your wife mean by saying I should have learned my lesson last time?'

The smug smile dropped from Rod Perry's face. 'She said that?'

He swallowed hard and shot a look at Norris, whose watery eyes focused on Karen as he raised his handkerchief to his nose.

'She did. She said it in the kitchen just before we went outside and found you.'

Rod shook his head and shrugged. His movements were over the top – exaggerated nonchalance – which told Karen she'd hit a nerve.

'I've no idea what she was going on about. You'll have to ask her.'

As Morgan asked the last few routine questions, Rod was more subdued and noticeably less smug – but sadly no more helpful than before.

CHAPTER SEVEN

When Karen and Morgan had finished interviewing Rod Perry, they returned to the open-plan office area. Karen headed towards her desk but stopped when she saw the superintendent standing by the glass door of Morgan's office.

She was used to seeing Superintendent Michelle Murray dressed impeccably in her work uniform of sober grey or navy skirt suits, together with her perfectly styled hair. Today, she wore casual clothes – faded blue jeans with a loose-fitting lilac T-shirt – and her hair was pushed back from her face and tucked behind her ears.

'Ma'am,' Morgan said with a nod. 'I didn't realise you were coming in.'

'This could be a complicated case,' Murray said in her soft Glaswegian accent. 'I wanted to see how you were getting on.'

'Well, we've been busy. We've interviewed the Perrys but haven't got much out of them. They're insisting they were doing the three men a favour by letting them stay in the garage. They're also denying the men worked at the pub.'

'That's to be expected, I suppose,' the superintendent said. She nodded to the nearest empty desk, and all three of them went to sit down. 'I've assigned another DI to cover the murder on Canwick Hill. DI Freeman. How far did you get with the murder investigation before you were sidetracked?'

Karen thought she detected a note of frustration in the superintendent's voice. Was she annoyed that they'd brought the Perrys in and focused on that enquiry at the expense of the murder investigation? Karen believed the two cases were likely to be closely related.

Morgan didn't protest at his lightened caseload. 'I think that's the most sensible course of action, ma'am. We haven't made much progress. We don't yet have an ID for the victim. I suspect we've stumbled on something that goes deeper than the Perrys.'

'So do I. We need to tread carefully, because we can't afford any screw-ups. If we want a strong case that ends in a successful prosecution, we have to do everything by the book. Now, fill me in on what you've learned about these three men.'

Karen told the superintendent what she'd managed to find out so far. She supplied the details she'd unearthed in the background checks, informing the superintendent that none of the men had criminal records and she had no reason to believe they were a danger to the public. 'The only one I've had trouble tracing is Vishal Salike. I can't find any records indicating when or where he entered the country. He says he was born in Nepal.'

'Then we need to inform border control.'

'Yes, I'll do that, but I was hoping to get your approval, ma'am, to keep him at the station overnight,' Karen said. 'I've arranged accommodation for Aleksy Iskow and Joe Rowland at a local rest centre, but I doubt border control will sanction that if Vishal is in the country illegally. We'll need to question him, so it makes sense to keep him here temporarily if everyone is amenable.'

The superintendent was silent while she contemplated the request. Then she mused, 'It would make life easier, wouldn't it?'

'It would. Of course, I'd explain the situation to Vishal, and he would be in the custody suite overnight.'

'That seems like a sensible solution for tonight at least, if all the agencies agree. We'll need to organise an advocate for him, too. Are you planning to question him tomorrow?' she asked, turning to Morgan.

'Yes, ma'am. Vishal and the other two men. After they've had a proper night's sleep and a hot breakfast, we'll start the questioning.'

'Good. These men are the best evidence we have against the owners of The Red Lion. Have you let the Perrys go?'

'Not yet, ma'am, but I don't think we have enough to hold them or charge them at this stage.'

'Neither do I. Let them go, and then you should both get a good night's rest yourselves. You'll have a busy day of interviews tomorrow.'

The superintendent spun her chair around to face Karen. 'You've had dealings with the Perrys before, haven't you?'

Karen glanced at her own desk, where she had the case file and her notes detailing the previous run-in with the Perrys. 'Yes, though I never thought it was as bad as this. The investigation didn't go well last time. I think we tipped our hand too early. All the evidence pointed to the fact the Perrys were exploiting undocumented workers, but when we searched the premises, they'd covered up before we got there. They must have known about the raid at least a week before it took place. When we visited the pub, we found they'd put staff on the books. Locals had insisted they'd seen Vietnamese women working at the pub, but the Perrys swore it was nonsense, and we never found a trace of the women.'

'Well, let's hope we have better luck this time. If we're right and the Perrys are part of a modern slavery ring, we want to catch everyone associated with it. Plus there will be a lot of public interest on this one and a lot of political points to be scored.'

'If you'll excuse me, ma'am, I need to check on the progress of the warrant,' Morgan said.

The superintendent dismissed him with a nod, and Morgan entered his office.

When the glass door closed, the superintendent got to her feet. 'Right, I'll ask DI Morgan to make sure everything is ready to hand over to DI Freeman. I think we should both go home. Busy day tomorrow.' She made to move but then stopped. 'Is everything all right, Karen?'

Karen hesitated. 'Yes . . . To be honest, I was a little unnerved by something Patricia Perry said.'

The superintendent sat back down, resting her elbows on the desk and leaning closer to Karen. 'What did she say?'

'That I should have learned my lesson last time.'

Superintendent Murray frowned. 'What did she mean by that? Did she threaten you last time?'

'No, not really.'

'"Not really"?'

Karen shrugged. 'There were a few vague "you'll regret this" comments, but no more than you'd expect when dealing with people like the Perrys.'

The superintendent was quiet for a moment, studying Karen so intently she felt like a specimen under a microscope. Eventually, Murray said, 'I've spoken to the chief constable, and he's pleased you're working this case with your first-hand knowledge of the Perrys. But if you feel uncomfortable, I could put you back on the murder case and assign another DS to work with DI Morgan on this one.'

Karen shook her head, not surprised the superintendent had spoken to the chief constable about the case already. A modern slavery case brought a lot of publicity. Karen *was* surprised the chief constable had mentioned her, though. 'No, ma'am, I'd like to see this case through. My previous experience with the Perrys could prove helpful.'

Despite the fact her stress levels were through the roof, Karen kept her voice calm. She had a bad feeling about the Perrys, but the last thing she wanted was to be shunted from the case. The Perrys had got away with their misdeeds last time. Karen wanted to make sure that didn't happen again.

'All right. But if they say anything else that could be construed as even vaguely threatening, you tell me.'

'Absolutely, ma'am.'

The superintendent ran a hand through her unusually messy hair. 'This hasn't been the most restful Sunday.' She smiled at Karen. 'Once Vishal is settled in the custody suite, go home and get some rest.'

'Yes, ma'am.'

Karen walked over to her desk.

'And Karen?' the superintendent called when she was halfway across the office.

Karen turned. 'Yes?'

'You can come and talk to me if you're finding it tough . . . I realise your first interaction with the Perrys came at a difficult time.'

Though she didn't say so overtly, Karen knew she was referring to the accident.

'Thanks, ma'am. I appreciate it.'

DI Morgan yawned and pushed himself back from his desk. Karen had gone home a couple of hours ago, but he'd wanted to stick around and make sure the warrant came through and was actioned.

He rubbed his hands over his face and contemplated getting another coffee. He didn't usually have any trouble staying bright and alert when he was working a case, but sitting in front of his computer and waiting for news on the warrant was sending him to sleep. He'd used some of the time to look up Vishal on the available databases, but like Karen, he'd found no evidence of him entering the country.

A quick trip to the custody suite to have a chat with Vishal didn't give him any answers either. Vishal was sullen and quiet. That was understandable. They were supposed to be helping the men, liberating them from exploitation, yet they'd put him into one of the cells overnight. Sure, it was cleaner and more comfortable than the garage, but he was still not able to come and go freely.

When Morgan entered the cell, Vishal regarded him with a mournful gaze. He'd brought a chocolate bar and a can of Coke, and Vishal took them without uttering a word.

'This is just for tonight,' Morgan explained. 'We need to assess how you got into the country before we can let you go.'

Vishal's steady gaze didn't waver.

'Can you tell me about how you got into the country? Did you have a visa?'

Vishal shrugged. 'It was a long time ago. I came because I have family here.'

'Right. Did you fly in?'

Vishal was quiet for a moment and then said, 'I can't remember.'

It was looking more and more likely that Vishal had entered the country illegally, which meant eventually it would be out of Morgan's hands.

He left Vishal munching the chocolate and went to check on the warrant again.

It had come back unauthorised.

He stared at the computer screen in disbelief. What had he done wrong? Filled in the wrong sections?

Morgan scanned through the document again, looking for his mistake, and then saw he'd filed without attaching the supporting information.

What was wrong with him? He groaned and leaned back in his office chair. That was hours wasted. It was a rookie error.

He wasn't looking forward to telling the superintendent, but he had to own his mistakes.

The phone rang for a long time before she answered.

Her voice was sleepy. 'Superintendent Murray.'

'Sorry to disturb you, ma'am, it's DI Morgan. I'm afraid I made an error filing the warrant. It's come back unauthorised.' He explained his mistake.

'Well, file it again, and DI Freeman will have to action the search when it comes through.'

'I'm sorry, ma'am, it's not like me to make an error like this.'

'I know it isn't. But you've had a busy week and had two demanding cases today. You need to get home and get some rest, so you'll be on better form tomorrow.'

'Yes, ma'am. Only . . .'

'Only what?'

'We've released the Perrys. They're going to know we'll be searching the property soon. It's highly likely they'll try to get rid of any evidence before the warrant is actioned.'

'It can't be helped,' the superintendent said. 'Besides, the best evidence we have is the three men the Perrys were keeping in their garage. I need you fresh tomorrow, because questioning them will influence the outcome of this case.'

Morgan thanked the superintendent and hung up.

That could have been worse. She was frustrated but hadn't taken it out on him. It had been a genuine mistake. Errors happened – but not usually to him. Not since the last time. He checked and rechecked his paperwork before filing, and was careful to fill in everything correctly.

But now, here in Lincolnshire, he had found himself relaxing, letting his guard down a bit, and that was probably why he'd screwed up.

Rubbing a weary hand over his face, he sighed. Then he checked the document three times, making sure every item of supporting information was attached before hitting 'Send'.

After turning off his computer, he reached for his jacket and switched off the light in his office.

He stood there for a moment in the dark, berating his sloppiness.

He had responsibilities. He couldn't afford to make any more mistakes like this.

CHAPTER EIGHT

Grace Baker stood at the kitchen window making herself a cup of hot milk. It was three a.m., and for the fourth night in a row she hadn't been able to sleep. Her little cat, Dolly, was at her heels.

She smiled fondly at the Burmese.

'Sorry, Dolly, no hot milk for you, I'm afraid.' She added a hefty slug of whiskey to the milk.

She'd never been much of a drinker before, but these days it seemed to be the only thing that got her off to sleep.

Grace moved over to the stove, her slippers shuffling against the stone tiles. Carefully, she poured the hot milk from the saucepan into her large 'World's Best Sister' mug.

Her sister, Jean, had given it to her three weeks ago for her birthday. She smiled.

Since her husband had died, she'd been growing closer to Jean. Despite the fact her sister had a large family and a stressful full-time job, she always made time for Grace. Jean didn't have much money, but she made the best of things, and she was always cheerful.

Funny how life turned out. They were complete opposites. Grace had plenty of money, the mortgage was paid off now, and the bills weren't too expensive. But Grace was always sad.

Since becoming a widow two years ago, she'd been thoroughly miserable. She'd expected it to get better as time passed. That's what people *said* was supposed to happen. But it didn't.

It wasn't so bad during the day. She could keep herself busy with gardening and crossword puzzles, and she always had a good book on the go. Books were the only things that made the darkness around her lift these days. Getting away from her own life and entering the make-believe world of fiction was a blessing.

'Thank goodness for books,' she muttered as she glanced down at the latest Lucinda Riley lying on the kitchen table. She planned on starting it tomorrow.

When the insomnia had first begun, she'd thought reading would make her sleepy and after a few chapters she'd drift off, but she found herself reading all night and feeling absolutely wretched the next day, dropping off and napping for twenty minutes or so at a time but never getting proper restful sleep.

So she'd given up on that idea and turned to whiskey. It wasn't immediate, but eventually had an effect.

Jean kept insisting she should go to her GP and ask for some tablets, but there was something terribly scary and artificial about sleeping tablets. Grace had decided she'd only take them as a last resort. Jean suggested that perhaps whiskey wasn't a wise choice and wasn't good for Grace's liver, to which Grace had replied she was sure that the tablets probably weren't very good for livers either.

She took a sip of the hot milk and looked through the patio doors to her little courtyard garden. She did enjoy spending time out there and had just spent two hundred pounds on new bedding plants. Poor Roger would be turning in his grave. He'd always been a frugal man. She had him to thank for the fact she was so comfortably off now. She didn't have to worry whether she could afford to buy new plants for the garden.

They'd intended to use some of the money they'd saved to go on holidays once Roger retired. Grace had always wanted to go to Tuscany. But it was too late for that now. She wouldn't enjoy travelling alone. It would only remind her how lonely she was.

She carried her hot milk through to the living room and settled on the sofa with Dolly curled up beside her. Within seconds, the cat was asleep.

'If only I found it that easy to drift off,' Grace said, stroking the cat's sleek fur.

She lifted her mug to take another sip of hot milk and noticed something very odd. Though the curtains were drawn, they didn't quite meet in the middle, and there was a sliver of night sky visible from where she sat. She eased herself off the sofa, trying not to disturb Dolly, placed her milk on the coffee table and then walked across to the window.

She pulled the curtains apart to get a better look.

Her driveway faced the main B1188. It was a busy road, but at this time of night was usually very quiet.

Directly opposite was the Premier Inn. It was quite popular with business travellers, and the attached Beefeater restaurant was busy most nights. As expected for three a.m., most of the lights in the building were out – apart from the security lights. All was quiet.

Behind the Premier Inn was The Red Lion pub.

She never went there any more. Back in the early days after they moved to Canwick, she and Roger had often gone for a couple of drinks and chatted to the locals, but when the pub changed hands about fifteen years ago, things went downhill. They'd taken to getting the bus into town or walking to Washingborough instead. The pubs there were nicer.

Now that Roger was gone, she didn't go to any pubs.

Grace didn't have a clear view from her living room window, but she could see the roof and the chimneys. It was the strange glowing light emanating from the top of the roof that had caught her attention.

Grace scrunched up her face and stared. She'd left her glasses upstairs, so she couldn't see properly, but from where she was standing, she could have sworn . . .

Fire.

Grace felt a stab of panic and turned, opening her mouth to call for Roger, forgetting that he couldn't hear her and would never hear her again.

Her pulse raced, and as she rushed out into the hallway she shook her head in disbelief that she was still doing that after all this time.

Picking up the phone, she tried to keep calm as she dialled 999.

It was still dark when Karen woke. She lay there, heart thudding in her chest, crumpled sheets twisted around her shivering body. After five years the dreams had lessened, but today's events had brought them back more fiercely than ever.

They always began with Tilly. Not a nightmare at the start, but a memory. Playing in the garden, reading her a bedtime story. Part of Karen never wanted the dreams to fade because she wanted to keep those fragmented memories. They were so real, so vivid. But they always ended with Tilly growing fainter and fainter as Karen desperately tried to stop her disappearing.

Karen stayed motionless in bed for a long time, too tired to get up, too anxious to go back to sleep.

At the first sign of dawn's grey light, Karen shoved back the sheets, untangling her limbs. She rubbed her face and dragged a hand through her short hair on the way to the bathroom. Purposefully, she turned away from the mirror. She didn't need to glance at her reflection to know she looked terrible. Her eyes were sore, and her body was crying out for rest.

Karen didn't want to see the dark circles under her eyes this morning. Stepping into the shower, she turned the temperature to hot and let the spray pummel her back and shoulders. The steaming water eased some of the tension in her muscles and she reached for the shower gel, playing through yesterday's events in her mind.

After her shower, Karen sat in the cold conservatory looking out at the garden. It was eerily quiet in the early-morning light. Her cup of tea sat on the coffee table beside her.

A blackbird began to sing, and hopped across the lawn.

Karen swallowed the last of her tea and carried her mug into the kitchen. Time for coffee now. She needed to get her mind straight for this case, but she couldn't get Patricia Perry's words out of her head.

Should have learned your lesson last time. Those words ran on a loop through Karen's mind as she made the coffee.

Was Patricia just trying to push her buttons? Very likely. It could have been nothing more than a way to wind Karen up. Something a little nasty, a dig, hoping to get at Karen – and it had worked. The last time she'd interacted with the Perrys had been just before Josh and Tilly died in the car accident on Canwick Hill, and though she'd tried to stop her mind from going to those dark places, it kept returning to linger on her bleakest thoughts.

Immediately after the accident, Karen had been too shocked to think clearly, but as the days and weeks had passed she'd become unhealthily obsessed with the idea that someone else had been involved in the crash – someone important, with power and influence, who'd used their sway to hide the facts. Karen had been desperate to believe it was a cover-up, wondering if someone high-up was involved, pulling strings to make sure it was hushed up. She had gone so far as to track down the whereabouts of the local councillors, MPs, even the chief constable. But her investigations had come to nothing.

Somehow, accepting it had been an accident had been harder than investigating a cover-up. It meant accepting there was nothing she could do to avenge their deaths. She couldn't search for justice. It was simply a random, pointless accident.

It had taken a long time to come to terms with her loss and accept the fact their deaths had been a cruel accident. Now, just when she'd turned the corner and pushed her obsession aside, Patricia Perry had to go and say something like that, sending Karen back into the spiral of constant questioning, constant wondering.

She blew over the top of her steaming-hot mug of coffee and then took a sip.

When she'd come home last night, she'd watched mindless television and eaten some of the leftovers from the barbecue. Then she'd had a bath, trying to relax and get her mind to settle. But the tension wouldn't leave her, and she barely slept thanks to the nightmares.

She opened the fridge and inspected the contents. Fruit meringue probably wasn't the best choice for breakfast . . . She shrugged and pulled out what remained of the meringue, and grabbed a fork from the cutlery drawer.

Perhaps the super had been right to suggest she work on the murder case with DI Freeman and get away from the Perrys, though Karen had a hunch both cases would be related. There was no denying the Perrys had triggered unwanted thoughts. Working with DI Freeman might be the sensible course of action, but deep down she wanted to keep working on this case. Not just because she wanted to see the Perrys punished for the exploitation that must have been going on for years, but because she wanted to get to the bottom of whatever Patricia Perry had been implying. If she had just been trying to wind Karen up, then she'd be able to put all that behind her and move on.

But on the other hand . . .

Karen's mobile rang. She saw from the illuminated screen it was now almost six a.m.

It was DI Morgan. She answered the phone.

'What's happened?'

'Sorry to wake you,' he said. 'There's been a report of a fire at The Red Lion pub.'

'A fire?' Karen quickly walked through the kitchen and headed for the stairs. She needed to get dressed. 'What about the search?'

Morgan sighed heavily. 'There was a hold-up with the warrant. The search was due to take place this morning.'

'You're kidding? The Perrys would have got rid of any evidence by this morning.' She ran up the stairs.

'It was my fault,' Morgan said. 'I screwed up the initial warrant application.'

'How?' Karen yanked opened her wardrobe door.

'I didn't submit all the relevant information. I resubmitted it before I went home, but when it came back, DI Freeman didn't action it. He probably thought it was too late at that point.'

Karen gritted her teeth. Two experienced officers, and neither had managed to action a warrant.

Trying to push aside her irritation and the niggling concern this could be more than a simple error, she pulled a blouse from a hanger. 'Are there any casualties? Do we think the Perrys set fire to the pub to cover things up?'

'I don't know anything at this stage. I'm going to head down there now. The fire crew have the blaze under control, but it sounds like the place is wrecked. Do you want to come?'

'Yes.'

'I'll be with you in ten minutes.'

CHAPTER NINE

Karen was shocked when she saw the state of The Red Lion. The fire had really done a number on the old building.

Two fire engines were parked outside. Smoke – or was that steam? – travelled upwards, leaving the roof in white streams. There was no sign of flames now. The fire brigade had the situation under control.

'What a mess. Looks like the place has been gutted,' Morgan said as he applied the handbrake.

'So much for our evidence,' Karen said. 'I wish DI Freeman had actioned the warrant last night.' She unclipped her seatbelt and reached for the door handle. 'If the search had gone ahead, this probably wouldn't have happened.'

'I think I need to share some of the blame for that,' Morgan said quietly as he got out of the car.

'I wasn't blaming you. It's just I thought if the warrant had been actioned—'

Morgan locked the car and turned to look at The Red Lion. 'I know. Let's find the officer in charge.'

Karen cringed as he walked away. That had been tactless. She hadn't meant to rub salt into his wounds. No one enjoyed getting things wrong, but Morgan was particularly sensitive when it came to mistakes. He'd confided in Karen not long ago about an error he'd made at work that had resulted in the death of a young boy.

She couldn't really blame DI Freeman for not actioning the warrant. He'd had the murder case handed to him on a Sunday night and then been tasked with following up on the warrant as well. It was just so frustrating to think the Perrys would escape punishment again, when Karen was sure they'd been taking advantage of workers for years.

She sighed and followed Morgan towards the pub. Perhaps they wouldn't be able to charge the Perrys for the exploitation, but they might be able to get them for arson.

The pub was in a terrible state. It wasn't a historic building, so it was doubtful it would be restored. It would likely be demolished. The red bricks were coated with soot. There was a gaping hole in the roof. Red tiles around the hole were stained grey and black from the fire.

There was a trickle of what sounded like running water. Steam and smoke continued to drift up from the roof and windows.

Fragments of glass lay on the ground. Had the windows shattered from the heat? Or had the fire brigade broken them in order to put out the fire? The air was heavy with a smoky bonfire scent, tainted with the acrid chemical smell of burnt plastic. The detached garage where they'd found the three men was untouched by fire. The extension at the back, supposedly used for B&B guests, looked structurally sound, but the walls were black with soot.

Morgan held out his identification to one of the fire officers, who asked them to wait a minute while he went to fetch his boss. They both stared at the pub while they waited.

Karen blinked, the lingering smoke making her eyes sting. 'They really did a number on it, didn't they?'

A heavy truck rumbled down the B1131 in the direction of Bracebridge Heath. Even at this early hour, the traffic was crawling along as drivers slowed their vehicles to rubberneck and get a good look at the destruction of The Red Lion. It did make quite a shocking sight.

'Mick Thyme,' a deep male voice said.

Karen turned to see a tall fire officer shaking hands with Morgan. He'd removed his hat and the dark hair beneath was mussed up.

After the introductions were out of the way, Morgan asked, 'What's the verdict? Arson?'

'Officially, I'll have to wait until the investigation crew finish. They can't go in yet. We need to wait until the building has cooled. There's likely to be severe structural damage, so there are safety protocols we have to follow. Unofficially, it's almost certainly arson. I think the fire started downstairs and some kind of accelerant was used.'

'Whereabouts downstairs?' Karen asked.

'The kitchen. We see a lot of fires that are started by electrical malfunctions in the kitchen, but I don't think that's the case here. I'd say we're looking for an arsonist.'

Karen gritted her teeth. She hadn't thought it possible for the Perrys to sink any lower in her estimation, but they'd managed it. By starting the fire, they'd put lives at risk. Brave fire officers, whose job it was to make sure no one was left inside the building. Karen turned to look at the garage. Why burn down the pub and not the garage? Perhaps they hadn't bothered with it because they knew that all that was inside was the men's belongings and a few dirty mattresses. Karen coughed as the smoke caught at the back of her throat.

'So no one has been inside the building yet?' Morgan asked.

'Two of my crew went upstairs with breathing apparatus. When we got here the fire was ferocious, but we had to check if anyone was still inside. Unfortunately we found three bodies.'

His words hit Karen like a punch to the stomach. 'Three bodies?'

Thyme's face was sombre. 'I'm afraid so. One still in a bedroom, the other two in the upstairs hallway. They were probably trying to escape when they were overpowered by smoke. They're still in there. We'll get the bodies out when the building is declared safe.'

'How long will that be?'

'Hard to say. Possibly only a few hours. If supports are needed, it could take longer.'

Karen wrapped her arms around her middle and shivered. Three bodies. Probably Rod and Patricia Perry and their fourteen-year-old son. That was the most obvious conclusion. Had the Perrys been overcome with guilt and set fire to the pub? Was it a case of murder–suicide? Or had someone else started the fire? Someone who was worried the Perrys might talk?

Barry Perry. Karen's stomach churned. She hadn't been able to recall his name yesterday until she'd looked through the old files. He was just a boy. The last time she'd seen him, he'd been a skinny nine-year-old with dimpled cheeks. He'd already been a mouthy little thing, taught to hate the police by his parents, but still . . . Fourteen.

The smell of burnt plastic was suddenly overwhelming. Karen fanned the air in front of her face, feeling sick.

She tried to focus on the rest of Morgan's questions, mentally filing away Mick Thyme's answers.

When the fire officer left them, Morgan turned to her. 'Are you all right?'

She nodded slowly. 'Shocked, really. I was so sure the fire was down to the Perrys, but if the bodies are Rod and Patricia and their son . . . then the fire wasn't their attempt to cover their tracks.'

Morgan ran a hand through his short hair. 'I think it *was* a cover-up. I think someone else wanted to get rid of the Perrys before they could talk.'

As they walked back to the car, Karen couldn't stop wishing DI Freeman had been able to put together the search last night. The police presence surely would have deterred the arsonist. Then a small worry wormed its way into her mind. First Morgan hadn't filed the correct information. Then the superintendent had insisted they both go home, telling DI Freeman to pick up the slack. And finally DI Freeman, for whatever reason, hadn't actioned the search when the warrant was approved. Was it really a run of bad luck? Karen couldn't push away her suspicions.

'This is obviously a much bigger case than we thought,' she said. 'If Mick Thyme is right and this was arson, it's likely someone targeted the Perrys. They didn't just want to destroy the building, they wanted to kill the Perrys.'

'Yes. I'm inclined to believe someone wanted to silence them.'

Karen hesitated for a moment before blurting out, 'Do you think someone on the inside could be involved?'

'The inside?' Morgan asked as he dug in his pocket and pulled out the key fob.

'A police officer. The thing is, the last time we had dealings with the Perrys they were tipped off. They knew we were coming, and they got rid of all the evidence and put their staff on the books to make themselves look legitimate. Now we take the Perrys in for questioning last night and *this* happens.'

Morgan was silent as they got into the car, and then as he started the engine, he said, 'I think that's quite a leap, Karen.'

'Yes, forget it. It's just my overactive imagination, I suppose.'

'Don't forget anyone passing by could have seen the Perrys taken away in a marked car. Plus, the Perrys' solicitor could have been the one who tipped off the arsonist. I suspect someone else was paying Norris's bill. In which case, he likely provided information on the arrest.'

Karen gave him a tight smile. 'That makes more sense.'

She needed to be careful and remember who she was talking to. Over the past few months, she'd grown closer to Morgan, even spending time with him outside work, but she needed to remember the past. She couldn't fall back into the trap of obsessing over coincidences and getting fixated on wild theories.

Morgan was right. His suggestion made a lot more sense. She didn't want him to believe she was jumping to conclusions. The last thing she wanted was to be taken off this case or perhaps shunted to a desk Job Indefinitely. She'd come close to that, last time. She knew some of her fellow officers had labelled her neurotic and unstable.

Some of her behaviour had been overlooked, as people gave her more leeway due to her circumstances. She had lost her daughter and husband, so it was understandable she'd be on edge. But five years had passed. People wouldn't be so understanding now.

She couldn't just accuse officers of corruption with no evidence. It was one thing to think it, but quite another thing to voice it to a fellow officer. As much as she admired and liked Morgan, he wouldn't understand. He took his job seriously, and if he considered Karen to be a liability to the investigation, he would remove her without hesitation.

She stared out of the passenger window as they drove away from The Red Lion, thinking about the past. It wasn't easy to remember the way she'd acted. For someone who'd always followed her instincts, she'd had to learn a hard lesson. She wasn't always right, and jumping to conclusions could cost her the job she loved.

Karen tensed as they drove along the B1188, passing the petrol station. She took this journey to work every day, passing the site of the accident that had killed Josh and Tilly, coping by keeping her eyes fixed straight ahead, ignoring the spot where the car had veered off the road.

Morgan hadn't noticed her reaction. As they headed towards Lincoln, Karen felt some of her tension ease. She was doing okay now. It hadn't been easy, but she'd come to terms with the accident and accepted the facts.

She owed a lot to two men in particular. DCI Anthony Shaw had been the officer who'd originally encouraged Karen to go for a promotion. Though he'd retired shortly before the accident, he'd visited her multiple times afterwards, listening to her crazy ideas without judgement. Then there was DI Freeman. When other officers had started to avoid her, sending her curious looks and gossiping behind her back, he'd actively sought her out and patiently listened to her theories of a cover-up before calmly explaining why she was wrong.

Not once had he dismissed her without listening. He'd never made her feel crazy or unbalanced as some of her colleagues had. It was thanks to his contacts with traffic that she was able to get a lot of the documentation and evidence, which finally convinced her that their deaths had indeed been an accident. Acceptance had taken a long time, and she couldn't throw all that away because Patricia Perry made a throwaway comment and a search had been delayed.

She might never get rid of her suspicions completely, but she could keep them to herself.

CHAPTER TEN

DI Morgan dropped Karen off at home so she could pick up her car. Within two minutes, she was back on the B1188 heading to Lincoln. She'd almost reached the Premier Inn when she spotted a pedestrian on the other side of the road, waving frantically.

Karen indicated and slowed her Honda Civic before pulling up to the kerb.

The woman seemed agitated and intent on flagging Karen's car down. She had blonde hair streaked with grey, styled in tight curls. Her full-length burgundy dressing gown matched her fluffy slippers.

Karen got out of the car and crossed the road. 'Is everything all right?'

The woman put her hand to her chest. 'Thank you for stopping. You're a police officer, aren't you?'

'That's right. DS Karen Hart.'

'I'm Grace Baker. I recognised you and your car. I know your neighbour, Christine.'

Karen glanced back at her car. It was causing a traffic tailback as cars tried to get past. Commuters would be cursing her. 'Is there a problem? It's just I have to get back to—'

'Well, yes. I need to talk to you. About the fire. It was me who called it in.'

'Ah,' Karen said. 'Do you live nearby?'

That was a silly question. Of course she lived nearby. It was unlikely she'd travelled far in her dressing gown and slippers.

'Yes, just along this road. You can park on my drive.'

Karen went back to her car and turned into the driveway the woman had pointed to. It was partially paved with the rest filled with stones, and the high laurel hedge at the front of the property gave it some privacy. The house was a cream chalet bungalow. 'Quaint' was the first word that came to mind. Large bay windows looked out in the direction of the road, but the view was partially obscured by the hedge. A crab-apple tree, still heavy with blossom, grew in the middle of the front lawn.

Karen parked in front of the garage.

'So what exactly did you see last night, Grace?' Karen asked as she followed the woman towards the house.

'It was the light that caught my attention. It was a very odd, orange glow. I knew something was wrong.'

She pushed open the door and was greeted by a welcoming purr from a Burmese cat. The cat wound its way around Karen's legs, demanding attention.

'That's enough, Dolly. That isn't how we greet visitors,' Grace said, scooping the cat up in her arms.

Karen reached a hand out to stroke the cat's head. 'What a cutie.'

'She is. Dolly is a little darling, very affectionate, and she likes attention.'

'My grandmother had a Burmese. Used to follow her all around the house.'

'Do you have any pets yourself?' Grace said.

Karen felt a pang of bitter awkwardness as Grace led her into the kitchen. She'd never owned a cat or a dog. They'd planned to get a pet when Tilly was older. But that wasn't what was making her uncomfortable. It was the question itself, the normalcy, the small talk . . . It was only a matter of time before Grace asked if she had children, and no matter how much time passed, answering *that* question never got any easier.

If she said she didn't have children, it was like denying Tilly had ever existed, but she couldn't say she did without explaining her loss and she really didn't want to get into that with a stranger.

Before Grace got too comfortable with the small talk, Karen took control of the conversation. 'No pets yet. I work long hours, and I'd feel bad leaving them at home alone all day. So, did you see anyone lurking about last night?'

Grace shook her head. 'Unfortunately not.' She lifted the kettle. 'Tea?'

'That would be nice, thanks.'

Grace flicked the switch on the kettle and then gestured to the kitchen table. 'Have a seat if you like.'

Karen pulled out a chair and sat down as Grace busied herself making the tea.

'I wanted to talk to you about other things as well. Not just last night. There have been all sorts of things going on up at that pub over the last few years.'

Karen thought back to the previous investigation into the Perrys. They'd spoken to some of the local residents, but she didn't recall speaking to Grace Baker.

'What sort of things?' Karen asked.

'There have been comings and goings at all hours. I don't mean the usual problems you get with pubs – loud music and drunk men staggering home – I mean lorries turning up in the middle of the night. I think the vehicles are from the haulage yard on Hectare Lane in Canwick. Do you know it?'

Karen nodded. She rarely went into the village itself, though she drove past Canwick every day on her way to work. It was a surprisingly quiet, small village for one so close to Lincoln. There was a golf club, though sadly she had heard rumours that it had gone into administration recently. She did recall a haulage yard, situated along the narrow lane that ran along the perimeter of the golf course. There had been a few local complaints, mainly because the large vehicles created potholes in the roads, and at times there had been grumbles about the lorries travelling through the village too fast.

'Well, sometimes the lorries stop at the pub at very odd times. The previous owners of The Red Lion were lovely. A Welsh couple, but when they retired the pub was sold to the Perrys and that's when it all started – the lorries, I mean.'

'And you're sure they're coming from the haulage yard?' Karen asked as Grace placed two cups of tea on the table and sat down opposite Karen.

'Pretty sure,' Grace said as she frowned at her cup of tea. 'I don't have a perfect view from my house. I can see through the gap between the Premier Inn hotel and the building next to it, which gives me a view of The Red Lion car park, but I can only see the tops of the lorries from downstairs. There's a better view from the upstairs spare room.'

'Do you see people loitering in the car park when the lorries arrive?'

'Sometimes, but like I said, the view isn't that good. After what happened last night, I wondered if it was connected. Unless the fire was just an accident . . .'

'We're not sure at this stage. We're still waiting for the report.'

'Were there any casualties? I heard the Perrys were inside.'

'I really can't talk about that, Grace. I'm sure you understand.'

'Of course,' Grace said quickly, then picked up her tea and took a sip. 'I suppose you think I'm an annoying, nosy woman with nothing better to do. I didn't mean to pry. The lorries could have just been dropping off deliveries, but I thought it was a funny time to be delivering anything. The last one turned up at two a.m.'

Karen agreed. It did seem suspicious. Why would they be visiting The Red Lion under the cover of darkness? It seemed likely they had something to hide.

She asked Grace questions about the late-night visits, focusing on timings and any details she could remember. After making careful notes, Karen thanked her.

'That's quite all right. I did bring the matter up at the parish meeting, but you never know if it's reported to the police, so I thought I'd better let you know directly.'

'Thank you, Grace. I am very glad you did.'

CHAPTER ELEVEN

Shortly after nine a.m., Karen arrived at the Lincoln Rest Centre on Monks Road. Wondering why it was called a *rest* centre, she rang the brass bell at the entrance, tapping her foot impatiently on the stone step. DI Morgan wouldn't appreciate being kept waiting.

'Sorry I'm late,' Karen said as the door opened.

'No problem,' the man in front of her said. He had a wide smile, dark skin and warm brown eyes. 'Your colleague is already here. I'm Theo Bailey, the centre director. Come in.'

He stood back, allowing Karen to enter the narrow hallway. The floor was tiled, and beside the entrance was a display case full of self-help leaflets. To her right, a large ornate staircase led up to the first floor. She'd read that the centre had been converted from three large terraced houses.

'We've taken Joe and Aleksy's photographs and added them to our system. They have access cards, so they can come and go as they please. I knew you were coming in this morning, so I asked them to stay at the centre. The translator arrived a little while ago.'

'Good,' Karen said, hoping they'd get more out of Aleksy with the translator's help.

Theo led the way into a small kitchen, where Morgan was standing holding a mug of coffee. He shot her a quizzical glance, no doubt wondering if she'd got lost on the way.

She'd explain about Grace Baker later.

'Want one?' Theo asked, pointing at the filter coffee machine on the kitchen counter.

'Yes, please.'

'Milk, sugar?'

'Just a splash of milk, please.'

'When you're both ready, you can use the communal room next door. I'll keep everyone else out, so you have some privacy. Unless you want to take Joe and Aleksy back to the station?'

'I think they might feel more comfortable talking here,' Morgan said. 'What do you think, Karen?'

'That makes sense. Have you spoken to the translator?'

'Yes, her name is Carolina Nowak,' Morgan said. 'I had a brief word. She's introduced herself to Aleksy. Unfortunately he was still stubbornly silent as of a few minutes ago. I decided to leave them alone for a few minutes in case it was my presence causing him to clam up. They're just next door.'

It was possible Aleksy had a deep mistrust of the police. He wasn't in the country illegally and had no criminal record, so there was no need for him to worry about being deported. Maybe his silence was due to trauma, thanks to his mistreatment at the hands of the Perrys and whoever else they'd been working with.

As Morgan led the way out of the kitchen and into the corridor, Theo said, 'There's a little bell in the entrance area. Ring that if you need to speak to me again. Otherwise, I'll leave you to it.'

He gave them Joe's room number so they could get him after they'd spoken to Aleksy. They thanked him, and Morgan rapped on the door before they entered the communal room.

They'd decided it was better to speak to the men separately. That way they could assess whether their stories matched, and there was also a chance they might not talk freely in front of each other.

It was a large room, with a grand mantelpiece over an empty fireplace. Two sagging beige sofas sat opposite each other near the bay window. Next to a large bookshelf was a worn, dented pine table. Aleksy sat on one side and the translator sat opposite him.

Karen judged Carolina Nowak to be in her fifties. She had the kind of smooth skin that didn't need make-up. There were faint lines around her eyes that crinkled when she smiled.

'Hello,' she said, holding out her hand to Karen.

'Hi, I'm DS Karen Hart. We're hoping to have a chat with Aleksy this morning – with your help, of course.'

Karen and Morgan both pulled up chairs to sit at the table.

Aleksy's hands rested on the table top. His fingers interlinked, he stared stubbornly down at them.

'I hope you had a good night's sleep, Aleksy,' Karen said.

Carolina rapidly translated, but Aleksy didn't reply. He didn't even look up.

This wasn't going to be easy.

Carolina and Aleksy both had mugs of coffee. Carolina's was almost finished, but Aleksy's was untouched.

'Can you tell me why you were staying in the garage belonging to Rod and Patricia Perry, Aleksy?' Karen asked, lowering her head slightly, trying to gain eye contact.

Aleksy's body was rigid. Was he scared?

'You're not under arrest, Aleksy. We just need your help in finding out what went on at The Red Lion.'

Again Carolina translated, but Aleksy said nothing.

Karen sipped her coffee as Morgan tried a variety of approaches to get Aleksy to open up. But he remained sullen and unresponsive.

'I'm sorry to tell you there was a fire at The Red Lion last night,' Morgan said.

Finally, that made Aleksy raise his gaze from the table. He stared at Morgan so intently that Karen felt unnerved, her senses on high alert.

78

'We think perhaps the fire was started deliberately,' she said. 'Do you know anyone who would want to do that?'

Aleksy switched his gaze to Karen, watching her warily as Carolina translated, but still he gave no response. After a further ten minutes of fruitless questioning, they finished up the interview.

Karen suspected something had happened in Aleksy's past that made him reluctant to communicate. He obviously didn't trust the police.

She checked her watch. They'd need to be getting back to talk to Vishal soon. She hoped they'd have more luck with Joe Rowland.

After thanking Carolina for her time and Aleksy for his, Karen went to fetch Joe Rowland. As she was climbing the stairs, she heard footsteps above her.

It was Theo. 'Getting on all right?'

Karen grimaced. 'It could be going better, to be honest.'

'He's still not talking?'

She shook her head. 'Has he said anything to you?'

'No, but . . . Look, if you have a minute, I'd like to show you something.'

Her curiosity piqued, Karen nodded. 'Okay. I was just on my way to get Joe Rowland, to begin his interview.'

'It won't take long,' Theo said. 'But we have to go to the top floor.'

She followed him up the next flight of stairs and into one of the rooms on the second floor that was furnished as an office. Theo walked up to the desk and nudged the mouse of the computer, making the screen light up. 'We have a security camera in the vestibule. Most of the men staying here just want peace and quiet and a chance to get off the streets, but occasionally we have trouble. So it helps to have a camera.'

'Very sensible,' Karen said.

Theo pulled out a chair so she could sit down in front of the computer. 'I looked through the security footage just now and noticed Joe and Aleksy both went out twice last night. Once at eleven, and they came back within forty-five minutes.'

The men weren't under house arrest and were perfectly entitled to come and go as they pleased. There was a risk they'd do a runner, but as both men were legally in the country, and hadn't committed any crimes as far as they knew, the police had no authority to restrict their movements.

Karen watched a fast-forwarded video of Aleksy and Joe walking across the black-and-white tiled hallway and leaving through the front door. 'Well, it seems Aleksy gets on well with Joe. He's choosing to spend time with him.'

'Yes, and they both went out again at two a.m.'

'Two a.m.? Isn't the centre locked at twelve?'

'It used to be. But now we have access cards, we don't tend to physically lock the front door. If any of the men want to leave, they can.' He selected another file and pressed play. It was a video of Joe and Aleksy in the hallway again, but this time the time stamp was 1.50 a.m.

'What I found particularly interesting about this video . . . Well, look, you can see for yourself.'

Karen stared at the screen. 'He's talking.' Although there was no sound on the video, Aleksy's lips were moving and Joe was nodding. It was quite clear that Aleksy was communicating with Joe.

'Yes. I can't lip-read, but I don't think Joe speaks Polish. It suggests Aleksy is pretending he can't understand your questions.'

It certainly looked that way. 'Thanks, Theo. Do you have any idea why they'd leave at two a.m.?'

'No idea. They were gone for almost two hours and returned together. Perhaps a late-night craving for a takeaway?' Theo suggested.

Karen frowned. It certainly didn't take two hours to get a fast-food fix, so what were they doing for all that time? An uneasy thought occurred to her. Were the men involved in the fire? Had they attempted to get revenge on the Perrys by setting fire to the pub?

'I don't want to cause any trouble . . .' Theo said. 'But I thought you should know that Aleksy seems to be capable of communicating when it suits him.'

'Thanks, Theo. That made very interesting viewing.'

They needed a tighter timeline. Grace Baker called to report the fire at ten past three. Canwick was very close to Lincoln. Aleksy and Joe could have reached the pub in about forty minutes, maybe thirty if they were walking fast . . .

Karen exhaled a frustrated breath. This case was growing more complicated by the hour.

CHAPTER TWELVE

Theo went to make a fresh pot of coffee while Karen fetched Joe Rowland. The translator had apologised, telling them she was needed on another job. Karen told her not to worry. It wasn't as though Aleksy was willing to communicate in English *or* Polish.

The security footage weighed heavily on Karen's mind as she walked to his room. All three men had gone through a health assessment last night, and Joe had been highlighted as a case needing specialist attention. Preliminary signs indicated he was suffering from anxiety. It wasn't clear whether the anxiety resulted from his bad treatment at the hands of the Perrys or if it was a long-standing condition. So a referral had been suggested.

Morgan and Karen had agreed that Joe might need help during his interview and a chaperone should be assigned. Theo said he would step in. He had a master's in social care and a diploma in counselling.

Karen knocked on the door of room twenty-two.

After a few seconds, it opened. Joe stared at her for a moment with wide eyes and then blinked, looking confused.

'Hello, Joe. Do you remember me from yesterday? I'm DS Karen Hart. I was hoping you could come downstairs for a chat.'

Joe hesitated and looked over his shoulder, back to the safety of his room.

His room was small with a large sash window and a single bed pushed up against one of the walls, which were painted light blue. There was a blue and grey patterned rug on the vinyl flooring. A small sink stood in the corner with a small mirror above it.

'I hope you slept okay here last night.'

Joe shrugged. 'All right, I suppose.'

Karen gestured towards the stairwell. 'Shall we go downstairs?'

Joe nodded slowly, then shoved his hand in his jeans, which looked several sizes too big for his skinny frame, then he shuffled forwards, closing the door behind him and joining her in the hallway.

Karen headed for the stairs. 'There's nothing to worry about, Joe. We're just going to have a chat with DI Morgan. Theo will be there too.'

He popped a piece of chewing gum in his mouth as he trudged after Karen, who led the way to the communal room.

'Here's DI Morgan. Remember him?' Karen said.

Morgan stood up. 'Hello again, Joe.'

Joe gave Morgan a lopsided smile. 'Hi.'

'Why don't you sit down next to Theo?' Karen pulled out a chair for Joe.

He sat down and rested his hands flat on the pine table.

Karen slid into her seat as Morgan began the interview, keeping his tone light and friendly. 'How long have you been living with the Perrys?'

'Few years,' Joe said. 'Can't remember exactly.'

Joe wasn't sullen and silent like Aleksy, but he wasn't exactly forthcoming with information either. Every line of questioning Morgan tried resulted in a dead end.

'Do you have any family you'd like us to get in touch with?' Karen asked, hoping the change of subject might get him to open up.

Joe lifted his gaze, his pale eyes meeting Karen's. 'My mum. I haven't seen her in a long time.'

'We can reach out to her and see if she'd like to come and visit you, if you'd like that?'

'Yes, please.'

'What's her name, Joe?'

'Linda Rowland.'

'Do you remember her address?' Karen asked. The woman may have moved since the last time Joe had seen her, but the address would give them a starting point.

'Number eight, Magnolia Crescent, North Hykeham.'

Karen made a note of the address as Morgan continued with the questioning.

'Did the Perrys pay you for the work you did for them, Joe?'

Joe shrugged. 'No. They were saving it up for me. I can't be trusted with money.'

'Who told you that?'

'Rod. He said he'd keep it for me, so I didn't waste it. He'd buy me some beers if I'd worked hard, though.'

'Were you happy with that arrangement?'

'What arrangement?'

'The Perrys not paying you the money they owed you?'

Joe rubbed the side of his nose. 'I asked them for it, but they always said no. Rod told me I'd have a room of my own when I worked for them as well as regular money, but . . .' He trailed off and shrugged again.

'How long were you living in the garage?'

'We weren't there all the time. Usually we had the rooms at the back of the pub, but we had to move to the garage whenever they—' He broke off abruptly, apparently realising he'd said too much. A flush spread over his cheeks.

'Whenever they what, Joe?' Morgan asked.

Joe shook his head. 'If they needed the rooms to be cleaned or something.'

Morgan changed tack. 'Were the rooms ever used for other people, Joe? Other workers?'

'I don't know.'

Morgan leaned back in his seat and Karen took over the questioning. 'What type of work did you do for the Perrys?'

'Cleaning or kitchen prep usually.'

'For The Red Lion?'

'Sometimes, or other restaurants or hotels.'

'Do you remember the names of the hotels and restaurants?'

'I'm not allowed to say.' Joe bit his lip.

'Did you work for anyone else, other than the Perrys?'

Joe looked down at the table and didn't answer.

Karen kept up the line of questioning, but Joe was adamant he couldn't give them any names.

'How did you first come into contact with the Perrys?'

'I was at the job centre. Rod was putting up a notice and we got talking. That's when he told me he had a job that would be perfect for me.'

'Did you ever try to leave?'

Joe's expression darkened. 'Yes, I tried to go and visit my mum, but Rod found me at the bus stop. He was very angry. He made me promise to never leave the premises without permission.'

'Were they ever violent?'

'Sometimes,' Joe said in a small voice.

Despite them asking him directly about other men and women he met during his time living under the Perrys' influence, Joe was very vague on the details. Karen wasn't sure whether that was because he was still scared of the Perrys or because he'd mentally blocked out the memories as a coping mechanism. They still didn't have a definite ID for the bodies found in the pub. Though it looked very likely the Perrys were dead and would no longer hold any power over Joe.

As they continued to talk about his day-to-day life, rather than focusing on names and locations, Joe seemed relaxed and comfortable with them, even if he wasn't providing as many details as they'd hoped.

When they informed Joe about the fire, he tensed but otherwise took the news well, and when they changed the direction of the questions, Joe seemed nervous, but not stressed.

'You left the centre twice last night, with Aleksy. Where were you going?' Karen asked.

Joe licked his lips, glanced at Morgan and then Karen, and shrugged. 'We went to get something to eat. We were hungry and decided we would like a kebab.'

He lowered his gaze to the table. His answer sounded rehearsed.

'You went out twice?' Karen asked.

Joe frowned. 'No, we didn't.'

'There's a security camera in the vestibule, Joe. It caught you and Aleksy leaving twice last night, once at around eleven p.m. and the second time at around two a.m.'

Joe lifted his head, his eyes darting around the room anxiously, like he was searching for answers or looking for somebody to help him.

'You're not in any trouble, Joe. We just wanted to know where you and Aleksy went last night. It was quite late.'

Joe wrapped his arms around his middle and leaned forward as though his stomach hurt.

'Are you feeling all right, Joe?' Theo asked, looking at him with concern.

'I just went out to get a kebab.'

Joe was intent on sticking to his story. He didn't want them to know where he and Aleksy had gone last night. It was looking more and more likely that Aleksy and Joe may have been involved in the fire that killed the Perrys.

Karen really didn't want to believe that. Joe was looking tense, but she decided to give it one more shot.

'So you went out for a kebab at eleven?'

'Yes.'

'Then you came back here, and two hours later, you went out again.'

'No . . . I don't know. We just went for a kebab,' he said, his voice rising.

Karen decided it was time to back off when suddenly Joe gave a grunt of anger. He pushed the table away in frustration, and the edge of the wood jammed painfully into Karen's ribs. She pushed back just in time as Joe gripped the edge of the table and lifted it, preparing to flip it over.

Morgan acted quickly, using his weight to manoeuvre the table back to the floor. 'Calm down.'

Theo put a hand on Joe's shoulder. 'Come on, Joe, mate. There's no need for that. Maybe we should take a break.'

Karen rubbed the sore spot on her ribs. 'Yes, I think we'll leave it there for now.'

Joe flopped back into his seat, trembling.

Once Joe had calmed down, Theo walked with them to the front door.

'I'm sorry,' he said. 'I really didn't see that coming. Joe struck me as a gentle bloke.'

'We were pushing him to answer questions on something he clearly didn't want to talk about,' Karen said. 'He didn't want to tell us where he and Aleksy went last night.'

Theo's face creased in a frown. 'Did something happen last night? Do you think Aleksy and Joe got themselves into some kind of trouble? '

Before Karen could reply, Morgan said, 'It's all part of the ongoing investigation.'

Realising they weren't going to provide any further information, Theo shrugged. 'Fair enough. I don't think you should question Joe again until he's had further psychological evaluation. He's had the mandatory health assessment, but I think he needs specialist help.'

'I agree,' Karen said. 'Is that something you can organise?'

'I have a list of approved medical professionals. I can contact one of them. Though if you do manage to get in touch with his mother, she'll know more about his medical history.'

Karen thanked him and then followed Morgan outside.

After Theo closed the door, and they were alone, Morgan said, 'That didn't go as well as I'd hoped. We have one witness who won't communicate and another who is clearly disturbed.'

'We still have Vishal to talk to back at the station,' Karen said, wincing as she turned and felt a sharp pain in her ribs.

'True. You should get that checked out if it's bothering you.'

'It's fine,' she said. 'Just a bruise. I should have moved out of the way faster.'

'I don't see how you could have. I wasn't expecting him to react like that.'

'No, me either. Joe Rowland is more traumatised than we thought. Which is obviously bad news for him, but also bad news for us. He's not going to be much help as a witness.'

Morgan nodded soberly. 'Let's hope Vishal can give us the information we need.'

CHAPTER THIRTEEN

DC Sophie Jones sat up straight behind her desk. Correct posture was so important because her job involved a lot of time sat in front of a computer.

Of course, she'd prefer to be out there on the street, questioning suspects, but over the past few months she'd realised a lot of the important investigative work was actually done at the station.

DC Rick Cooper had teased her constantly since she'd started trying to improve her posture. He said she looked like a puppet on a string. On one occasion he'd used a more obnoxious description, and said she looked like she had a ruler stuck up her backside.

She liked him, but sometimes he could be very irritating. They were both competitive in a friendly way, but Rick had had his nose put out of joint when Karen had trusted Sophie to investigate the history of the three men found in the Perrys' garage.

Recently there had been articles about modern-day slavery cases in the press, and if she was honest, Sophie had to admit she was quite excited about working on one herself. It could be a career-defining case. Perhaps it could lead to an early promotion.

She tapped on the keyboard, bringing up more information about Aleksy Iskow, and quickly read the report.

Interesting. That could be a possible lead, she thought, and made a note.

Behind her, she heard Rick say, 'Morning, Sarge . . . Boss.' When she turned around she saw DS Hart and DI Morgan walking into the open-plan office area.

DI Morgan headed straight for his office, and Karen approached Sophie's desk.

Sophie beamed, tucking her light brown curls behind her ears.

'How are you getting on, Sophie?'

'Quite well,' Sophie said. 'I think you'll be pleased.' She shuffled together the pieces of paper she'd printed out and presented them to Karen.

'Aleksy Iskow was reported missing by a member of staff at the Helping Hand night shelter in Lincoln. The man's name was David Allen. We don't have any pictures or many details, but I thought it might be worth talking to Mr Allen.'

'You're right.' Karen turned. 'Rick, get the address from Sophie. I want you to go and speak to David Allen and find out what he knows about Aleksy Iskow.'

'Sure thing, Sarge,' Rick said with a grin.

Sophie pursed her lips. Rick knew very well she was hoping to follow up this lead herself. She considered protesting and asking Karen if she could go instead, but then she remembered the talk they'd had a little while ago. Karen had reiterated the importance of steady background work. It might not be the most exciting part of policing, but it was essential. And Karen was sure to remember that it was Sophie who had come up with the lead in the first place.

'What about Vishal Salike and Joe Rowland?' Karen asked, pulling over a chair from the desk next to Sophie's and sitting down.

'Nothing on Vishal, I'm afraid. I did check on him this morning. I think he's getting a bit fed up being stuck in the custody suite.

As for Joe Rowland, I got your text message and tracked down his mum. According to the records we have available, she's still living at the same address. I could call her and let her know we found Joe. She reported him missing five years ago.'

Karen smiled. 'Yes, give his mum a ring. Hopefully she'll be very happy to hear from him. We think he might have some mental health problems. Maybe she can tell us if Joe has had previous problems, or whether this is something that has recently developed due to his mistreatment by the Perrys.'

Sophie nodded enthusiastically. 'Absolutely, I can do that.'

She gave Rick a sideways glance as he approached the desk.

He gave her a wide smile in return. 'If you've got that address, Soph, I'll head there now.'

Sophie scribbled the address on a piece of paper and handed it to Rick. Then handed him a printout. 'This is a copy of the original missing persons report David Allen filed.'

'Thanks, see you later,' Rick said cheerfully, and walked away whistling.

Sometimes, he really was unbearable.

He acted like he had no worries in the world, but Sophie knew better. The cheerful laddish front was just that – a front. The carefree, cheeky attitude most people saw hid the real Rick Cooper. He was more sensitive than he let on, but she still found him annoying at times.

'Good work, Sophie,' Karen said, but she sounded distracted, looking in a different direction.

Sophie followed her gaze and saw DI Freeman had entered the office area with DC Shah.

Karen's eyes had narrowed, a small furrow appearing between her eyebrows – the start of a frown – and Sophie shivered. She recognised that look.

It appeared one of them was in Karen's bad books. She'd been on the receiving end of a dressing-down by Karen in the past and was glad it wasn't her earning that look today.

She wondered what they had done to earn Karen's wrath.

'DI Freeman, could I have a word please?' Karen asked after striding up to the officers.

DC Farzana Shah's dark eyes darted to her boss and then she made an excuse to disappear.

'Of course, Karen, what can I do for you?' DI Freeman replied with a smile.

He looked tired. Frank Freeman was in his fifties. He had a pale face with dark red hair, open expressive eyes and a ready smile. He was a good officer and Karen had always got along well with him in the past, which made it harder to understand why he hadn't acted on the warrant last night.

'I suppose you heard about the fire at The Red Lion?'

The smile disappeared from Freeman's face. 'I did. Awful. Three bodies, wasn't it?'

Karen nodded. 'Yes, likely to be Rod and Patricia Perry and their fourteen-year-old son.'

Freeman's face crumpled. 'Horrific.'

'DI Morgan filed a warrant to search the premises yesterday. We thought the search would be initiated last night.'

Freeman tensed. 'I don't like where this conversation is heading, Karen.'

'I just want to understand why the search wasn't actioned.'

DI Freeman sighed heavily. 'That was down to me. I thought it would be fine to wait until the morning. There were problems getting the search team organised so late. Look, I'm juggling a lot of balls right now. I've got a murder case to investigate, I can't do everything. If I could turn back time and action that search, I would. I had no idea it would end up like this.'

He looked like he was genuinely sorry. And he had a point. How was he supposed to know The Red Lion would go up in flames last night? He'd been handed a heavy caseload.

It struck Karen as odd that the superintendent expected DI Freeman to cover everything. He'd certainly got the short straw last night.

'You're right. I know you would never have intended this to happen.'

He ran a weary hand through his short red hair. 'I really thought it would be fine to wait until this morning. It was a judgement call, and I made the wrong one. I can only apologise.'

The search may have only delayed the inevitable. Though they would have had more evidence to bolster their case against the Perrys, Karen was sure someone had wanted the Perrys silenced.

'How are you getting on with the murder enquiry?'

'Not well, I'm afraid.' He shook his head. 'We're doing some door-to-door enquiries around Canwick today. Though I'm not sure anyone would have seen much. We think he was killed in situ, and the area is well hidden from view. We're looking at traffic cameras and hoping someone saw the victim before he went on to the South Common.'

'It sounds like it's going to be a difficult case. Any progress with an ID?'

'The post-mortem isn't taking place until later today. You never know, I suppose, but right now it's looking like our murder victim arrived out of nowhere. What about your case? Any hope of salvaging evidence from the fire? Are the men talking?'

'The pub itself is a wreck. The garage was untouched, though. We haven't got much from the men yet, but it's early days. We're hoping to dig and find how deep this network goes. It's unlikely the Perrys were working alone.'

She was about to mention the fact that a haulage firm in Canwick was seen making regular stops at the pub, but she stopped when DC Shah approached.

'Sorry to interrupt, DI Freeman. You asked me to remind you about the post-mortem. It's nearly time.'

Freeman glanced at his watch. 'Ah, yes. Sorry, Karen. I'd better get going.'

'Sure.'

She watched him leave the office and felt a pang of sympathy. He really did have a lot on his plate at the moment, including trying to identify the murder victim. If she'd been in his position, would she have made the right call? If there weren't enough officers for the search, it made sense to postpone it until the following day.

Every officer thought their case was the most important. They all believed they needed rush jobs in the lab and fast-tracked warrants. She couldn't blame him for not chasing up the search. There was no way he could have known what was going to happen.

She turned to head back to her desk when she realised DC Shah was still watching her. Karen met her gaze with a quizzical glance, and the young officer quickly bowed her head and turned away. Karen sat at her desk and tried to focus, but a tingle at the back of her neck told her she was still being watched. She swivelled in her chair, but Farzana's head was dipped, and she was staring intently at a file on her desk.

CHAPTER FOURTEEN

Karen was deep in thought when DI Morgan came out of his office. 'Ready?' he asked.

'Sorry?'

'Our interview with Vishal?'

'Oh, yes, of course. I'll just get my notes and meet you there. Interview room two, isn't it?'

Morgan frowned. 'Yes.'

Karen rushed back to her desk. She needed to get her act together and not allow herself to be so easily distracted.

Morgan was sitting opposite Vishal when Karen entered the interview room.

She nodded at Morgan and then said, 'Good morning, Vishal. Sorry to keep you waiting.'

Vishal's dark eyes regarded her steadily. 'Good morning,' he said quietly.

'Before we start, you should know you are entitled to legal representation at any point. We are not gathering evidence to charge you with a crime, but because we can't track how you entered the country, border control have been informed.'

Vishal's shoulders slumped and he curled forward, making himself seem even smaller. 'I entered the country legally,' he said with quiet insistence.

'Can you remember where and how you entered the country?' Karen asked.

Vishal shrugged. 'It was a long time ago.'

They'd decided not to push too hard in this direction today. Their priority was finding the people responsible for the worker exploitation. It was likely Vishal, Joe and Aleksy were only the tip of the iceberg.

They could really use Vishal's help to find out more about the people running this operation – since it seemed clear that the Perrys hadn't been working alone.

Morgan had decided not to tell Vishal about the fire until the end of the interview. He didn't want anything to discourage the man from opening up. Vishal might be even more reluctant to talk if he knew the Perrys had been targeted.

It was possible the Perrys had set fire to the property themselves and then were overcome by the fumes and smoke before they could get out of the house, but Karen thought that was unlikely.

It seemed certain that someone else had started that fire. Right now Aleksy and Joe were both suspects. They had a motive – exploited workers out for revenge. But it could also be someone involved in the people trafficking network, silencing the Perrys before they could tell the police anything. The only thing they knew for sure was that Vishal wasn't involved in starting the fire. He'd been in the custody suite all night. The perfect alibi.

'Can you tell us what type of work you used to do for the Perrys?' Morgan asked.

Vishal cleared his throat. 'I used to work in the kitchens and also cleaning jobs sometimes.'

'How long did you work for them?'

'A couple of years. I used to go where they need me. Sometimes at the pub . . . sometimes other places.'

'Did you work for anyone else other than the Perrys?'

Vishal considered the question carefully, staring down at his hands. 'I don't remember.'

'Did you only deal with Rod and Patricia Perry? Or did you have dealings with others during work hours?'

Vishal shrugged. Then he looked up, his dark eyes bright. 'If I talk, does that help me with my case to stay in the UK?'

'It could,' Morgan said, 'but I have to be honest and tell you that I don't have any personal influence over your case.'

Vishal sighed.

'By helping us, Vishal, you'll be helping others who are being forced to live and work in bad conditions,' Karen said. 'What the Perrys were doing wasn't legal. People have a right to be paid a minimum wage.'

Vishal looked at her as though she were stupid. He shook his head. 'It doesn't work like that. Not for someone like me.'

'Who else did you work for, Vishal?'

'Not sure.'

They tried again, but now he remained stubbornly unhelpful. Although he wasn't quite as good at stonewalling them as Aleksy, Vishal only gave short answers to their questions and refused to give them any names.

They needed to build up a level of trust. But they couldn't lie to Vishal and tell him he'd be allowed to stay in the UK if he cooperated with their enquiry, because they didn't know what would happen.

'Let's start at the beginning,' Karen said. 'Where were you born?'

Piece by piece, they managed to extract the bare minimum of information from Vishal. He'd been born in Nepal in 1976. He was open about the place of his birth, and where he'd grown up and the jobs he'd worked. He could remember those details clearly enough.

But when it came to his entry into the UK and the names of people he'd worked for, his good memory disappeared.

◆ ◆ ◆

After parking at the new multi-storey car park near the bus station, DC Rick Cooper made his way to the Helping Hand night hostel in Lincoln. He didn't use the buses much, but in his opinion the new bus station was a vast improvement over the old one.

The night hostel was a non-profit organisation located on Montague Street. The hostel offered safe emergency accommodation for the homeless and had a strict no-drugs-or-alcohol policy.

At eleven a.m. on the dot, Rick rang the bell and stood on the stone step, enjoying the warmth of the sun on his back. The weather forecast was good for the next week or so – that was, if you could ever believe the long-term forecast in England – and the fine weather had put him in a good mood. It was hard not to be cheerful when the sun was shining.

His mum was doing well these days. The consultant had told them her upturn likely wouldn't last very long, so Rick was determined to make the most of it. Maybe he could even take her away for the weekend, somewhere on the coast – maybe Mablethorpe. His mum and dad had taken him and Laura there when they were kids. She might like that, it could possibly even bring back a few good memories.

Perhaps he'd ask Priya if she could go with them. His mum had taken to Priya, her carer, very well, and Rick was rather keen on her, too.

The door buzzed and a distorted voice sounded over the intercom. Rick leaned closer to the box by the door and gave his name.

'Come in,' a crackly voice replied as the door unlocked.

Rick went inside. Ahead of him was a tall man striding along the hallway. The man held out his hand.

'I'm Dave Allen,' he said. 'We spoke on the phone.'

'Thanks for seeing me, Dave,' Rick said. 'I shouldn't take up too much of your time.'

'Not a problem. Come through to the kitchen. Coffee?'

Rick followed him down the corridor. 'No thanks, I just had one.'

The kitchen was long and thin, with white cupboards and worktops. A long, high table ran along one wall and a series of kitchen stools were tucked beneath.

Dave Allen pulled out one of the stools and sat down. Rick did the same.

'How can I help?' Dave asked.

'It's about a chap called Aleksy Iskow.'

Dave nodded. He seemed to brace himself for bad news. 'Is he . . .'

'He's all right,' Rick said, quickly realising what Dave was thinking. 'We think he's been working for some people who have been exploiting homeless and vulnerable individuals.'

Dave let out a relieved sigh. 'To be honest, I thought you were going to tell me you'd found his body.'

'Why do you say that?'

Dave shrugged. 'I'm afraid a lot of the men who stay here have various problems. Aleksy had issues with alcohol. When I first reported him missing, I wondered if he'd drunk himself into a stupor and got into an accident. As time went on, I imagined the worst.'

That was understandable. It also might explain why Aleksy had gone missing last night. If he had a drinking problem, perhaps the drive to find alcohol had sent him out looking for some.

Though that didn't really explain why Joe Rowland had gone with him.

'What can you tell me about Aleksy?'

'He was a regular here. I was trying to help him. We managed to get him a job clearing tables at a coffee shop just around the corner, but it didn't last too long. Unfortunately they know they're not allowed to stay here if they're drunk or on drugs, so often the people I try to help just don't come back. They're ashamed. So they go back to the streets. But with Aleksy, it was different. I really thought he'd turned a corner. That's why I was so surprised when he disappeared. I'm not sure the police took me seriously when I reported him missing.'

'We treat every missing persons report seriously,' Rick said.

Dave gave him a sceptical look. 'I have to admit I didn't get that impression. And truthfully, I thought the drink had taken him. I wasn't expecting him to turn up again. I suppose I was right in a way. He didn't come back here.'

'When did you first meet Aleksy?'

Dave frowned. 'We keep records, the names of men who stay here, at least, the names they give us. We don't check ID or anything like that. I could look and give you a firm date, but I think it was about five years ago. He was here for a good eight months. Then on and off for another three and then he returned almost full-time for another six months.'

'Did you get on well with him?'

'Yes, he's a friendly chap. We used to play cards – not for money, of course, just as a way to pass the time.'

'So you were on good terms? I wonder if you might be able to come and have a chat with him?' Rick asked. 'He might feel more comfortable talking to you.'

'I'd be happy to. Be nice to see him again, actually.'

'Great. Could you make it this afternoon?'

Dave pulled a face. 'I'm afraid not. Sadly for me, I've got a root canal scheduled, but I could do it tomorrow. I'd put the dentist off, but my tooth has been killing me.'

'Tomorrow will be fine,' Rick said, hoping that talking to someone he knew would get Aleksy on side. If Dave could persuade him to confide in them, it might be the first step in gathering some firm evidence against the Perrys and whoever else was involved.

Rick held out his hand. 'Thanks very much for your time, Dave. You've been very helpful.'

Both men stood up.

'Not a problem,' Dave said, leading the way out of the kitchen. 'It'll be really nice to see Aleksy after all this time.'

'It would be fantastic if you could get him to open up. We've had no luck, even with an interpreter.'

Dave turned abruptly before they reached the front door. 'Interpreter?'

Rick nodded. 'Yes, we have a number of people we can call on if we need help translating during interviews.'

Dave frowned and folded his arms over his chest. 'That can't be right.'

'Why do you say that?' Rick asked.

'Because Aleksy speaks English fluently.'

Rick wasn't surprised. This confirmed it wasn't a language barrier that stood in the way. He simply didn't want to talk to them because he was either afraid or hiding something. And that problem couldn't be solved by bringing in a translator.

He could only hope that Dave Allen would manage to get Aleksy to talk. Maybe he'd succeed where the police had failed.

CHAPTER FIFTEEN

Sophie put the phone down and smiled with satisfaction. It wasn't often in this line of work she managed to deliver *good* news to relatives. Joe Rowland's mother had been moved to the point of tears when Sophie told her they'd found her son. She couldn't wait to be reunited with him and thanked Sophie profusely when she arranged for Linda to visit Joe at the centre later that day.

She'd been on a high after the phone call and had launched straight into attempting to reconnect Aleksy Iskow with his family, too. He'd been reported missing by his daughter Lucja, who lived in Poland. Lucja had also been overjoyed to learn her father had been found.

All in all it had been a very satisfying morning's work. She'd acted on her own initiative and the outcome couldn't have been better. She grinned as she tidied the papers on her desk, imagining just how impressed Karen would be when she told her the news. On days like today, she loved her job.

When Karen returned to the office, flipping through paperwork as she walked, Sophie stood up to get her attention. 'Sarge?'

Karen looked up and then headed over to Sophie's desk. 'Everything all right?'

Sophie beamed. 'Yes. Joe Rowland's mother can't wait to see him again. They're going to be reunited later this afternoon at the centre.'

Karen smiled. 'That's good news.'

Sophie sat down and leaned back in her chair, her smile widening. 'While I was on a roll, I decided to contact Aleksy's family too. His daughter reported him missing three years ago after he stopped contacting her. She's over the moon. She was crying tears of joy when I spoke to her.'

The smile slipped from Karen's face, and Sophie shifted uncomfortably. Had she done the wrong thing?

'She was really pleased . . .'

Karen sighed and pulled over a chair to sit down beside Sophie. 'I'd asked Joe's permission to contact his mum. He said he was happy to see her. I know Aleksy went missing, and you'd like to bring the family back together for a happy reunion. But he might not want that. We really should have asked his permission before contacting his family.'

Sophie's face fell. She'd messed up, but she'd only wanted to help.

Running a hand through her brown curls, she looked miserably at Karen. 'What should I do? Should I contact her again . . . ?'

Karen shook her head. 'Look, it was an error, but your heart was in the right place. I know you're trying to be helpful. But in cases like these you need to be sensitive. When people leave their families and their old lives behind, there's often a reason.'

Sophie swallowed hard. 'Why did Aleksy leave his family?'

'That's just it, I don't know. And until he starts talking to us, we're unlikely to find out.'

Sophie put her fingertips to her temples, to massage away the tension headache that had started to build. A moment ago, she'd been feeling on top of the world. 'So what can I do to make it right?'

'Aleksy might be happy to get in contact with his daughter again. It might even encourage him to open up to us, so don't be too hard on yourself. Rick has asked David Allen to pay Aleksy a visit tomorrow, so once we get Aleksy talking, we can ask him about his family. Hopefully he'll be happy to be back in touch with his daughter.'

Sophie nodded dejectedly. 'Right. Sorry.'

Karen stood and put a hand on her shoulder. She was about to say something when Harinder walked into the main office. He scanned the room and then his gaze fixed on Karen.

Still feeling slightly miserable, Sophie couldn't even manage a smile for the handsome tech analyst. Not that it mattered. He barely noticed her.

'Karen, can I have a word?' Harinder asked. His normal charming, easy smile was missing.

'Of course.' Karen followed him out of the office, presumably to go to the technical department.

Sophie watched them leave, tapping the end of her pen on the notebook in front of her.

Harinder had seemed very serious. Had he discovered something important about the case they were working on? If so, why hadn't he shared the information with her?

She couldn't help feeling a little put out.

She glanced over at Rick's empty desk, wondering what time he'd get back. If he were here, he would have been invited to the tech department, too. He had more experience than Sophie, who was always given the mundane jobs. She was tempted to make an excuse to go downstairs and see if she could eavesdrop on their conversation, but she gave herself a mental shake.

For goodness' sake. She wouldn't get anywhere like this. She'd already messed up once today. Karen was going to get tired of her if she didn't knuckle down and stop making such basic mistakes.

'This is all very cryptic, Harinder,' Karen said as they left the main office and headed to the lab.

Harinder smiled. 'Sorry. There's a piece of evidence from DI Freeman's case I thought you might find interesting. I know you're not working the murder any more . . .'

'I'm intrigued.'

Harinder held open the door for Karen to enter the lab ahead of him.

'It's on the bench.' He pointed to the long white workbench in the centre of the room.

'The notebook?' Karen asked.

An A4-sized navy-blue notebook sat on a tray in the middle of the bench. It looked old and well thumbed. It had a hardback cover coated in dirt and grime.

'Yes. It was found buried not far from the murder victim.'

'Are you sure it's linked to the case?' Karen asked, her mind wandering back to the man they'd found on Canwick Hill. His fingers had been caked with mud, and earth had been embedded under his fingernails. Had he buried the notebook? Is that why he'd been scratching around in the dirt?

'The victim's fingerprints are all over it. He definitely handled it at one point.'

Karen frowned. 'Why would he bury it?'

Harinder shrugged. 'Maybe he was trying to hide it from someone.'

'Yes, I suppose that's the only thing that makes sense. Are you any closer to identifying the victim?'

'Unfortunately not. His fingerprints and DNA aren't in the database . . .' He let out a long breath and shifted his weight from foot to foot.

'Out with it, Harry. There's obviously something else you want to tell me.'

'Not exactly . . . I just wondered if DI Freeman or DC Shah had told you about the book.'

'No, they didn't. I spoke to DI Freeman this morning, but he didn't mention it. Why?'

'It's strange. I would have thought they'd want to involve you. I'm no detective but—'

Karen finished his sentence for him. 'But when you've got a dead body with a beer mat from The Red Lion, along with what looks like a modern slavery ring centred at the same pub, the cases are likely linked.'

Harinder met Karen's gaze and nodded. 'Well, yeah.'

'I agree.'

'I asked DC Shah about it this morning, but she said DI Freeman dismissed the link as tenuous. Anyway, I'm sure they would have told you about it eventually. I just thought you might like to see it.'

Some police officers could be notoriously tight-lipped when it came to their cases, but Frank Freeman was generous and open, usually willing to share information and help colleagues out whenever he could. Why hadn't he mentioned this? Tenuous or not, it was still a link.

Harinder was watching her carefully, waiting for her reaction. He'd thought it was odd that Freeman hadn't passed on the information, too.

'I know DI Freeman is incredibly busy at the moment,' Karen said. She wasn't going to make a big deal over this until she had all the facts and had spoken to Freeman. 'He was probably going to tell me about it later.'

'Yes, probably.'

'Any clues inside?' she asked, not wanting to touch the notebook and contaminate the evidence.

'Yes, it's already been processed.' Harinder pulled on a pair of tight blue vinyl gloves and opened the book. 'There's a table, a list of dates, and payment amounts with some kind of code or codename next to each one. I wondered if it's a record of payment for illegal activity.'

Karen looked at the list. 'No real names though. Shame. That would have made our job much easier.'

At first glance, she couldn't make sense of any of the codes, but the book could be a crucial piece of information for the case if they could work out what these payments were for.

'Thanks for coming to me so quickly, Harinder. I think this could be really important.' She gave a wry smile. 'That is, if we can make sense of the codenames. Could you copy the pages for me, so I can take a proper look and give a copy to DI Morgan?'

Harinder smiled. 'I thought you'd ask for that. I've already scanned it. I'll email you and DI Morgan a copy.'

Karen focused on the pages again, her eyes scanning the codes. 'Thanks again, Harry. If you have any clever ideas as to what these codenames mean or how we could link them to real people, come to me straightaway.'

'Will do. Happy to help.'

Back upstairs, on her way to speak to Morgan and tell him about the notebook, Karen spotted DI Freeman leaning over DC Shah's desk, shuffling through some paperwork. 'Frank?'

He looked startled and put the paperwork down quickly. Pushing it to one side, he turned around. 'Yes?'

He wore his usual friendly smile. Karen wasn't sure if it was her imagination, or if she could detect an element of guilt in his expression.

She glanced down at the papers, but he shoved them behind his back and shifted his position, blocking Karen's view. 'Everything all right?' he asked.

'Yes. I've just been down to see Harinder in the lab. He told me about the notebook found buried on the South Common.'

He looked harassed as he ran a hand through his short red hair. 'Yes, the notebook. I was going to tell you and DI Morgan about that. Sorry, things have been a bit manic.'

Karen's suspicions began to ebb away. She was reading too much into the situation. Frank Freeman was one of the officers Karen had always got on well with. He'd proved himself trustworthy. He had a lot on his plate at the moment so it was understandable he hadn't had time to share the development with them yet.

'Have you managed to make any sense of the contents yet? It looked like some kind of payment schedule.'

Freeman sighed and shook his head. 'No, not yet sadly. It's all gobbledygook to me.'

'We've got a few visits to do this afternoon,' Karen said, 'but I'll take another look and see if I can make sense of it.'

Freeman smiled. 'I appreciate that, but don't let me take you away from your own case. I know you're busy. I think the superintendent believes we each have three brains, eight legs and ten arms.'

Karen smiled. The superintendent did have high expectations. 'It's strange that he buried it there. I presume you're thinking he was hiding it from someone?'

'I can't think of another reason why he'd bury it. I'll be honest, Karen, this case has me stumped at the moment.'

'I think there's a chance the murder is linked to our current case – payment for people trafficking perhaps, or payment for low-paid staff? It makes sense to keep the records on paper rather than on computer, so it's harder for us to track them.'

Freeman frowned. 'I considered the possibility, but it's not really a strong connection, is it, Karen? I mean, the murder happened close to The Red Lion, but the only real link between the pub and our murder victim is the beer mat in his pocket. It's not exactly conclusive evidence.'

Karen thought about arguing the point, but she decided better of it. Freeman was experienced, and she was sure he wouldn't rule anything out without a proper investigation.

'Keep me updated if you do find out what those codenames mean,' Karen said.

'Of course,' he said, but he was looking past Karen now. His body stiffened, then he eased himself up from where he'd been perched on the side of DC Shah's desk.

Karen turned to see Farzana Shah marching towards them. She looked at her boss, and then her eyes travelled down to the paperwork then back up to him. She didn't even glance at Karen.

'The superintendent would like a word, sir.'

'Right.' He turned to Karen. 'Sorry, I'd better go. I'll keep you updated.'

After Freeman had rushed out of the office, Karen turned to DC Shah, who was carefully going through the papers on her desk.

'Everything all right?'

She looked up, distracted, as though she'd only just realised Karen was still there. 'Yes, fine. Just a bit busy at the moment. Everything okay with you?'

She'd asked a question, but Karen wasn't certain she expected an answer, because she'd already turned her attention back to the papers.

'Got a minute?' Karen asked, sticking her head around DI Morgan's open office door.

He checked his watch. 'Yes, though I'm thinking of heading out. I thought we should visit the haulage yard on Hectare Lane. If

Grace Baker is right, and the owners or possibly some of the HGV drivers are involved in the transportation of people, it's best we talk to them today.'

'I agree. But before we go, I've just spoken to Harinder. A notebook was found on the South Common, buried a short distance away from the murder victim. The book has the victim's fingerprints all over it.'

Interest sparked in Morgan's eyes. 'What was in the notebook?'

'It looks like dates, payment amounts and codenames of some sort. Harinder's sending us both a copy of the scanned pages.'

Morgan reached for the mouse on his desk and clicked 'Refresh' on his email.

Karen moved behind his desk as he opened Harinder's email and clicked on the image files. 'I think the notebook relates to what was going on at The Red Lion, but I'm not sure how we can identify people from the codenames. There are no bank account numbers.'

Morgan pointed at the screen. 'These names are under a column headed 999. That's interesting.'

'I wonder if it's a list of police officers taking bribes?'

The suggestion left Karen's mouth before she thought to censor it. Her colleagues were aware of her previous claims of a cover-up after the accident. She'd sensed they were waiting for her to come up with conspiracy theories again and spiral out of control.

Morgan frowned. 'Yes, possibly, or it could be contacts only to be used in emergencies? Why would they be writing this stuff down in a notebook?'

'It can't be hacked, and it's easy to dispose of if things go wrong. It's hard to wipe a computer completely; much easier to burn a notebook.'

Morgan nodded thoughtfully, and then his eyes narrowed as he stared at the computer screen.

'What is it? Have you figured out the codes?' Karen peered at the screen hopefully, but she couldn't make any sense of it.

He continued to stare at the screen intently and didn't reply straightaway.

'No,' he said eventually. 'I thought one of the codenames looked familiar, but I have no idea what it all means.' He closed the file and shut down his computer. 'Let's head to the haulage company. We can take another look at this later.'

CHAPTER SIXTEEN

As DI Morgan drove from Nettleham to Canwick, he was deep in thought – not in the mood for conversation. Thankfully, Karen seemed to be content with her own thoughts as she gazed out of the passenger window. That was just one of the many reasons they worked well together. He could relax and be himself, without worrying about fending off questions and inane small talk. It was quite different when he took a journey with Sophie or Rick.

Rick could talk for England. He was always chatting away about random facts, or the football game he'd watched the previous night, or the type of car he wanted, or even commentary on the pedestrians they passed during the journey.

And Sophie . . . Well, Morgan had actively started to avoid being in a car with Sophie for any length of time.

At the station, it was different. He could shut his door if he needed peace and quiet to mull over a case. But in the car there was no escape. Her questions were endless. It was a bit mean. Sophie was eager to learn and hard-working, but at times her enthusiasm wore him out.

The drive from Nettleham took twenty minutes. They had to travel through the centre of Lincoln, but the traffic wasn't too bad considering it was just after lunch. The journey gave him time to think, but it wasn't long enough to reach a conclusion.

He'd been shocked when he'd viewed the list of codenames scanned from the notebook because one seemed familiar.

Rameses1979.

Alarm bells had rung when his gaze reached the name, but a few seconds had passed before he remembered where he'd seen it before.

Rob Miller had used that name on an old police internet forum. He'd once told Morgan he used the moniker because his teammates on the five-a-side football squad had called him 'The Ram'. He said it was short for Rameses, but Morgan suspected he'd got the label due to his tendency to ram people out of his way on the pitch, much the same as he did in life. In his conceit, Rob had probably made up the Rameses bit himself, liking the idea of comparing himself to an all-powerful Egyptian pharaoh.

What were the chances that someone else would be calling themselves Rameses and following the name with the exact same digits – the year of Rob Miller's birth? It was an obscure name, but not that obscure. No doubt there were a few people using Rameses for usernames for various things on the internet. Perhaps it wasn't as distinctive as he'd first thought. Besides, why would Rob have his codename in the notebook?

Rob Miller had been Scott's old boss when he'd worked in the Thames Valley. He wasn't a pleasant person, and if Morgan was going to suspect anyone of being corrupt, Rob would be pretty high up the list.

That said, he couldn't jump to conclusions. He'd warned Karen about that before.

When she'd mentioned the lines of code words beneath the heading *999* as representing police officers involved in corruption, he'd played it down. Not because it wasn't a sensible idea, but because he knew a little of what Karen had been through over the past five years.

Other officers talked, and the superintendent had filled in the blanks for him. Karen herself had told him about the death of her husband and daughter and how she'd struggled to come to terms with the fact it had only been an accident.

The superintendent had told him about Karen's prior obsession with the idea that the officers investigating the accident were covering something up. The Karen he knew was sensible and pragmatic. Yes, she went with her gut more often than Morgan would without solid evidence, but she wasn't reckless. She wasn't a loose cannon. Despite that, the superintendent's words rang in his mind.

Come to me if you think Karen is having any problems.

He shot a sideways glance at Karen, who was still staring out of the window, lost in thought. She seemed fine to him. He'd been about to tell her about Rob Miller's old forum handle, but had held back, not wanting to add fuel to a potential fire.

Once they'd passed the cemetery and the petrol station, Morgan said, 'The turning to Hectare Lane is coming up soon, isn't it?'

Karen blinked. 'Oh, yes, sorry. It's the next turning.'

Morgan indicated and turned left. It was a narrow road – more of a country lane. It was covered with tarmac, but large potholes pitted the surface and the tarmac crumbled at the edges. Probably thanks to the HGVs regularly travelling back and forth.

There were only a few houses dotted along the right-hand side of the lane, each with a neat garden. On the left were fields.

'Not much here,' Morgan said, surprised at how quiet it was now they'd left the B road.

'It's a quiet village.'

The B1188 cut Canwick village off from the Premier Inn, The Red Lion and the International Bomber Command Centre. It was peaceful, and for a village so close to Lincoln, surprisingly countrified.

Morgan slowed as the car juddered over some potholes. Ahead of them loomed a large white sign with blue writing. *Cook's Haulage.*

'This is it,' Karen said. 'We might want to talk to the people who live in the houses along the lane, too. They might have seen something.'

'It's worth a try,' Morgan said, thinking that if the owners of the haulage company were smart, they would never bring anything incriminating back here. They'd dump people at places like The Red Lion, making sure there was no evidence at the property they owned.

The large, rusted iron gates at the front of the property had been propped open with heavy pieces of wood. Morgan drove through the gates and into the yard.

Containers were lined up at the far side of the yard and there were three lorries parked close to the small, squat, red-brick building, which he imagined was the hub of the operation. A large Alsatian patrolled the side of the building behind a wire fence. It barked as they got out of the car.

Before they were able to take a single step, a man in blue overalls appeared from behind one of the lorries. He had black grease marks down the front of both legs.

'Can I help you?' he asked, suspicion lacing his tone.

'DI Morgan and DS Hart of the Lincolnshire Police,' Morgan said, holding up his ID.

Karen did the same.

The man paused a few feet away from them and folded his arms over his chest. 'What brings you here?'

'We're hoping to speak to the owner.'

'That's Eric. He's in the office.' The man jerked his thumb in the direction of the building.

'What's your name?' Karen asked.

'Terry Kidd.'

'Do you drive these?' she asked, gesturing to the parked HGVs.

'No.' He shook his head. 'Not me. I don't drive them, I just maintain them.' After giving them another assessing stare, he said, 'I'll take you to see the gaffer.'

Morgan detected a London accent and wondered what had brought Terry up to Lincolnshire. Usually it was the other way around. There was more work in the south-east than there was up here.

But the fact he was from London wasn't necessarily suspicious. After all, Morgan had moved to Lincolnshire from the south-east, craving a change.

They followed Terry into the building. The door was white UPVC and the bottom was covered with black marks. Inside, the floor was covered with dark-grey nylon carpet tiles. Morgan judged the walls along the entrance hall to be merely partitions, almost as thin as single-width plasterboard. He wondered whether this had originally been a residential property, converted by the Cooks for their business.

Terry led them into a large office that smelled of stale coffee.

A short, bulky man sitting behind the desk looked up. He had a ruddy face and a low brow, which gave him a stern appearance. He ran his hand through his thick, dark hair as his eyes narrowed at the interruption. He held a wad of paper in one hand and clutched a Biro in the other.

'Sorry to trouble you, boss,' Terry said. 'We've got two police officers wanting a word.' He turned to Karen and Morgan. 'I'll leave you to it.'

After Terry had left the room, Eric leaned heavily on the desk and pushed himself up. Though he was a short man he was powerfully built, with wide shoulders and thick arms. He hitched up his trousers and walked around the desk, holding his hand out.

'Eric Cook. How can I help you, officers?'

They introduced themselves, and Eric invited them to sit down. As they all took a seat, Morgan explained the purpose of their visit.

Eric listened patiently with his fingers interlinked and his hands resting on the desk.

When Morgan finished talking, he said, 'I'm sorry, but I can't help you. I didn't know the Perrys. I've popped into The Red Lion once or twice for a pint or two, but I wouldn't recognise them if I passed them on the street.'

Morgan studied the man's ruddy face and watery brown eyes but couldn't see any evidence that he was hiding the truth.

'Is this a family business?' Karen asked.

Eric grinned. 'It is. It's me and my son Charlie who run the place. Well, mostly me. I'm hoping Charlie will take over one day, though.'

'Is Charlie around? I'd like to ask him if he knew the Perrys.'

Eric grimaced and shook his head. 'No, sorry. He's gone away for a few days. He tells me he's working on getting us a new contract. But I'll believe that when I see it.' He rolled his eyes and chuckled.

'We have a witness who believes your heavy goods vehicles have been stopping at The Red Lion in the early hours of the morning.'

Eric frowned and scratched his head. 'Who said that?'

'I'm afraid we can't tell you that, Mr Cook.'

'Call me Eric. Well, all I can say is your witness must be mistaken as far as I know. I mean, there's a possibility one of the drivers might stop at the pub for a spot of dinner, but I'm not sure why they'd stop so close to the haulage yard when they could come here, get paid and go home.'

'So it's possible one or more of the drivers have stopped there?'

'Well, I suppose I can't rule it out. But I can't see why they would, especially not in the early hours.'

'Could we talk to the drivers?' Morgan asked.

'Of course you can, Detective. Feel free. There's no one here at the yard right now, but I'd be happy to give you names and contact details of all of my drivers. I heard about the fire. Horrible business. You're thinking arson?'

'We're still waiting for the fire officer's report.'

'Canwick's usually such a safe place.' Eric gave a low whistle and shook his head. 'Sorry I couldn't be more help. You're welcome to take a look around the yard if you like . . . I know you don't get much thanks in your line of work, so if there's anything I can do to make this investigation go more smoothly, just let me know.'

Morgan shook Eric's hand.

Eric Cook was being very open and very helpful. That either meant the man had absolutely nothing to hide or – perhaps more likely – he knew they wouldn't find anything here because he'd been extremely careful to cover his tracks.

Eric asked Terry to escort them around the haulage yard. Terry even showed them the two bedrooms in the building that were made up for the drivers. He said they were there in case the drivers 'needed a kip before heading home. Safety first. Drivers are only allowed to be on the road a certain length of time before they have to take a break. Eric is a good boss. He lets them stay the night before if they need to. We have drivers based all over the country.'

It was a very detailed tour, with Terry determined to show them every inch of the haulage yard, and there was nothing to indicate Eric Cook was involved in anything illegal.

'Very friendly and helpful, weren't they?' Karen asked dryly as they got back into Morgan's car.

He smiled. 'I suppose you're thinking what I am.'

'That they were far too helpful.'

'Exactly. Makes me think they were hiding something. Tell you what, after we speak to the residents on Hectare Lane, why don't we go and have a word with Grace Baker again? Let's see how certain she is that the lorries she saw at The Red Lion were from this haulage yard.'

CHAPTER SEVENTEEN

Apart from a few general grumbles about noise and vibrations from the HGVs travelling along the lane at all hours, Morgan and Karen didn't get much out of the residents they visited on Hectare Lane. Hoping to have more luck with Grace Baker, they left the village and pulled on to the main road.

Morgan parked behind Grace's blue Fiesta on the drive. As they got out of the car, a grey squirrel scampered across the stone driveway, across the lawn and then up on to the bird table beside the crab-apple tree, where it began helping itself to the nuts and seeds Grace had left out for birds.

'Cheeky thing,' Karen said. 'I've got holes all over my lawn thanks to grey squirrels.'

'I don't have that problem,' Morgan said with a grin. The garden at the front of his house had been converted into a driveway, and the small square rear garden had been paved over. Though Karen loved her big garden, she envied Morgan his freedom from the lawnmower.

Grace opened the door, and her eyes widened when she saw Karen and Morgan standing on the doorstep.

'Oh, hello again,' she said to Karen. 'I wasn't expecting to see you so soon.'

Karen introduced DI Morgan and then said, 'We have a few more questions for you, Grace. Is now a convenient time?'

Grace opened the door. 'Of course, come in. I wanted to ask how the investigation's going. I've heard some terrible rumours.'

'Unfortunately we can't say much about that yet. The investigation is still ongoing.'

'Oh, I see. Well, come in. I was about to make a pot of tea, if you'd like a cup?'

Karen and Morgan said they would, and Grace led them through to the living room, where Karen made a fuss over Dolly, who purred and rubbed her cheek against her hand.

When Grace returned with a pot of tea and a plate piled high with custard creams, she was full of more questions.

'Have you talked to that lot at the haulage yard? I'm sure they're involved, you know. It's not normal. They do it in the middle of the night, so nobody sees. But they didn't expect me, with my insomnia, to be there at the window watching them, did they?'

'Actually, Grace, we did have a word with the owner of the haulage yard. We didn't mention your name, of course, but we did tell them their vehicles had been seen at The Red Lion.'

Grace sat down in an armchair and gave a satisfied smile. 'And what did the owner have to say for himself?'

'He denied it. He said to his knowledge none of his lorries made stops at The Red Lion.'

Grace's forehead puckered in a frown, then she said, 'Well, I suppose he would say that. He was hardly likely to come right out and admit it, was he? If all criminals did that, you'd be out of a job.'

'Quite,' Morgan said. 'It must be difficult to see The Red Lion car park clearly from here. Is it possible you made a mistake?'

Grace bristled with irritation. She put her cup and saucer on the coffee table and looked at Morgan. 'I did *not* make a mistake.'

'Is it possible the lorries were from another haulage yard, Grace?' Karen asked. 'There are a few in the area.'

'No. Because the others don't have that blue colouring, and they don't have *Cook's Haulage* plastered on the side in white letters. I'm not daft, you know.'

'We have to double-check these things, Grace, and make sure you're absolutely positive they were from Cook's Haulage. We really appreciate your help.'

Grace settled back in her armchair, seemingly mollified. 'I suppose you do have to be thorough in your investigation.'

'Yes,' Morgan said. 'I don't suppose you made a note of the exact dates and times the lorries stopped at The Red Lion?'

Grace's face fell. 'No. I gave DS Hart estimates, but I didn't think to do that. But . . .' She suddenly brightened. 'Wait here! I'll be right back.'

When Grace left the room, Morgan and Karen exchanged a quizzical look.

'What's this all about?' he asked.

'I have no idea.' Karen reached for a custard cream.

A minute later, Grace returned, holding a small camera. 'Now, it's not the best quality because it was at night. This is my late husband's camera. I haven't used it much, but I tried to record a video of them.'

She turned the camera around so they could see the square screen on the back and pressed the button on the top right. The video began to play.

At first it looked like an out-of-focus shot of the rooftops of the Premier Inn hotel, but then the image zoomed in on the space between the buildings, focusing on a section of The Red Lion's car park. As Grace had said, there was a lorry with a blue container on the back.

There were a few figures around the lorry, but the video was shaky and blurred. There was no clear view of the number plate either. Harinder might be able to do something with it – sharpen the image or improve the resolution somehow. He could work magic with electronic media.

'I don't know if you can see the lettering clearly there, but I saw it from another angle, and it definitely said *Cook's Haulage*,' Grace said proudly.

'Do you know, I think it does,' Karen said, focusing on the slightly blurry letters on the side of the lorry. 'Well done, Grace. That's incredibly helpful. Could you send me a copy of the video? If you still have my card, it's got my email address.'

Grace frowned. 'I'm afraid I don't know how to do that. Like I said . . . it's my husband's camera, and, well . . .' She shrugged.

'May I?' Morgan asked, and he held his hand out for the camera.

Grace gave it to him.

'It looks like the data is on an SD card.' He released the small black plastic square from the camera. 'With your permission, Grace, I'd like to take this so we can make a copy of the video. We'll return the SD card as soon as we're finished with it. We shouldn't need to hang on to it for too long.'

'Of course,' Grace said. 'Happy to help. You can keep it as long as you need.'

◆ ◆ ◆

By the time they got back to the station, Eric Cook had sent through the list with his drivers' contact details, as promised. Karen would need to go through and speak to each driver. There were over twenty of them, so she'd need to make a start on that soon. But her first task was to touch base with Rick and Sophie. Both were sitting at their desks, heads bent over paperwork.

'Sophie, how are you getting along with the background research into Cook's Haulage?'

Sophie looked up, her cheeks flushed. 'I'm still working on it. Eric Cook is a widower. He only has one son – Charlie Cook, who is married to Meghan Cook. They live in a large house in Blankney. Eric lives in Ruskington now. He used to live in Canwick, in a fancy house that backed on to the golf course.'

'They've closed the golf course now, haven't they?' Rick asked.

'Yes, I think I read something about that,' Karen said.

'It's going into administration, I think. Shame.'

Sophie frowned at Rick's interruption. 'Anyway, as I was saying, Eric's a widower. His only other living relative, apart from his son and daughter-in-law, is his brother, Harry Cook – who, interestingly, operates a haulage company in Shinfield, Berkshire.'

'Now that is very interesting,' Karen said. 'Does Harry Cook have a family?'

'He's a bachelor, never married, no children. From what I can find out online, it seems Harry Cook's yard is bigger than Eric's. I've got the address here. You can see the size of it from the satellite map.' She handed Karen a printout.

'Good work, Sophie. Continue looking into the Cooks. I think we might be on to something with them. I'm sure they're involved in this somehow.'

Sophie's cheeks dimpled at the praise.

'How about you, Rick? How did you get on with the chap who reported Aleksy missing?'

'Pretty well. Dave Allen was helpful. He's agreed to come and meet Aleksy tomorrow. Apparently they had a pretty good relationship. And – this is interesting – he said Aleksy spoke extremely good English. So his refusing to communicate with us is not due to the language barrier.'

'Good to have that confirmed. Perhaps Dave can help us get Aleksy to open up a bit. If you've got time, give Sophie a hand with the background research into the Cooks. I'm particularly interested to see if they've had any run-ins with border control in the past. I'm going to spend the afternoon on the phone, talking to drivers working for Cook's Haulage.'

'Will do, Sarge,' Rick said.

'Good work, both of you.'

Karen walked over to her own desk. Despite not getting anywhere with Aleksy, they were now making some progress on the case. If the Perrys had been working with the Cooks to traffic and exploit vulnerable individuals, Karen was determined to find the evidence to prove it.

CHAPTER EIGHTEEN

At nine p.m. Grace Baker parked her Fiesta on the drive and lifted her shopping bags from the back seat.

She'd spent the early evening cleaning and hadn't intended to go out this evening, but she was running low on teabags. Besides, sitting alone in the house with nothing to do but think about the arson at The Red Lion was sending her stir-crazy, so she'd decided to go to Waitrose and stock up on a few things.

She'd bought a ready meal for her dinner – paella – something she never did when her husband was alive. Then she had enjoyed cooking, but now it was only her and it seemed such an effort to prepare meals from scratch. Besides, she'd checked the nutritional information and the fat content wasn't too high, so it couldn't be that unhealthy, could it? She'd also bought a bag of salad to accompany it, so surely that would make the meal practically healthy.

With the shopping bags looped over her arms, she took a deep breath, inhaling the fresh green scent of the garden. One of her neighbours must have been mowing the lawn, because the smell of freshly cut grass was heavy in the air. The sun had almost disappeared, the last of its glow tinting the clouds a dusky pink. She enjoyed this time of year, when the evenings were getting longer. Listening to the shrill alarm calls of the blackbirds as they darted into the hedge, Grace selected her front door key.

She held up the key to the lock, but her arm dropped to her side when she realised the door was already open.

How strange. Had she not shut the door behind her when she'd left? That was very unlike her. The front door locked automatically when it was shut, but it was possible the door hadn't clicked into place.

She peered into the hall and noticed the kitchen door was wide open. Something was definitely wrong. To keep Dolly away from the freshly washed kitchen floor, she'd shut it before she'd left to go to the shop.

Grace's heart began to beat double-time. Someone had broken in. *Dolly!*

Trembling, she stood in the doorway and called out, 'I've called the police!'

No sounds from inside. Had the burglar left? She should go next door, ask them to call the police, but Dolly . . . What if the cat was hurt?

She rushed inside, dumped the bags on the doormat and called out for her cat. But what she saw at the end of the hallway made her freeze.

There was a line of small paw prints – bright red, the colour of blood.

No! Grace ran towards the kitchen, breathless and terrified. 'Dolly? Where are you?'

She would normally wait for Grace at the front door when she heard her return. What could have happened? Had somebody hurt Dolly?

When Grace ran into the kitchen, she let out a gasp. In the middle of the room, pooling over the tiles, was a puddle of bright red liquid. Dolly sat beside it, sniffing the liquid and tapping it with her paw.

'Dolly, no, don't do that! Are you hurt?'

Grace patted the cat all over, looking for injuries, but she seemed to be completely unharmed. She scooped the cat up, clutching her against her chest, not caring that some of the bright red liquid transferred from Dolly's paws on to her blouse.

Breathing rapidly, she edged her way cautiously around the puddle, not wanting to get anywhere near it.

She was almost out of the kitchen and back into the hallway when she noticed the table top. There, crudely written in large letters in the same red liquid, was a single word.

Grass.

Grace was so shocked that she loosened her grip on Dolly, and the Burmese squirmed out of her arms, jumping to the floor and racing for the stairs.

'No!' Grace shouted, coming to her senses.

Whoever had written that word on the table could still be here. They could be lurking upstairs. She'd always felt safe in her chalet bungalow, but today it felt like a house of horrors. She wanted to run, to leave and drive as far away as she could, but she couldn't do that without Dolly.

Mouth sour with fear, her blouse sticking to her torso from sweat and the red liquid from Dolly's paws, she slowly made her way up the stairs.

Please, don't let anyone be hiding up there . . .

'Dolly,' she hissed. 'Come here.'

The cat ignored her. Why had Dolly gone upstairs? Had she heard something? Smelled something? A cat's senses were sharper than a human's.

Grace's body was shaking as she took the final step and looked around the hall. Everything seemed normal. The door in front of her which led to the bathroom was shut. Just as she had left it. The doors to the bedrooms were open. She crept towards the nearest room, cringing as the floorboards creaked beneath her feet.

Slowly, her hands gripped into fists, she walked into the room.

She let out a rushed breath of relief when she saw Dolly curled up in the centre of the bed. 'Oh, thank goodness.'

Taking a quick glance around the room to make sure she was alone, she decided it was safe. She grabbed Dolly and, without bothering to take anything else, headed downstairs.

The shopping was still on the floor, but Grace walked straight past it, only pausing to grab her handbag and keys. She slammed the front door behind her and ran towards the car.

With Dolly safely in the back, she got behind the wheel, locked all the doors and then buckled her seatbelt. She reversed, pressing the accelerator so hard that the wheels spun on the stones.

She pulled out in front of a taxi on the B1188. Waving her hand in apology at the driver's angry blast on the horn, Grace slowly got her breathing back under control.

When she was waiting at the lights near the petrol station, Grace looked down at the state of her blouse. Her fingers shook as she touched the red stain.

Tentatively, she pinched the fabric between her thumb and forefinger and lifted it to her nose. It didn't smell like blood. It smelled like paint.

That didn't make her feel much better, though. Someone had still been in her house and had wanted to scare her. Well, it had worked. She was terrified.

Grace gripped the wheel tightly and accelerated as the lights turned green, then she looked in the rear-view mirror and saw a large car behind her, too close to her bumper. It was a black Range Rover. Didn't Charlie Cook have a Range Rover?

She stifled a sob and turned on to a side street.

It was just after midnight when Karen awoke with a start. A sofa cushion fell to the floor as she sat bolt upright, heart hammering. Tilly had been calling for her, but she hadn't been able to move. She'd watched, paralysed, as Patricia Perry had snatched Tilly, taking her off into the darkness. As she'd dragged Tilly away, Patricia had laughed and said Karen should have learned her lesson last time.

Her breaths came in gasps. She leaned forward, cradling her head in her hands, trying to regain control.

It was just a nightmare. She closed her eyes and inhaled deeply. *It's over.*

But she knew it wasn't. Not really. It was all starting again.

She collapsed back on the sofa, feeling disorientated. The remains of her dinner and half a glass of red wine sat on the coffee table in front of her. Netflix had stopped playing. There was a message on the screen, asking if she was still watching.

Karen groaned. Scattered on the floor around her were the scanned images of the notebook. She'd printed the pages out before heading home, intending to spend the evening studying them and trying to make some sense of the codenames.

She hadn't made much progress.

She rubbed her hand against the back of her neck, trying to massage away the tension. *That's what you get for falling asleep on the sofa*, she thought.

Her head was still filled with images from the dream, and try as she might, she couldn't get Patricia Perry's face out of her head.

With a sigh, Karen took her plate and wine glass through to the kitchen.

She scraped off the remains of her stir-fry into the bin and poured the rest of the wine down the sink. She was tempted to finish it off, but she needed to make an early start tomorrow, and it was already after midnight. She wasn't going to risk a muzzy head in the morning. She needed to be sharp.

The fact she couldn't find a strong connection between the notebook and The Red Lion was frustrating. She sensed they were close, and in her mind it seemed obvious the codenames under *999* were police officers, but she probably shouldn't have been so forceful on that theory to Morgan. Not that she would stop looking into it. She just wouldn't go on and on about it to the point where people started believing she was obsessing again. It was unfair, but once you got a reputation, it seemed to stick.

They still had the date and time on the beer mat. There had to be some significance to it. A meeting? Perhaps a transport of people into the country, or a transport of exploited workers around the country?

Karen walked back through to the sitting room, collected up the sheets of paper and stacked them on the coffee table.

She wasn't getting anywhere tonight. She needed sleep if she was going to function tomorrow.

She shivered, remembering the nightmare. After turning off the lights, she headed upstairs, hoping for a dreamless sleep this time.

CHAPTER NINETEEN

The following morning at nine a.m., Karen returned Vishal to the custody suite after treating him to a full English breakfast in the staff canteen. She intended to try to make more time for him today, so they could build up some mutual trust. It was hard to gain the man's confidence when they were keeping him locked up all day.

They hadn't talked about the case over breakfast. Instead, Karen had tried to get him to talk about himself. He'd surprised her by mentioning he loved books, particularly crime novels, and Karen had promised to get hold of some for him, to help pass the time.

Agents from border control would be coming to the station in the afternoon. Karen hoped they'd allow Vishal to stay at Nettleham for the rest of the day at least, rather than take him straight to the Immigration Removal Centre, which would make interviewing him more difficult.

After dropping Vishal back at the custody suite, she headed to the rest centre to talk to Aleksy and Joe. Theo Bailey greeted her at the door, as he had last time.

'Joe's mother is here,' Theo said with a wide smile.

'That's good news,' Karen said, following him down the hallway. 'How did the reunion go?'

'Really well,' Theo said. 'I was a little worried after his outburst yesterday. I wondered if he had a violent streak, but he's been very calm in the presence of his mother. I'm planning to have a chat with her before she leaves, to ask about his medical history.'

'I suppose I should talk to Aleksy first then. I don't want to interrupt Joe and his mum getting reacquainted.'

Theo bit his lower lip. 'There might be a problem with that.'

'Why?'

'Aleksy went out again last night.' Theo nodded at the coffee machine as they entered the kitchen. 'Want one?'

Karen shook her head. 'No thanks. Do you know where he went?'

Theo grimaced. 'No, and to make matters worse, he hasn't returned yet.'

'He's not here?' That was not good news. Although Aleksy and Joe were free to come and go, they were important witnesses, and Karen couldn't afford to lose touch with them.

'I'm afraid not. Like I said before, we don't keep them under lock and key here. He might come back later today.'

Karen sighed and looked up at the Artex ceiling. 'I can't believe it.'

But she could believe it. She already knew Aleksy didn't want to talk to them, and as much as she would have liked to keep him at the station, legally they couldn't hold him. Even if she suspected he and Joe may have been involved in the fire at The Red Lion, she had no proof, no reason to detain Aleksy.

'I feel a little bit responsible,' Theo said, as his large shoulders hunched up in a shrug. 'But I don't have any right to tell them when they can leave or where they can go.'

'It's not your fault.' Karen looked at the coffee pot. 'I think I've changed my mind. I could do with a caffeine boost.'

'Sure,' Theo said, grabbing a mug from the cupboard and pouring her a cup of coffee.

'It's a pain, though, because we arranged for someone who used to know Aleksy to come in and have a chat with him today. I should probably cancel that.'

'Don't be too hasty,' Theo said. 'He might still come back this morning. I doubt he's got anywhere else to stay.'

That was a good point. He couldn't return to The Red Lion, so where would he go? Who would he turn to for help? But while she wished she shared Theo's optimism, she didn't. She had a feeling Aleksy wouldn't be coming back.

There was a movement in the hallway, and Karen turned to see Joe shuffling along the corridor, followed by a short woman with grey hair. Her eyes shone with tears, but she had a wide smile on her face.

'Ah, DS Hart, this is Joe's mother, Linda Rowland,' Theo said.

'It's good to meet you,' Karen said.

'Thank you so much for finding my son. I'd started to give up hope. I thought I'd never see him again.'

Joe fidgeted uncomfortably.

Theo handed Karen her cup of coffee and then said, 'Why don't we make your mum a cup of coffee, Joe, while she has a chat to the detective.'

'All right,' Joe said, entering the kitchen.

Karen and Linda stepped out into the hallway. After Joe's mother had thanked Karen yet again, she answered some of Karen's general background questions.

'When did Joe go missing?'

'He first started going off on his own about ten years ago, but usually he'd only stay away for a few nights. He's always been easily influenced, too trusting. He was drinking too much, and gradually his disappearances got longer and longer and eventually turned to months. I was terrified that something was going to happen to him, but he always turned up in the end. So when he went missing the last time, I thought he'd come back eventually, but months turned into years, and I started to think I would never see him again.'

'We believe Joe was living with a couple in Canwick, and we suspect they were coercing him to work for them and live in awful conditions. Do you know Rod and Patricia Perry?'

Linda Rowland shook her head. 'No, I don't think I do. Their names don't sound familiar.'

'What about The Red Lion pub in Canwick?'

Linda's eyes grew wide. 'Yes, I know the pub, but I've not been there for years. Is that where Joe was found?'

'Yes.'

She put a hand to her mouth. 'I don't believe it. After all this time, he's been living only a few miles away. I thought he must have gone to London or Manchester . . .'

'We believe the Perrys may have been exploiting other individuals as well as Joe. We're trying to build a case so we can stop this happening to other people, so if you or Joe think of anything that could be pertinent to our investigation, we'd really appreciate your help.' Karen gave the woman her card.

'Of course, I'll talk to Joe. He's never been very communicative. He's struggled with learning disabilities and can get quite frustrated at times. He's easily led. Very loving, but sometimes things get a bit too much for him, you know?'

Karen nodded. 'Is there a doctor or healthcare professional who could help, maybe someone who knows Joe? We had a doctor run some health checks, but we think he could use some extra help. He may feel more comfortable with someone he's seen before.'

'Yes, I'll take him back to our GP. She was always very good with Joe and has referred him to a centre just north of Lincoln in the past. He loved it there, really came out of his shell for a while. Unfortunately his funding was cut back and he lost his place. Ironic really, he couldn't go any more because he was doing so well. But he was only doing well because of the centre. I'm not even sure the programmes are still running, but our GP should be able to help.'

'That sounds like a sensible way forward,' Karen said.

'I was wondering if I could take him home? I mean, it's very nice here, and Mr Bailey seems like a nice chap, but it's not the same as him being at home, is it?'

'Do you feel able to cope with Joe?'

'Of course.' Linda seemed taken aback at the question.

'I ask because Joe got quite upset when we last talked to him, and though he wasn't physically violent towards any of us directly, he did try to flip over the table. I know he's your son and you want him home, but I want you to be safe.'

A flicker of indecision played over the woman's face, but then she pursed her lips and shook her head firmly. 'Joe has never been violent towards me. He is my son and he belongs at home.'

'I understand. We have your address if we need to follow up with more questions. I hope things work out for you. I really do.'

Linda's tightly pursed lips relaxed into a smile. 'Thank you.'

◆ ◆ ◆

Back in her car, Karen connected her mobile phone to the hands-free system and scrolled through her contacts for DI Morgan. She wasn't looking forward to this call. But she had to tell him Aleksy had gone missing. There was still a chance he would turn up, but Karen wouldn't have put money on it. Before she'd selected Morgan's number, the phone lit up with an incoming call.

Sophie.

Karen pressed the answer button. 'Sophie, what have you got for me?'

Sophie's voice shook. 'I'm really sorry. I should have thought this through.'

'What is it?' Karen asked. She could do without more bad news this morning.

'Well, you know I contacted Aleksy Iskow's daughter yesterday?'

'Lucja? Yes, but we discussed that. It was a mistake. You'll learn from it. We just need to put it aside and move on.'

'I wish I could. The thing is, Lucja must have been incredibly thrilled at the news. So thrilled she's flown from Poland to the UK. She just called to tell me she's arrived at East Midlands Airport and is heading over to Nettleham to be reunited with her father.'

Karen closed her eyes.

'Hello? Are you still there?' Sophie asked.

'Yes, I'm still here. Is she making her own way to the station?'

'Yes, she's hiring a car. I know I should have told her that I haven't yet spoken to Aleksy, and we don't know if he even wants to see his daughter again, but she sounded so excited on the phone, and I didn't know how to phrase it properly.'

'Sophie—'

'I know, it's my mistake. I should have owned it, but do you think you could talk to her instead? I just feel awful.'

'I'm afraid you're going to feel worse,' Karen said. 'I've just been to the centre and Aleksy isn't there. He's gone missing, and I'm not sure he'll be back.'

Now it was time for Sophie to fall silent.

'Look, never mind. It's a mess, but we'll sort it. I'm heading back to the station now.'

'Okay,' Sophie replied in a small voice.

When Karen arrived at Nettleham HQ, she didn't have a chance to talk to Sophie straightaway because she was intercepted by Rick as soon as she walked into the office.

'The super wants to see you. DI Morgan has already gone up.'

Karen thanked him, shrugged off her jacket and hung it over the back of her chair.

'Rick, we need to tell David Allen we don't need his help today after all. Though we may have to call on him again if Aleksy ever turns up. Can you let him know?'

'Will do, Sarge.'

On her way back out of the office, she caught a glimpse of Sophie's forlorn face over the top of her computer monitor.

She felt a pang of sympathy for the young officer. She really had been trying to help, after all.

'We'll have a chat as soon as I get back,' Karen said in what she hoped was a reassuring tone.

Sophie nodded and attempted a smile.

Hurrying up the stairs, Karen tried to ignore the tension headache building behind her eyes. She'd already told Morgan that they had no idea where Aleksy had gone. He'd taken the news in his usual stoic fashion, but Karen had a feeling the superintendent was going to be more vocal in her disappointment.

She didn't see how they could have avoided this outcome, though. They weren't allowed to keep Aleksy Iskow or Joe Rowland under lock and key, but then again, maybe she could have tried harder to reach out and get Aleksy to trust them. That was difficult, though, when he had refused to talk.

She smiled at Pamela, Superintendent Murray's assistant.

'You can go straight in. She's expecting you.'

Karen raised her eyebrows. 'That sounds ominous.'

Pamela gave her a sympathetic look. That was not a good sign.

She rapped on the superintendent's door, stepped into the large office and was surprised to see it wasn't only Morgan here with the superintendent. There were two other people sitting in front of the desk.

Superintendent Murray glanced up at Karen and then gestured to the final empty seat.

'This is DS Karen Hart,' the superintendent said, and nodded at Karen. 'And this is DC Olivia Webster and DI Rob Miller. They're from the Thames Valley and think we have an investigation in common.'

Karen didn't recognise either of them, but she did recall the name Rob Miller. Wasn't that Morgan's old boss?

As the superintendent explained the situation, Karen tried to process the information while shooting a surreptitious glance at Morgan, but he stared stonily ahead, his expression unreadable.

The superintendent obviously expected them to work with these officers from the Thames Valley police service, and Karen couldn't help wondering how Morgan would handle that considering the history between him and Rob.

DC Olivia Webster, smartly dressed in a trouser suit and wearing what Karen considered very impractical high heels for a police officer, had dark brown hair, carefully styled and pinned in a perfect pleat. Not a strand was out of place. Self-consciously, Karen ran a hand through her own hair.

'Harry Cook operates a yard in Shinfield,' DC Webster said. 'We've been looking into him for a while. He's a much bigger fish than his brother Eric, and we believe he operates a network across the UK.'

Karen leaned forward, interested to know what they'd learned about the Cook family. 'We came across Harry's side of the business while we were looking into Eric. We did wonder if the brothers were working together, transporting low-paid workers and immigrants around the country.'

'I think the best way forward is to work together on this,' the superintendent said. 'We don't want to step on any toes, or inadvertently mess up other investigations. I've asked DI Morgan to brief

DI Miller and DC Webster so they can be brought up to date on our investigation.'

Rob Miller gave her a smarmy smile. 'Of course, we'll share our intel, too. Harry is the top dog. He's a big-time player.'

Karen was tempted to point out that DI Miller sounded like a character from an American TV police drama, but decided that probably wouldn't get them off on the right foot.

'Right, well, I'll let you get on with it. Keep me updated,' the superintendent said in dismissal, and then bowed her head to focus on her paperwork.

Karen stood up and tried to get a read on Morgan's mood, but he didn't meet her gaze. He strode briskly out of the office. To anyone else, he might have appeared unfazed by the abrupt arrival of his old boss, but Karen had noticed the way he'd clenched his fists when Rob had been speaking. He was more upset by this development than he was letting on.

CHAPTER TWENTY

On the way back from the superintendent's office, Karen popped in to see Harinder and collected Grace Baker's SD card. She intended to return it later that day. When she got back to the main office, she saw Olivia, Rob and Morgan standing beside Rick's desk.

Olivia stretched her mouth into a fake smile. 'We thought you'd got lost.'

'Sorry, were you waiting for me?' Karen asked.

'Yes.' Olivia's voice was cold.

Karen hadn't taken more than five minutes. She'd assumed Morgan was handling the task of updating the Thames Valley officers. 'I'm here now.'

'We thought we'd hold a briefing for the whole team.'

'Fine.'

'We can use meeting room one,' Morgan said.

As the others were walking away, Karen took the opportunity to have a quick word with Sophie. 'Has Lucja Iskow arrived yet?'

'Not yet. I've told the desk sergeant I'm expecting a visitor, so when she shows up he'll let me know right away.' Sophie looked at the retreating backs of the newcomers from Thames Valley. 'Do I have to attend the briefing?'

'No, you can stay at your desk and wait for Lucja to arrive. Come and get me when she's here.'

'That's all right. I should handle it. It was my mistake, after all.'

Karen frowned. 'Are you sure?'

Sophie took a deep breath and nodded.

'Okay then. I'd better get to this meeting. I'm sure Olivia won't be impressed if I keep her waiting again.'

Sophie smirked. 'She does seem to be quite a . . . forceful personality.'

Karen was surprised to see Rob Miller standing in front of the whiteboard when she entered the meeting room. It seemed he'd taken charge of the briefing. Karen tried not to make snap judgements about people, but with Rob she was prepared to make an exception, especially as she knew his background with Morgan. Olivia was almost as bad – condescending and haughty. She was a detective constable so Karen outranked her, but that wasn't reflected in her attitude. Still, it was early days. They'd find a way to work together somehow. They'd need to if they wanted to solve this case.

◆　◆　◆

Sophie squared her shoulders and took a deep breath before holding her card to the lock. The door released with a buzz followed by a click, and she walked out into the reception area.

Sitting on one of the green chairs was a slim woman of about Sophie's height, with wispy pale blonde hair. She looked up as soon as the door opened, her dark blue eyes anxious.

Sophie cleared her throat. 'Lucja Iskow?' she asked.

The woman hastily got to her feet. 'Yes.'

Sophie caught the eye of the desk sergeant and murmured a quick thank you, then turned back to Lucja. 'I'm DC Sophie Jones, we spoke on the phone.'

Lucja smiled. 'I was thrilled to get your phone call.'

That made Sophie feel even more guilty. 'I'm very glad you speak excellent English. It means we won't need a translator.'

'No, we won't. I understand English very well.'

'Let's go upstairs where we can talk in private.' Sophie led the way into the main part of the police station. She'd booked an interview room to talk to Lucja, but she wasn't looking forward to breaking the news.

She waited until Lucja had taken a seat in the interview room and then offered her tea or coffee, nervously clasping her hands.

Lucja shook her head and rested her elbows on the table. 'No, thank you. I'm eager to hear about my father. When can I see him?'

Sophie pulled out a chair to sit opposite Lucja. This was even harder than she'd anticipated. Maybe she should have asked Karen to come along for moral support. But no, she'd messed this up and it was down to her to make it right. Besides, Karen had enough to deal with. This case couldn't be easy for her.

There was no point putting it off. It was like a plaster. Rip it off. Get the bad news out of the way.

'Actually, there's been a development.'

Lucja's brows drew together in a frown. 'A development?'

Sophie swallowed. Her throat felt so dry. She looked around for water but there was none. 'Yes. Your father was staying in a rest centre, but unfortunately he went out last night and hasn't come back yet. So, you see, I'm not really sure where he is now.'

Lucja blinked in confusion, staring at Sophie. 'You mean he's missing again?'

Sophie held up her hands. 'Well, yes, I guess you could put it like that.'

Lucja promptly burst into tears.

'Oh, don't cry,' Sophie said, feeling wretched. 'I'm so sorry. It's my fault. I shouldn't have called you.'

'No, I'm glad you did,' Lucja said through her tears. She wiped her eyes with the back of her hand. 'I'm sorry. It's just the disappointment. I really thought, after all this time, I was about to see him again.' She shook her head. 'I haven't seen him for seven years. The last time I spoke to him was over three years ago. I don't even know if he looks the same as I remember . . .' She searched through her handbag and then pulled out a pack of tissues.

'There's still a chance he could turn up. He may go back to the rest centre tonight.'

Lucja blinked at Sophie. 'Do you really think so?'

'It's possible.'

Sophie wished there were something she could do to give Lucja more hope. But she sensed Aleksy wasn't coming back. He hadn't wanted to talk to them. Maybe he had something to hide. Was that the reason he didn't want to see his daughter? Perhaps he was ashamed of something in his past.

Sophie was close to both her parents and couldn't even imagine her dad going missing for so long.

'I'll tell you what I can do,' Sophie said. 'While he was staying at the rest centre, he had some photographs taken. I know it's not the same as seeing him in person, but perhaps you'd like to see the pictures.'

Lucja sniffed, wiping her eyes, and said, 'I'd like that very much. Thank you.'

Sophie left her in the interview room and went to go and get some hot drinks. At times like this, a cup of tea was in order.

On her way back, she stopped by her computer to print off copies of the two photographs of Aleksy the rest centre had used for their records.

They weren't the best shots. In the first one, Aleksy was glaring at the camera. Now that she looked at the photographs again, she could see it was hardly a surprise he'd done a runner. He looked angry and resentful.

Tucking the printouts under her arm, Sophie carried the teas back to the interview room.

She pushed open the door with her foot and smiled as she set the teas down on the table. 'Milk, no sugar,' she said.

She handed the printouts to Lucja and returned to her seat. As she lifted her cup, about to take a sip, she caught the incredulous expression on Lucja's face.

'What is it? Is something wrong?'

Oh, don't say I've messed up again!

She really thought Lucja seeing her father again, even though it was only a photograph, would help. Sure, they weren't very flattering pictures, but one of them was a full-length shot and the other was a close-up. He wasn't smiling, but . . .

In a hoarse voice, Lucja said, 'DC Jones, this isn't my father.'

'Oh.' Sophie got up from her seat and leaned over the table to get a better look at the images. 'Well, it's been seven years. I suppose he's changed a bit?'

Lucja shook her head stubbornly. 'This is not my father.'

'It's not Aleksy Iskow?'

Oh no, what if she'd messed up . . . Was Lucja's father a different Aleksy Iskow? But the date of birth had matched, and the details from the missing persons report. And though they didn't have a good image of Lucja's father – just an old driver's licence photograph – he definitely had the same colouring and a similar jawline.

'Are you absolutely sure?'

'Of course.' Lucja gave her a scathing look. She pointed at the full-length picture of the man Sophie had assumed was her father. 'He's missing his tattoo.'

'Tattoo? Maybe he had it removed . . .' Sophie was aware of how weak her explanation sounded even as she said the words. Then she felt a sharp jolt of clarity. 'Your father had a tattoo?'

Lucja nodded. 'Yes, on his forearm, there.' She pointed at the photograph.

Sophie's skin prickled. 'It wasn't an infinity symbol, was it?' She held her breath.

'Yes!' Lucja said, her features brightening again. 'So you have seen him?'

Sophie fell silent.

Things had suddenly got a whole lot worse.

Yes, she'd seen him. At least, she definitely remembered seeing a tattoo of that same symbol – on the murder victim found in Canwick.

CHAPTER TWENTY-ONE

Karen thought her day had gone badly, but that was nothing compared to the emotional rollercoaster Lucja Iskow had experienced. She'd arrived in the UK believing she was about be reunited with her father, but instead would end up taking a trip to the morgue to identify his body.

DI Freeman was pleased to now have an ID for his murder victim. Now they knew Aleksy Iskow had been bludgeoned to death on the South Common in Canwick, they had more questions. Who was the man they'd discovered in the Perrys' garage along with Vishal Salike and Joe Rowland? Why would he feel the need to impersonate a dead man?

Was he in the country illegally and had decided to give Aleksy's name so he wouldn't be found out? Did he know Aleksy was dead? Was he the killer?

The whole team, even Rob and Olivia – who liked to think they were on top of everything – were shocked by the news.

They sat in Morgan's office, debating options.

'I think it's important we speak to Joe Rowland and Vishal Salike as soon as possible,' Karen said. 'We need to determine how long that man was impersonating Aleksy. Did they really believe he was Aleksy Iskow, or were they in on the deception?'

Rob turned away from Karen and spoke as though she hadn't uttered a word. 'I think we need to talk to the other two men found in the garage. Olivia and Karen can go and speak to Joe Rowland. I'll talk to Vishal Salike with DI Morgan. It'll be like old times, won't it, Scotty?'

Rob grinned, and Morgan may have intended to smile back, but it looked more like a grimace to Karen.

Rob continued. 'Sophie, you can babysit Aleksy's daughter. She's had a shock, but you might be able to get something useful out of her. DC Cooper,' he said, turning to Rick, 'can you chase up the fire department? I want to know how their side of the investigation is going. We need to find out if they're any closer to a definite ID on the three bodies.'

Rick looked slightly surprised at being assigned work by DI Miller. He looked at Karen and then at Morgan and said, 'Is that all right with you, boss?'

Morgan paused for a beat before replying. 'It sounds like a sensible plan of action. I'd also like you to organise a team to go over Aleksy Iskow and Joe Rowland's rooms at the centre. We need to look for evidence that could link them to the fire, traces of accelerant and so on.' He glanced at Sophie. 'Are you happy to continue with Lucja?'

Sophie looked shaken. She was a hard-working officer, but she was young and this case had knocked her for six. It didn't help that she felt responsible for misleading Lucja and letting her believe she would be reunited with her family.

Olivia folded her arms over her chest and peered at Sophie. 'What's the problem? I'm sure she can handle it.'

Sophie lifted her chin. 'Of course I can.'

Karen wished she could take some time to talk to Sophie and offer the young officer more support, but right now it was more important they questioned Joe and Vishal as quickly as possible. They needed to discover what they could about the man falsely identifying himself as Aleksy Iskow.

The fact that Aleksy had turned up dead a few hours before they discovered the men in the garage surely couldn't be a coincidence. Karen was sure these cases were related now.

'Aleksy Iskow . . . I wasn't expecting that,' DI Freeman said as he walked into Morgan's office. Noticing them all squeezed into the small room – and the tense atmosphere – he raised his eyebrows. 'Sorry, am I interrupting?'

'Not at all,' Olivia said. 'We're just allocating tasks.'

Karen saw a way to help Sophie and acted quickly. 'Aleksy Iskow's daughter is here – Lucja. She's agreed to identify the body.'

'I'll ask DC Shah to liaise with her.'

Sophie shot Karen a grateful smile. 'I'll talk to DC Shah,' Sophie volunteered. 'I can help her with the victim identification. I've been speaking to Lucja, and she trusts me, I think. Continuity is probably important here.'

'I agree,' Morgan said.

'This is good news for my case, I suppose, but a complication for yours. Any idea who the man pretending to be Aleksy is?'

Morgan shook his head. 'No, not yet. But we need to find out quickly.'

◆ ◆ ◆

Karen was just washing her hands in the ladies' toilets when Michelle Murray walked in.

'How are things going?' the superintendent asked.

Karen rinsed the soap from her hands. 'Not great,' she said, deciding to be honest.

The superintendent raised an eyebrow. She'd been kept updated by Morgan, but Karen doubted he would have mentioned the strain between him and Rob Miller.

'I know we have to work with DI Miller and DC Webster, but they're not making it easy.'

The superintendent leaned against the sink and faced Karen. 'In what way?'

'They're undermining DI Morgan. DI Miller is bossing us all around, and Olivia Webster has an attitude problem.'

The superintendent blinked, and Karen thought perhaps she'd been a little too honest.

'Karen, I can't come in waving a big stick just because they're being mean to you. You're going to have to sort it out for yourselves.'

'Of course, we'll be professional, but they're annoying. They think we're country bumpkins and they're so much better than us.'

Superintendent Murray's eyes twinkled. 'Of course they do. They're from the Thames Valley. It's a big force. You have to work hard and show them what we're really made of up here.'

The superintendent disappeared into one of the cubicles as Karen dried her hands.

This case was turning out to be a confusing one, and to top it off, she had to put up with the company of DC Olivia Webster for the next few hours.

◆ ◆ ◆

'What do you make of DI Morgan?' Olivia asked as they walked across the tarmac towards Karen's car.

Karen shot her a sideways glance as she dug around in her handbag looking for her car keys. 'What do I make of him?' She shrugged. 'He's a good boss.'

'Not been here long, has he?'

Olivia's voice was high-pitched, and the drawn-out way she delivered her sentences made all her comments sound snide. Karen hoped they'd only be working together for a short time.

'He's been here almost a year,' Karen said, pressing the fob to unlock her Honda Civic.

'He used to work for Thames Valley Police, did you know that?'

'I did,' Karen said shortly, opening the car door and getting behind the wheel.

'He left under a bit of a cloud, I heard,' Olivia said, walking around to the passenger side.

'I wouldn't know about that.'

'Oh, yes. There was quite a fuss. He'd screwed up an investigation, apparently. I never got the full story.'

'If you don't have the full story, maybe it's not a good idea to speculate,' Karen said cuttingly.

A small smile appeared on Olivia's face, and Karen realised she'd been played. Olivia was just trying to get a rise out of her. She was that sort of person.

'What's this?' Olivia said as she tugged at a white carrier bag that had got stuck beneath the passenger seat.

'Oh, sorry, I'll put those in the back. They're paperbacks. I've read them and was intending to drop them off at a charity shop but haven't had time.'

Karen reached over to take the bag of books, but Olivia yanked the bag at the same time, sending one of the books toppling into the footwell. Karen leaned over and put the bag on the back seat as Olivia picked up the book that had fallen out.

It was a Lesley Pearse book, one Karen had really enjoyed.

'Lesley Pearse,' Olivia said, holding the book between her thumb and forefinger to study the cover.

'You're welcome to read it if you like. It's a really good one.'

Olivia wrinkled her nose. 'No thanks. I haven't read fiction since school. I can't understand why anyone would read made-up stuff for fun. Escapist nonsense, if you ask me.'

She tossed the book on to the back seat.

Karen started the car. 'Don't you watch TV?'

'Not dramas. I only like reality shows – real people, real situations.'

Karen bit back a reply as she reversed out of the parking space. As far as she was concerned, most reality shows were just as scripted as dramas.

When they got to the rest centre, they ran into yet more bad luck.

Joe's mother was there, getting Joe ready for his move back home. Linda Rowland had spoken to their GP, who'd suggested Joe not talk to the police again until he'd had an appointment with another doctor.

'Mrs Rowland, I know you only want the best for your son,' Karen said as they sat in one of the communal rooms. 'But people have died, and we really need Joe's help.'

'I'm sorry. If it was me, I'd be happy to talk to you, but Joe . . . He's had problems, he's vulnerable, and the GP suggested he could be easily led so it isn't a good idea to talk to the police until he's been assessed properly.'

'Well, perhaps you could get Joe an urgent appointment to see the doctor,' Olivia said. 'Then we can speak to him afterwards.' She didn't keep the impatience out of her voice.

Joe's mother straightened in her seat, visibly bristling. Karen was tempted to roll her eyes.

'I'm afraid that won't work. He's a priority case, but he needs to see a specialist and the appointment could take days to come through. There's too much demand on the NHS.' She glared at Olivia as though she held her personally responsible.

Olivia huffed, leaning back in her chair and looking away, as though wiping her hands of the whole business.

Karen wasn't ready to give up. 'What if we talk to Joe in your presence? If you're not happy with any of the questions, then you can ask us to stop.'

Linda considered that for a moment but then shook her head. 'I'm sorry, dear. You seem like a very nice young woman, but you never know. You might try to make Joe confess to something he didn't do.'

'I would never do that,' Karen said. 'And you'd be present during the interview to make sure that doesn't happen. We can keep it very informal, just a chat over a cup of tea.'

Joe's mother looked like she might be wavering.

Karen pressed on. 'One of the men we found with Joe gave us a false name. He gave us the name of a murder victim. We think Joe might be able to tell us who that man really was. It's incredibly important.'

Joe's mother studied her hands, twisting her silver rings. 'I don't know. I'm not really sure it's a good idea.'

'Perhaps Joe knew who the man was?' Olivia suggested, leaning forward in her chair. 'Is that why you don't want him to talk to us? You know he's hiding something. You believe he's involved.'

Linda looked startled. She blinked rapidly. 'No, that's not it . . . I'm just concerned for Joe.'

Karen couldn't believe it. Olivia was putting pressure on at the wrong time. Surely she could see that was a bad idea. Was she deliberately messing this up?

'Please, Linda. It's really important,' Karen said, sending a warning glance Olivia's way.

But Olivia didn't take the hint. 'We can do this the easy way, Linda, or we can apply for a warrant for Joe's arrest.'

Linda paled.

'We're not going to do that,' Karen said.

There were rules and strict procedures for dealing with subjects with mental health issues. They couldn't simply arrest Joe because he might have some information.

'Right, I see. So you're going to treat Joe with respect and kindness and not put any pressure on him, and yet you say that sort of thing to me. I'm afraid that tells me all I need to know,' Linda Rowland said, gathering up her handbag and coat. 'You won't be speaking to Joe, not if I have anything to do with it.'

Karen stood up at the same time as Linda. 'Please, Mrs Rowland. I respect your decision, but could you talk to Joe on our behalf? We need to identify the man who told us he was Aleksy. We want to know if Joe knew the real Aleksy Iskow.'

Linda hesitated, her lips pursed and eyebrows knitted together in a heavy frown. Eventually, her features softened and she conceded. 'I'll have a word with him and let you know if he tells me anything.'

After Linda left the room, Karen turned on Olivia, furious. 'What was that about? We can't arrest a mentally ill individual to question him.'

'Of course we can. We just need permission from the appropriate psychologists or psychiatrists. We can't kowtow to a pushy mother.' Olivia uncrossed her legs and got to her feet. 'I'm surprised you ever get anything out of interviews if you give up that easily.'

CHAPTER TWENTY-TWO

Karen was still fuming when she phoned Morgan with an update. She wanted to tell him exactly what she thought of Olivia's methods, but it was difficult with the woman sitting beside her in the car.

Unfortunately, Morgan and Rob hadn't made much progress with Vishal either.

'He refused to tell us what he knows. He's not going to talk unless we guarantee he can stay in the UK when this is all over. I told him we didn't have the authority to do that, but he was insistent. The border control agents will be interviewing him this afternoon. I don't know how lenient they'll be. I've asked the superintendent if there's anything she can do, but it doesn't look promising.'

Karen didn't think they could afford to wait until the afternoon. Border control could and likely would take Vishal to the Immigration Removal Centre. 'Do you think he knows something, or do you think he's trying to use this as leverage?'

DI Morgan sighed. 'Honestly, it's thrown me for a loop. He doesn't seem to trust us. That's the trouble.'

Karen watched Olivia slowly scrolling through emails on her phone. 'It's the same with Joe Rowland's mother. She's very protective, understandably so. She won't agree to let us speak to him until after he's had an appointment with a specialist. I've spent a bit of time with Vishal – not enough to build a genuine level of trust, but he knows I'm sympathetic to his plight. I think I should have a word with him.'

Karen tried to ignore Olivia's indiscreet snort.

'It couldn't hurt,' Morgan said. 'Are you heading back to the station now?'

'Yes, just about to leave.'

'All right. Come and see if Vishal will talk to you. You might have more luck than us.'

Karen hung up and started the engine. She hoped Vishal would help. Surely it was time for their luck to change.

◆ ◆ ◆

When they got back to Nettleham, Karen stopped at Sophie's desk. The young DC was looking very sombre.

'Everything all right?' Karen shrugged off her jacket. 'I know it's been a tough day.'

'Only down to me making mistakes,' Sophie said.

'We all make mistakes from time to time,' Karen said. 'There's no way you could have predicted this course of events.'

Sophie fidgeted with a piece of paper on her desk. 'Yes, I really wasn't expecting . . .' She shook her head. 'It certainly has been an eventful day.'

'How did the ID go?'

'It was quite straightforward. Obviously Lucja was very upset and wants to know when we'll be able to release Aleksy's body. She wants to take him back home for the funeral.'

'Understandable.'

'I couldn't give her a date yet, but she says she wants to stay in the country until we get some answers.'

'I hope for all our sakes that won't be long, but . . .'

'I know,' Sophie said. 'I did tell her that sometimes investigations run for a long time but I hoped we'd get some answers soon. She's going to be staying at the Premier Inn for the next few days at least. She wants to help in any way she can.'

'Poor kid. Is there any other family?'

'Lucja's mother. She's been estranged from Aleksy for over fifteen years, and Lucja's got lots of family back in Poland. Both Aleksy's parents passed away several years ago.'

'At least she has her family to support her. She'll need it.'

'Yes.' Sophie turned in her chair to face Karen fully. 'Are you okay?'

'Me?'

'Yes. I know this can't be an easy case for you, focusing on the Perrys and The Red Lion again.'

'You weren't around for the original investigation,' Karen said softly. 'I take it people have been talking.'

'Well, a bit, but not in a bad way. We're all worried about you, that's all.'

Karen smiled and put her hand on the younger officer's shoulder. 'I'm all right. There's no need to be concerned.'

Before Sophie could say anything else, Karen glanced at her watch and called Rick over.

'Yes, Sarge?'

'Any updates from the fire department?'

'Two males and one female died from smoke inhalation before the flames got to them. There's still no formal ID on bodies yet, though I can't see it turning out to be anyone but the Perrys. The preliminary report confirms an accelerant was used in the kitchen to start the fire, but the early test results haven't indicated the type of accelerant. It'll be another couple of days until they issue a more detailed report.'

'Okay, good work. I'm going to have a word with Vishal Salike now and see if I can get any information from him. We need to identify the man who was pretending to be Aleksy as a matter of urgency.'

Sophie leaned forward, elbows resting on her desk. 'Do you think he knew Aleksy was dead? I mean, that would make sense if he was planning to steal the name.'

'Possibly. We need to know why he assumed Aleksy's identity. Was it because he's been convicted of crimes in the past, or was he in the country illegally? We can't rule out the possibility he was hiding his identity because he murdered Aleksy, and so Aleksy was the first name that came to mind when we found him in the garage.'

'Do you think he's even Polish?' Sophie asked. 'He couldn't talk English, but maybe he was just pretending.'

'I think it's very likely he was pretending. We had a translator who spoke perfect Polish, and he wouldn't communicate with her either. I think he picked the name Aleksy Iskow in a panic when we arrived at The Red Lion.'

'But why didn't he do a runner earlier?' Rick mused, rubbing his chin. 'I think it's interesting he left the centre with Joe at two a.m. the night of the fire.'

Sophie nodded slowly. 'So our mystery man could be the one who set fire to The Red Lion?'

'Well, neither our mystery man nor Joe Rowland have an alibi yet,' Karen said. 'It's a good theory, but we don't have the evidence to prove it. Rick, could you take another look at the CCTV around the rest centre? Let's see if you can track him around the city, make a note of any places he visited or anyone he spoke to.'

Sophie brightened. 'I can help with that.'

Karen had asked one of the officers on duty in the custody suite to bring Vishal Salike to interview room two.

She opened the minuscule window to try to get some air into the stuffy room. Her stomach rumbled as she sat down. She should have picked up a sandwich but hadn't had time. She'd get something to eat as soon as she managed to get something out of Vishal.

The interview room door opened, and Karen turned, expecting to see Vishal and his escort, but instead Olivia Webster walked into the room.

'DI Miller thought it would be a good idea if I sat in. You don't mind, do you?' she asked in a sickly sweet tone.

'Not at all,' Karen said.

She tried to put her irritation with Olivia out of her mind as she went through her notes, looking at the list of questions she'd brainstormed earlier in an attempt to organise her thoughts.

Did Vishal know the man in the garage with him had been pretending to be Aleksy? Did Vishal know the real Aleksy Iskow?

Olivia settled herself in the seat beside Karen, peering over her shoulder at her notes.

The door opened for a second time, and Vishal shuffled in. His mournful dark eyes fixed on Karen and then shifted suspiciously to Olivia.

Having her here was a mistake. Karen had built up some trust with Vishal, but bringing in an outsider had wiped that out.

He sat down.

'Vishal, we need your help,' Karen said without preamble.

Vishal looked solemnly at Karen.

'This is DC Olivia Webster. She's also working on the case.'

Vishal looked at Olivia but didn't speak.

Karen continued, 'The man we found with you in the Perrys' garage is not Aleksy Iskow.'

Vishal said nothing.

'Did you know that?'

Again, Vishal was silent.

'Vishal, you're not helping yourself. We're trying to help you and—'

'No, you're not. You've just locked me up, and I've done nothing wrong. I've not committed any crimes.'

'Vishal, you won't tell us how you got into the country. That means you need to be investigated by the border control authority. We've been through this.'

'Fine. If you don't help me, then I'm not helping you. I already spoke to the other police officer. I told him, and I'm telling you, that unless you can offer me asylum and the ability to stay in the UK, then I'm not talking.'

'That's not in my power, Vishal. You're going to be talking to the border control authorities this afternoon and I hope they'll be able to help you. But right now I'm trying to solve a murder and want to stop more people like you ending up in this predicament. Did you know Aleksy? Was he your friend?'

Vishal flinched.

'He was brutally murdered, Vishal. No one deserves that.'

Vishal turned his head away to stare at the door.

During this exchange, Olivia remained silent, watching things unfold.

'Do you know the man who was in the garage with you and Joe? You must do. What was his name?'

Vishal shrugged. Karen could understand why he was being difficult. He was in a precarious situation, trying to protect himself from being deported, but his flippancy got under Karen's skin. A man was dead, and Vishal simply shrugged.

'This is an extremely serious situation, Vishal. And we can't guarantee your safety if you don't cooperate with us. Someone set fire to The Red Lion because they wanted to silence the Perrys. Perhaps somebody wants to silence you too.'

Vishal's eyes widened. 'What do you mean?'

'Somebody obviously doesn't want the truth coming out. A murder has been committed, an arson attack resulting in the death of three people, one just a fourteen-year-old boy. Maybe they want to silence everybody involved.'

Vishal shook his head rapidly. 'I wasn't involved.'

'So you say.'

Vishal took a deep breath and then exhaled. 'No, you're trying to trick me. You're trying to make out I'm in danger unless I talk to you, and it's not true.'

'The Perrys are dead, Vishal.'

As Karen said those words, she felt a chill run up her spine. Everything seemed to be linked, yet she couldn't quite connect the dots.

She could almost smell the cigarettes on Patricia Perry's breath as she remembered her saying Karen should have learned her lesson last time. She suppressed a shudder. What if the Perrys were responsible for the death of her husband and daughter? Had it been a warning to keep her nose out when she'd been investigating them last time? Or were more powerful people than the Perrys behind it all?

Karen put a hand to her forehead. It was so stuffy in the airless little room.

Her thoughts were hazy and unfocused. She needed to concentrate on getting the truth from Vishal.

'Is everything okay, DS Hart?' Olivia asked, her voice dripping with fake concern.

'Perfectly fine.'

'Perhaps you could tell us what you expect, Vishal. What do you think we should do for you?' Olivia asked.

'I want protection and I want asylum.'

'I'm afraid we've already told you we can't offer you that,' she said, sounding bored. 'I suspect you don't really know anything worth knowing anyway.'

Vishal looked smug. 'You must think I do, or you wouldn't be here asking for my help.'

'Aleksy was reported missing by his family because they were worried about him,' Karen said. 'They've been separated for years but they hadn't forgotten him. You must know what that's like. Did you leave family back in Nepal?'

Vishal's eyes widened. He gripped his hands together.

'Your parents?'

Vishal looked away.

'A wife?'

He tensed. Karen had hit a sore spot.

'What if your family were looking for you? Wouldn't you want someone to help them?'

He covered his face with his hands. 'I can't . . .'

'For goodness' sake, Vishal. I'm getting tired of this,' Karen snapped. 'You tell me right now if you knew Aleksy. Otherwise I'll ask his daughter to come in here, and you can look her in the eye and tell her why you're refusing to help.'

Olivia gave a muffled cough and Vishal turned to Karen, his mouth gaping open.

For a moment, no one spoke.

Then Vishal's eyes filled with tears.

It had been a gamble. She wasn't sure that he had known Aleksy, but if he had, if they'd been friends, then refusing to help an emotional relative was very different to fobbing off the police.

His eyes were shiny as he looked down at his hands. 'No, I . . .'

'You knew Aleksy, didn't you? The real Aleksy Iskow?' Karen's voice was gentle.

For a long time Vishal was silent, his head bowed, but then finally he said, 'Yes, I did. If I talk to you, will you try to put in a good word for me with border control?'

'I'll do everything in my power to help you, but I can't guarantee anything.'

Vishal cleared his throat, then said in a shaky voice, 'The man you found with us was not Aleksy. He was pretending. The man's name is Charlie Cook.'

'Charlie Cook?' Karen stared at Vishal as she repeated the name, recognising it. 'From Cook's Haulage?'

Olivia leaned forward with interest and made a note on a sheet of paper.

Vishal nodded. 'Yes, he took payments from the Perrys in exchange for us working at the pub, and he would transport workers around Lincoln to various restaurants. Sometimes he took me around offices as part of a cleaning team. When you turned up, he told us to hide, but you found us and he said he was Aleksy. I don't know why. We were shocked, but Joe and I couldn't say anything. We were scared.'

'What was he doing when we arrived? Why was he in the garage?'

'He was looking for something. He was going through Aleksy's possessions. He said Aleksy had stolen something.'

'And what happened to Aleksy? Had he been staying in the garage with you?'

'Yes. We hadn't been in the garage for long. The Perrys moved us there because they were expecting a new shipment of people so they needed to use the rooms in The Red Lion.' Vishal rubbed his face with his hands. 'Aleksy was a good man.'

'What happened to him?'

Vishal shook his head and said sadly, 'I don't know what happened. He just disappeared the night before you found us.'

'Did somebody come to collect him? Charlie Cook?'

'No, Aleksy tried to run away. He told me he was getting out of there and said he knew a way to make sure we all got out eventually. The Perrys told us we'd get free accommodation and a good salary when we worked for them, but we never got paid. They said any money we earned was used for our food and accommodation. When we threatened to leave, they were violent and threatened to tell the Cooks.'

'And it was the Cooks who took you to the Perrys in the first place?'

'Yes, a long time ago. Most of the people they use are brought into the country illegally and they have no way of getting a good job. The Cooks lied to us. They said we would be paid fair wages, but it wasn't true, and they monitored us all the time. We couldn't even go for a walk alone.'

'Did you ever try to leave?' Olivia asked.

'A few times. Years ago. But I soon learned there was nothing I could do. Nowhere I could go to earn money, nowhere I could legally get shelter. I was stuck.'

'And how long have you been in the UK?' Olivia asked.

'Ten years.'

'And you were brought in by the Cooks?'

Vishal stared down at the table dejectedly. 'No. I made a payment to a man in Nepal who organised my transport. I paid him my savings, then he got me to the UK, but I had no way of getting a job or finding somewhere to stay. I was living in a doorway when a man approached me and said he could get me a job without papers. He introduced me to the Cooks. I thought it sounded too good to be true. It was.'

As Karen and Olivia continued questioning Vishal, they learned more and more about the elaborate system the Perrys and the Cooks had used. From Vishal's description, the Perrys had been only a small part of the business, receiving cheap, exploited labour.

Karen wrote down the numbers that had been printed on The Red Lion beer mat and pushed them across the table to Vishal. 'Do these numbers mean anything to you?'

Vishal looked down at them and shook his head. 'I don't think so.'

'We think Aleksy wrote them on a beer mat.'

Vishal peered at the numbers again. 'Is it a date?'

'It could be a date and time. Do you know why that would be important to Aleksy?'

'No. I don't know why he would have written that down.'

'Could it have been when the Cooks were expecting to transport more people, or maybe a meeting . . . ?'

'I really don't know. We didn't usually hear about new deliveries unless they needed to use our room. We just heard the lorries turning up at The Red Lion. They kept us outside because we knew better than to try and escape, but the new ones – they always tried to escape, so they liked to keep them in the main building where they could be watched. The building was alarmed.'

Vishal looked like a broken man. Karen forced away the niggling guilt, knowing she'd pushed too hard. She'd needed answers, not just for this case but also for her own sanity.

When they finished talking to Vishal, Karen took him back to the custody suite. It was nearly time for his interview with border control and Karen wished him good luck.

She meant it. He deserved a fresh start.

CHAPTER TWENTY-THREE

Olivia and Karen went to look for Morgan and Rob Miller. They found both men in Morgan's office. Karen was pleased to offer some good news for a change.

'Vishal's started talking,' she said as she took a seat next to Rob.

'Excellent,' Morgan said. 'How much did he know about the Perrys' operation?'

'Quite a lot,' Olivia said before Karen could answer. 'Once he started talking, it all came out. To summarise, the man pretending to be Aleksy Iskow is Charlie Cook. He is a key player and organises transportation for the work in Lincoln. He was in the garage when you and DS Hart turned up because he was looking for something Aleksy had taken from him.'

Morgan looked at Karen. 'The notebook?'

'That's my guess,' Karen said. 'Though Vishal didn't know what he was looking for.'

'So Cook's Haulage is definitely involved?' Rob asked.

'Yes, though Vishal only had dealings with Charlie,' Olivia said. 'He says he doesn't know what happened to Aleksy.'

'Aleksy took the notebook. Maybe he was planning to use it as evidence against the Cooks,' Karen suggested. 'Either that or a way to blackmail them. I wonder—'

'It's one possibility,' Rob said, cutting her off before turning to Olivia. 'Excellent work.'

Olivia patted her perfectly coiffed hair, quite happy to take all the credit.

'That makes sense, Karen,' Morgan said. 'I imagine Charlie would have been very keen to get the notebook back.'

'We don't know for sure it was the notebook Charlie was looking for,' Olivia said. 'Still, I suppose it's one option.'

'Let's call a briefing,' Rob said. 'I think we need to update everyone, including DI Freeman and his team. I'll pop upstairs to ask your superintendent if she wants to attend.'

Karen watched as Rob Miller swaggered out of Morgan's office, followed by Olivia. She was tempted to moan about Olivia to Morgan but remembered the superintendent's words. The best way to handle officers like DI Miller and DC Webster was to show them exactly how capable the Lincolnshire Police were.

The superintendent came downstairs with DI Miller for the briefing. When Karen spotted them walking along the corridor to the meeting room, Rob was smiling and chatting away to the super as though they'd been friends for years.

Karen held the door open for them, and though the superintendent nodded her thanks, Rob breezed past as though she wasn't there.

She pulled out a chair and sat at the large table beside Sophie. Then she felt the small, square memory card in her pocket. She'd been intending to go back to Grace Baker's house to return the camera card, but it didn't look like she'd have time today. Hopefully Grace wouldn't mind waiting a little longer.

When the super sat down at the head of the table, Olivia and Rob scurried into the seats to her right and her left.

'Rob told me Charlie Cook was the man pretending to be Aleksy Iskow. Excellent work,' the super said, kicking off the briefing.

Karen couldn't help noticing Murray looked at Rob as she spoke, though he hadn't done much to help uncover the new information.

Rob Miller clearly thrived on attention, and it seemed he and Olivia weren't above taking credit for other people's work.

Frank Freeman hurried into the meeting room. 'Sorry, ma'am, everyone,' he said, putting a hand to his chest and sinking down into one of the chairs. 'I just had to finish up a phone call.'

'Anything to report, DI Freeman?' the superintendent asked.

Freeman took a deep breath. 'Lucja formally identified her father, Aleksy Iskow, as the man bludgeoned to death on the South Common. We asked her about the notebook, but she has no idea what it relates to.'

'We think Aleksy had taken the notebook from the Cooks and buried it on the common to hide it,' Karen said. 'It's probably what Charlie was looking for when we found him in the garage with Vishal and Joe.'

'Well, we don't *all* think that,' Olivia Webster said. 'That's one theory, certainly.'

They went round the room, with everyone providing the super-intendent with updates. Afterwards Murray said, 'We need to speak to Charlie Cook as a matter of urgency. Has he been located yet?'

Morgan shook his head. 'Not yet, ma'am. We've got an alert out for his car, but he's not at home. His father said Charlie's working away this week.'

'Did he say where?'

'He isn't sure exactly. Just that he thinks he's somewhere in the south-east.'

'Right, then we need to find him.'

'Perhaps we should organise a warrant to search the Cooks' haulage yard, ma'am?' Karen suggested. 'After all, Eric is very likely to be involved in this, too.'

'Hang on, we can't just rush in and show our hand like that. There's a lot riding on this investigation,' Rob said.

Although she felt like snapping back, Karen waited patiently for an explanation.

'We don't want to raid Eric Cook's haulage yard and tip off his brother, Harry. Harry's yard is where we think most of the action is going down. If we do a raid, we need to do both yards simultaneously. But, honestly, I don't think we have enough for a warrant at this stage. We only have the word of an illegal immigrant who would say anything to stay in the country.'

'My gut feeling is Vishal was telling us the truth . . .' Karen said.

'People lie, especially when they have a strong motive,' Olivia said.

'I appreciate that, but the longer we hold off, the longer the Cooks have to cover their tracks. Someone started the fire that killed the Perrys. It was no accident. If we act too late, more lives could be at risk.'

'That's a worrying prospect,' the superintendent said, 'but if we want to get every member of this operation, we need to play the long game. Build up a strong case with surveillance and undercover work.'

'I really think we need to speak to Eric and Meghan and apply some pressure. They must know where Charlie is,' Karen said. She understood the superintendent's point of view. The last thing they wanted was to rush in and lose their chance of catching some of the bigger players.

'Meghan is Charlie's wife, correct?' Murray asked.

'That's right, ma'am. She's not answering her phone, but if we went to the house we might get her to talk.'

The superintendent looked thoughtful.

'And we still have the time and date written on the beer mat,' Morgan said. 'If that's related to a transport, perhaps that's why Aleksy wrote it down.'

'Yes, I will authorise surveillance of the haulage yard tomorrow at three,' the superintendent said. 'Make sure the risk assessments are done today.'

Morgan nodded.

'And I'll chase down Charlie Cook,' Karen said. 'Aside from his involvement in the modern slavery ring, he's our prime suspect for the murder of Aleksy Iskow.'

'We really don't have strong enough evidence to call him our *prime* suspect,' Olivia said. She let out a light, tinkling laugh that set Karen's teeth on edge. 'We can't rush in like a bull in a china shop.' She faced the superintendent. Her eyes were sly. 'I'm not sure now is the best time to bring this up, but I was shocked at how Vishal was manipulated this afternoon. He didn't want to talk and . . . pressure was applied. Let's just say we might have to brace ourselves for a potential lawsuit once Vishal gets a human rights lawyer on his case.'

'What happened?' the superintendent asked, frowning.

Karen took a deep breath. 'I applied some emotional pressure, ma'am, but I thought it appropriate. We couldn't speak to Joe Rowland, and Vishal was our only hope of identifying the man who was pretending to be Aleksy. And it worked. Vishal did open up.'

'The ends don't always justify the means,' Olivia said archly.

Karen tried to explain her approach. 'I was gambling on the fact Vishal and Aleksy would have known each other. I suggested Vishal might want to talk to Aleksy's daughter.' Karen felt her cheeks flush. It had been an underhanded tactic, but she didn't regret it. She was tired of tiptoeing around, not getting answers.

'Karen thought it was the right way forward. In my opinion, she did the right thing.' Frank Freeman looked around the room. 'I've worked with DS Hart for a long time, and if she thought it was right to put pressure on Vishal, I support her decision. She managed to get information from him. If she hadn't, we'd still be feeling our way in the dark. But now we have a name, and I have a suspect.'

Karen shot Frank a grateful look.

'I see,' the superintendent said, her expression stern. 'I'll review the tapes this evening.'

Morgan handed out case files. Karen flicked through her copy. He'd included printouts from the notebook, the post-mortem report on Aleksy Iskow, and the background information Rick and Sophie had unearthed on the Cook family.

Rob, who had been fiddling with his mobile, gave a low whistle. 'You have been busy,' he said. 'You always did like your paperwork.'

'I like having all the information to hand,' Morgan said flatly. No matter what jibes Rob threw at him, he remained unruffled.

He led them through a summary of the case so far, suggesting ways events could be linked, but it wasn't long before Rob interrupted again.

'Sorry, could I say something?'

Morgan put his file flat on the table. 'Go ahead.'

Holding up his mobile, Rob said, 'Apologies, I don't normally use my phone during briefings, but I was waiting for a message from one of my informants. An *important* message.'

He left a dramatic pause, and Karen smothered the urge to tell him to get on with it.

When he was sure they were all hanging on his every word, he continued. 'Word on the street is Charlie Cook was expendable.'

'Expendable?' Karen asked. 'You mean he's dead?'

Rob nodded. 'It looks likely. There was a price on his head.'

'Who's the informant? Can they be trusted?' Morgan asked.

'You know better than that,' Rob said with a smile. 'It's confidential. Need-to-know only. I *can* tell you his information has always been reliable in the past. I've no reason to doubt him.'

'I'm sure you'd understand if I spoke to your boss about this confidential informant,' Superintendent Murray said coolly.

'Absolutely, ma'am. I'm sure he'll provide any information you need.'

Morgan leaned forward, picking up the file to continue with the briefing. 'If you could all look at page seven. This is a copy of one of the pages from the notebook. There is a list of what we assume are identifiers. Codenames. But they have me stumped. You can see *999* has been written at the top of the first column. We've wondered if it could be emergency contacts, or police officers' contact details.' Morgan paused and looked directly at Rob Miller.

But he didn't notice. He glanced down at the file and smothered a yawn.

Morgan waited for a beat and then continued. 'Any ideas what these codenames could represent?'

'Customers? Or a way to track payments?' Sophie suggested. 'It's a shame there isn't a key in the back.'

Morgan smiled. 'Yes, that would have made things a bit easier. Well, if anyone comes up with any bright ideas or recognises a codename, let me know.'

Rob took it upon himself to outline the action points and tasks for the days ahead, blatantly ignoring the fact Morgan should be leading the investigation. But Morgan didn't protest. He stayed quiet, and Karen couldn't read his mood. She knew how she would feel in his shoes, but his stony expression gave nothing away.

Was he frustrated at having to work with Rob? Annoyed at the way Rob was leading the investigation? Karen couldn't believe he was happy with the situation, but Morgan wasn't one to show emotion.

Karen had the opposite problem. She struggled not to show how she was feeling in certain situations – particularly now, when she'd like to tell Rob Miller to sit down and be quiet.

She enjoyed working with Morgan because she liked and, more importantly, respected him. Rick and Sophie, both eager, hard-working officers, might have their problems at times, but Karen never doubted their dedication to the job. She couldn't say the same for Rob Miller or Olivia Webster.

DI Freeman was very laid-back about the whole thing. He leaned back in his chair, fingers interlinked, hands resting on his stomach. He'd been working a murder case, handed to him on top of his already-heavy workload, and now he was part of the team investigating the modern slavery case, but he didn't look stressed or anxious. He was perfectly relaxed and amenable.

That was the best word for him. Amenable. He didn't take life too seriously and was always pleasant to be around. Karen envied him.

Rick and Sophie had both been pretty quiet throughout the briefing. They gave the superintendent their verbal reports in a few short sentences, and then remained watchful and silent for the rest of the meeting. Karen suspected they weren't enjoying the changes in working conditions either.

◆ ◆ ◆

'He's a very confident chap, isn't he?' Frank Freeman wore a mischievous smile as he nodded at Rob, who was walking along the corridor in front of them after they'd all filed out of the meeting room.

'That's one way of putting it,' Morgan said dryly.

Frank laughed and slapped him on the shoulder before heading off to the canteen.

Morgan walked slowly back to the office area. He wondered whether he was letting his past history with Rob Miller get in the way of this case. He liked to think he was a practical man, that he could put truth above everything else, but he had to admit Rob had a way of getting under his skin. No one else seemed to have a problem with him. The superintendent liked him well enough. Outwardly, he projected the image of a confident and competent officer.

Morgan was happy here in Lincolnshire. He had a good team and enjoyed his job, finally starting to put his past mistakes behind him. But now Rob Miller had turned up on his patch, trying to take control, he felt like he was slipping backwards.

Maybe he was being unreasonable. After all, Rob had been his boss a year ago. Perhaps he assumed he deserved the role of SIO. Did it matter if Rob was top dog? The most important thing was solving the case, and if he had to work with officers from the Thames Valley to do it, then that's what Morgan would do.

An uncomfortable thought at the back of his mind pushed its way forward. Did he dislike Rob being here because he didn't think he was a good officer, or was he resentful? No one else saw through Rob's charm. Was bitterness clouding his judgement?

It wasn't like him to be resentful of anyone. He looked on success – other officers rising through the ranks ahead of him – as inspirational;

something he could work towards. But when the superintendent had praised Rob, Morgan had felt a spark of indignation.

'Is Eric Cook's haulage yard the only place we're going to watch?' Karen asked as she caught up with him.

Morgan noticed Olivia ahead of them, her posture changing slightly as she tilted her head. She was listening. 'I think we're assuming whatever is going to happen will go down at the haulage yard.'

'What if it doesn't, though? What if it's a different location we should be watching?'

'Where?'

Karen smiled. 'I wish I knew.'

Olivia stopped walking and turned to face them. 'There wasn't a location written on the beer mat, correct?'

'That's right,' Karen said. 'Just tomorrow's date and three p.m.'

'Then it's not a good lead anyway. We should focus on something more productive.'

'I don't think we should just ignore it,' Karen said.

'I wasn't suggesting that, at all,' Olivia replied. 'I'm saying you need to prioritise. Patience and strategy would go a long way in this case.'

'I agree with Karen,' Morgan said. 'It's a lead we have to follow up tomorrow. We don't have a location, but the obvious place to keep watch is the haulage yard. Though we should investigate every business the Cooks are involved in.'

'Good luck with that,' Olivia said with a sniff. 'Is your superintendent really going to approve the manpower to stake out every one of the Cooks' businesses?'

Olivia's mobile rang. She answered it and walked off.

Karen shook her head. 'How long did the superintendent say we had to work with them?'

Morgan smiled. 'Unfortunately, she didn't specify an end date.'

CHAPTER TWENTY-FOUR

When she reached the main office, Karen stopped by Rick's desk. 'Fancy coming with me to speak to Meghan Cook?'

Rick looked up from his computer. 'We're going to talk to her in person?'

'We haven't had much luck calling her. I thought face-to-face she might be persuaded to tell us where Charlie is.'

Rick glanced around the office to see if anyone was listening. 'You don't buy what DI Miller's informant said then, Sarge?'

'I'm not ruling anything out, but I'm not going to stop looking for him just because the word on the street is he's been taken out. We spoke to Eric Cook. If he knew or suspected Charlie had been murdered, he would have been a mess. He wasn't. Maybe they've hidden Charlie somewhere until it all cools down, but I can't see Eric going along with his own son's murder.'

Rick reached for his jacket. 'I agree. I did wonder if the Cooks would try to get Charlie out of the country.'

'I think that's more likely than them sanctioning his death, but even if that's the case, we're not going to stop looking for him.'

They walked out of the station and headed for Karen's car.

'I've got to make a quick stop en route in Canwick. I want to drop off Grace Baker's SD card. Harinder transferred the record-ing, and I promised to return it. Plus she's the type of neighbour to keep an eye on things. I'm interested to hear if she has anything new for us.'

The journey from Nettleham to Blankney, where Meghan and Charlie Cook lived, usually took twenty minutes. They had to travel through the centre of Lincoln, and then drive straight past Grace Baker's house on the B1188.

When Karen pulled on to the driveway, she muttered a curse under her breath.

'What is it, boss?' Rick asked, looking up from his phone where he'd been busy typing in some notes.

'Grace's car isn't here. So we won't learn anything new from her today. I won't be a minute.'

Karen left the car and knocked on the front door. There was no movement inside the property.

As the sun went behind a cloud, Karen shivered.

She walked back to the car. 'She's not home. I don't suppose you have an envelope on you, do you?'

She didn't think Rick was going to say yes, but he surprised her.

'As a matter of fact,' he said, pulling his black messenger bag from the footwell, 'I think I do.' He unzipped the front compartment and pulled out two white envelopes, handing one to Karen.

'I'm impressed,' Karen said, putting the SD card into one of the envelopes and sealing it.

'You know me, boss. Always prepared.'

Karen shook her head but couldn't help smiling as she pulled a pen from her pocket and scrawled a quick message on the back of the envelope, thanking Grace for her help.

She put the envelope through the letterbox, leaning down as she did so. She shivered as the breeze picked up, rustling the leaves of the crab-apple tree. A movement to her right startled her – a grey blur darted along the lawn. Turning, she saw a squirrel leap on to the bird table, and she let out the breath she'd been holding. Why was she so jumpy?

Grace was probably just out. All the same, Karen crouched down, lifted the letterbox cover and peered into the hall. She couldn't see much through the strands of the draught excluder. Feeling a bit silly, she stood up. There was no reason to think Grace was in danger. Her line of work made her too suspicious sometimes. Dolly was probably curled up in a warm corner of the house, sleeping, and Grace had gone to visit a friend or popped to the shops and would be back soon. That was the most likely explanation.

Reluctantly, Karen went back to the car and drove away from Grace's home.

Rick whistled as they drove into Blankney, passing the busy golf course. 'I wonder how much it costs to be a member here,' Rick said. 'I bet it's a packet.'

'I've no idea. It's nice to see it so busy, though. It seems like quite a few golf clubs have closed recently.'

'Have you ever played, boss?'

'A couple of times, but I was awful. Don't have the patience for it. Or the skill. How about you?'

Rick shook his head. 'I've always fancied a go. Maybe I will one day if I ever win the lottery or get a promotion, hint hint.'

Karen grinned. 'If you want a promotion, you know what you have to do.'

Rick pulled a face. 'I know. Exams.'

'You could do it. I have every faith in you.'

'That's more than I have in myself,' Rick said. 'Anyway, my home life is a bit hectic at the moment so I'm not looking to commit to anything soon.'

'How's your mum doing?' Karen asked. She'd worked with Rick for a long time and believed the light-hearted, Jack-the-Lad persona he showed the world. It wasn't until events had come to a

177

head this year that she understood Rick's struggles. His mother had dementia, and he and his sister shared her care.

'Not bad at the moment, actually. She seems to have rallied a bit. The doctor says that can happen sometimes but not to get our hopes up. More than likely, she'll have a downturn pretty soon.'

'I'm sorry. It can't be easy.'

'No, it isn't. I thought maybe I could do something while she's more aware of everyone and everything. Maybe a little holiday. I do have some leave.'

'That's a nice idea. Where would you go?'

'Somewhere local. Probably on the coast. She loves the sea.'

'Then put in a request for the leave,' Karen said. 'Don't put it off.'

'I don't like to book time off when we're so busy at the moment with this slavery case. It's a huge deal for the whole department.'

'We'll cope.'

'Well, maybe I'll put in for leave next week. See if I can book something last-minute.'

'Good idea.'

'Would you look at that,' Rick said, staring wide-eyed at Charlie and Meghan Cook's residence. 'Clearly, business is booming.' He leaned forward and peered out the windscreen. 'That is some house.'

Karen agreed. The house was huge. It must have had at least six bedrooms and was a new build. The bricks were a light sandy colour. The windows were light green UPVC and must have cost a bomb. Karen had recently had a couple of quotes to put new windows in her own house and had been shocked at the prices. She'd decided to put the replacements off for another few years and just cope with the draughts. But it looked like money wasn't as hard to come by for Charlie and Meghan.

The front garden was huge, with a long paved driveway. A black Mercedes was parked in front of the house.

'They've even got their own fountain,' Rick said, nodding incredulously at a white marble fountain in the centre of a turning circle in the drive.

Karen pulled on to the driveway, slowly heading towards the house.

'Did you tell Meghan Cook we were coming?' Rick asked.

'No, I thought we'd surprise her. I was half hoping we might stumble across Charlie Cook, to be honest.'

Rick pulled a face. 'I doubt we'll get *that* lucky. Rob Miller's informant might be wrong, but Charlie would be a fool to stay here.'

'Criminals are often not the sharpest tools in the box,' Karen said, though she thought Rick was right. Their chances of finding Charlie Cook at home were very slim indeed.

The front door was opened by a tall, slim woman with heavily highlighted, wavy brown hair. She wore black eyeliner that flicked up at the corners of her eyes, which were a startling pale blue.

'Can I help you?' the woman asked.

Karen held up her ID. 'DS Karen Hart and DC Rick Cooper. Are you Meghan Cook?'

Her eyes narrowed. 'Yes.'

'We hoped you might have time for a chat.'

She stepped back, waving a manicured hand. 'I suppose you'd better come in. I expect this is about Charlie?'

They both made their way inside, wiping their feet carefully on the mat so as not to traipse dirt on to the pristine white carpet. It had to be the most impractical colour for a hallway.

Rick looked down at his thick-soled black shoes. 'Do you want me to take my shoes off?'

Meghan shook her head. 'No, you're all right. Come through to the kitchen.'

She led the way into a huge open-plan kitchen-diner. It was styled with shiny white cupboards – the sort with no handles that you pressed in a certain spot and they opened themselves. Karen's sister, Emma, had them at home, but she didn't understand the appeal.

Even the worktops were white and shiny. Dark grey tiles covered the floor, so highly polished they reflected the spotlights. At the far end of the kitchen was an imposing dining table with metal legs and a smoky glass top. It looked like something pieced together from a junkyard, but perhaps that was the in thing these days. It had probably set the Cooks back a fair wad of cash. The table was fully set, with crystal glasses and a white table runner, as well as a vase of white roses that looked too perfect to be real.

'Sorry, were you planning dinner?' Rick said, nodding at the place settings.

'No, we never use it really. Just for show. The interior designer set it up. Charlie loves it. Personally, I think it just collects dust. What's wrong with putting plates in a cupboard?'

Karen could see her point. She watched Meghan as she scooped up a half-full glass of white wine from the island in the centre of the kitchen.

She took a sip, leaving a smear of pink lip gloss, set it back down on the worktop and said, 'Can I get either of you a drink?'

'No thanks, we're fine,' Karen said, answering for both of them.

'So, what's Charlie done now?' Meghan asked, tapping her pink nails on the counter.

'Is it all right if I sit down?' Rick asked, pointing to the stools beneath the island.

'Go ahead,' she said.

Both Karen and Rick pulled out stools and perched on them. They were surprisingly uncomfortable. The kitchen must have cost a bomb; surely they could have made the stools slightly less hard.

The cushions felt like they were fashioned from concrete. This house was all style over comfort.

'Do you know where Charlie is, Meghan?' Karen asked. If Charlie really was dead, as DI Rob Miller had suggested, then it didn't look like Meghan had heard the news. She was far too relaxed.

'I'm afraid not. He doesn't tell me much. He said he was going down south. Something to do with work.'

'Does he go away a lot?' Rick asked.

'All the time. Even more frequently lately.'

'It's a big place for you on your own.'

'Yeah, well, we plan to have kids one day.'

'We wanted to speak to Charlie about an investigation we're running at the moment.'

Meghan let out a little snort and wrinkled her nose. She had small lines around the bridge of her nose but nowhere else on her face, which made Karen suspect she'd used Botox.

'That doesn't surprise me. Charlie's always doing something to get himself in trouble. Although, to be fair, he hasn't been in trouble with the police for a while.'

'You don't sound local, Meghan. Where are you from originally?' Rick asked.

'Maidenhead. Charlie was working with his uncle in Berkshire when we met in a nightclub. He was a flash so-and-so.' She smiled. 'I fell hook, line and sinker. I always was a fool when it came to men.'

'Things not going well between you then?'

She took another sip of wine. 'Everything's fine. I'm just not so keen on his family.'

'How so?'

'They . . .' Meghan trailed off as though coming to her senses. She shrugged. 'It's nothing. Just the normal in-law issues.'

They hadn't come across a record for Charlie Cook, but Meghan's words suggested he'd had run-ins with the law before.

'Has Charlie been arrested in the past, Meghan?' Karen asked.

'He was taken in a couple of times, for different things. Helping the police with their enquiries.' She made quote marks with her fingers as she spoke. 'I don't think he was ever *charged* with anything, though. He's not a bad bloke really. He can be easily led.'

'It's really important we talk to him as soon as possible, so if you do hear from Charlie, can you tell him we need to speak to him as a matter of urgency?' Karen took out a business card and pushed it across the island to Meghan, who glanced at it fleetingly. 'Have you ever heard of a man called Aleksy Iskow?' Karen studied Meghan closely as she asked the question, but Meghan betrayed no signs she recognised the name.

'No, never heard that name before.'

'Charlie didn't mention him?'

She shook her head.

It was difficult to know how much to tell Meghan. Any questions they asked could lead to her tipping off Charlie or another member of the Cook family. But they desperately needed information. Karen decided it was worth the risk.

She reached for the business card and scrawled the same date and time on the back as had been on the beer mat found in Aleksy Iskow's pocket when his body was discovered in Canwick.

'We have reason to believe that this date and time could be significant to Charlie. Do you know anything about that?'

Meghan looked down at the date and time and blinked. She glanced at her phone and then studied her nails. 'No, I can't think what it could mean.'

'It's really important, Meghan. Even if you're not sure, give us your best guess.'

Her light blue eyes met Karen's, and she gave a minute shake of her head. Her hand trembled as she reached for her wine.

'If you have any ideas, it would really help us out,' Rick said, smiling.

Meghan set down the wine glass and picked up her mobile phone, which was covered by a glittery gold case. She tapped the screen, swiping through apps.

Karen guessed that meant their time here was over. But she wasn't ready to give up just yet.

'We think Charlie's got himself involved in something very big, Meghan. Something that could get people killed. I don't know how much you know about Charlie's business, and that's not my main concern right now. I'm not trying to get you into trouble. But I need to know what's happening tomorrow at three p.m.'

Meghan hesitated for such a long time that Karen was sure she was going to tell them something, but in the end she just put her phone down on the counter. 'Sorry, I need to go to the bathroom.'

Rick watched her leave the kitchen, but Karen's attention was drawn to the woman's phone. She'd left it unlocked, and the screen was illuminated.

It was open on the map application.

Karen frowned, then pulled her own mobile phone from her pocket and took a quick photograph of the screen just before it turned black.

Had Meghan intentionally left her phone unlocked so they'd see the address?

'What was that?' Rick asked in a whisper.

'An address. It's a property in Lincoln. Looks like a nail salon.'

Rick shook his head in confusion. They sat in silence, waiting for Meghan to return.

When she walked back into the kitchen, she picked up her phone and put it in the back pocket of her jeans.

'Are you sure there's nothing more you want to tell us, Meghan?' Karen asked as they stood to leave.

Meghan shook her head. 'No, sorry, I can't help you.' She picked up her wine glass and swallowed the remaining contents in two gulps.

CHAPTER TWENTY-FIVE

They had just pulled into the car park at Nettleham station when Karen's mobile rang. She parked up before answering.

'DS Hart.'

'Hello, you don't know me. I'm Grace Baker's sister, Jean.'

'Is Grace okay?' Karen struggled to undo her seatbelt while holding the mobile.

'Not really. She's in a terrible state. She turned up at my house last night almost hysterical with panic. She'd gone shopping, and when she got home the front door was open and there was red paint pooled on the floor in the kitchen. Someone had written *Grass* on the table in paint. She panicked and came here.'

Karen nodded at Rick when he signalled he was going to head inside. Then she leaned back in the car seat and closed her eyes. Someone had found out Grace had been talking to them, but who and how? Was someone from inside the investigation sharing information with the Cooks? 'Does Grace have any idea who broke in?'

Jean's voice was cold. 'It's probably got something to do with that haulage yard. I don't know how you live with yourself, putting innocent people in danger. Didn't it occur to you to check on Grace? After she'd given you the information you needed, you left her to cope with the threats alone!'

Karen didn't deny Jean's assertion. The woman was angry because she was scared for her sister. 'Have there been previous threats?'

'Not that I'm aware of.'

'Did you report it to the police last night?'

'No. She was so upset, my first priority was getting her settled. Grace gave me your card and told me you were the one she spoke to . . .' There was no missing the accusatory tone in Jean's voice.

'I'm really sorry this happened. Can I talk to Grace?'

'No, she's sleeping. I took her to see my GP because she was overwrought. He prescribed some tablets to help her relax and rest.'

'Okay. I'm going to get a crime scene unit over to Grace's house as soon as possible. We might be able to get some fingerprints. Now, about accessing the property – where are you at the moment?'

'In Louth. But Grace's neighbour, on the right-hand side, number ninety-six, has got a spare key.'

'What's the neighbour's name?'

'Sylvia Markham.'

'All right, Jean. I'll get a team over there as soon as possible. Is Grace going to be staying with you for a few days?'

'I think that's for the best. I can't imagine her ever wanting to go home again after this.'

'I'm really sorry this happened. Grace was a real help to us.'

'I wish she'd never got involved.'

'She was trying to do the right thing,' Karen said.

'It wasn't the right thing for her, though, was it?'

In Karen's opinion, the law didn't treat home invasion with the severity the crime deserved. But unfortunately she wasn't in charge of the sentencing or doling out justice. Her role was to catch the criminals, not to punish them. But seeing how a break-in affected innocent people, how it made them feel like their home wasn't safe any more, made Karen's blood boil.

'We'll do everything we can to find out who did this,' she said, trying to sound reassuring.

When Jean hung up, Karen stared at her phone for a moment, wishing there was something more she could do. She was doing everything she could in the scope of the law, but sometimes that just wasn't enough.

◆ ◆ ◆

It was almost three p.m. when Morgan was summoned to see the superintendent. When he got to her office, he wasn't surprised to find that Rob Miller was already there, making himself comfortable.

'Scott,' the superintendent said, 'take a seat.'

He sat down, feeling awkward. They'd been talking about him. Not that he had anything to hide from the superintendent. She was fully aware of his track record at Thames Valley. He hadn't hidden anything from her and couldn't have even if he'd wanted to.

'Superintendent Murray thought you should be included, DI Morgan,' Rob said with a trace of a smile. 'We're going to pay Harry Cook a visit tomorrow. Things are progressing quickly on this case and we think it's the right time to act.'

'A raid?'

'Nothing so dramatic. We're just going to have a word with him. Keep it simple, make him think we're on to his brother. Hopefully, that will force him to make a move.'

'I'm not sure it's a good idea to talk to him so soon,' Morgan said. 'We think something is going down at three p.m. tomorrow. A visit might cause him to panic and cancel the plans, wasting our surveillance operations.'

'I don't think a scrawled date and time on a beer mat is a solid enough lead to put off talking to Harry. We've heard mumblings of a new shipment and we want to apply some pressure. If he thinks we're on to them, chances are he'll move them and that's when we'll catch him. Don't you agree, ma'am?' Rob asked, looking at the superintendent.

'I do. We'll keep the surveillance on the haulage yard in Canwick tomorrow, but we can't put off the investigation on the off chance that will produce a result.'

'What's the shipment?' Morgan asked.

'People. They've been brought into the country illegally, and according to my informant it's a large group this time.'

Morgan thought it through. He wasn't sure paying Harry Cook a visit at this stage was a good idea, but he didn't appear to be leading this investigation any longer.

'I'd like you to come with us to talk to Harry.'

Morgan looked up in surprise. The invitation had come out of the blue. Why would Rob want him there? Surely it wasn't because he believed Morgan could bring something to the investigation that he couldn't? Rob liked to think he could do everything single-handed. What did he gain from having Morgan present at the interview? Or was it simply a way to rub salt in his wounds? Rob liked lording it over people, especially when he sensed a weakness.

'I'm not sure—' Morgan began.

'Actually, I think it's a very good idea for you to go,' the superintendent said. 'You've spoken to Eric Cook already. It's time to learn more about his brother.'

'Yes, ma'am,' Morgan said.

After arranging the details, Murray dismissed them. As they were leaving the room, she called Morgan back.

'Is everything going all right?' she asked, assessing him with a penetrating gaze.

There was no point lying. 'To be truthful, ma'am, I've never got along well with DI Miller.'

'You don't strike me as the type of officer to let personal griev-ances get in the way of the case.'

'I'm not, ma'am. But in DI Miller's case, we've worked together before, and I don't think he's a good police officer.'

As far as Morgan was concerned, that was probably the worst thing he could say about a colleague.

'Interestingly, he spent five minutes before you entered my office singing your praises,' she said. 'I'm well aware you have his-tory with him, DI Morgan. I'm also aware that DI Miller was your senior officer during the joyriding case. He still believes in you and wants you to be involved in this case. I suggest you put your differ-ences aside and learn to work with him.'

The superintendent was making it very clear she felt he was being petty, and maybe he was. Rob Miller singing his praises? He found that hard to believe. Unless Rob had an ulterior motive.

Morgan nodded. 'Yes, ma'am.'

'I'll let you go now, DI Morgan. You'd better pack your over-night bag.'

CHAPTER TWENTY-SIX

Morgan sat in the back seat of Rob's car. Olivia had claimed the front passenger seat, saying she suffered from car sickness if she sat in the back. Morgan didn't mind. It would be a long journey to Shinfield, and he preferred to be left alone with his own thoughts.

Rob pulled out of Nettleham station on to Deepdale Lane and then headed towards the A46. The journey would take them around three and a half hours, depending on how heavy the traffic was around Newark. So Morgan would have the pleasure of spending a minimum of three hours in the car with Rob and Olivia. He wondered if he could make an excuse to avoid them tonight and get something to eat on his own.

They would pay Harry Cook a visit first thing in the morning. They'd booked rooms at the Holiday Inn on the Basingstoke Road, which was close to Harry Cook's haulage yard in Shinfield and not too far from the Lower Earley police station.

As Olivia and Rob chatted away, Morgan tuned them out. He had a lot to think about. Two things had been bothering him, the first of which was the codename Rameses1979 that had been in the notebook.

He'd purposely mentioned the list during the briefing, watching Rob closely for any signs of guilt, but he hadn't reacted – or if he had, he'd played things very cool. It made Morgan doubt his memory. A long time had passed since he'd seen the name on the forum, and even if it *was* the same username, it could be a coincidence.

The other matter concerning him was why Rob wanted him present when they talked to Harry Cook. Did he want Morgan there as a cover, a way to appear legitimate? Was he using Morgan because he thought he could be manipulated?

When they hit the section of the A46 that crossed the River Trent, the traffic slowed to a crawl.

'It's not even rush hour yet,' Olivia said with a sigh. 'Is it always this bad around here?' She turned and looked at Morgan through the gap in the seats.

'It can be. It should clear up again once we get past this single-lane stretch of road.'

'How are you finding working up here?' Olivia asked. 'It must be quite a change.'

'It is, but a good one. I've got a good team, and the people are friendly.'

Olivia nodded, but didn't look convinced. 'It's very . . . rural, isn't it?'

'In some areas, yes, but Lincoln itself is a busy city.'

'It seems a bit *different* up here,' Olivia mused. She looked at Rob. 'Don't you think?'

'Yes, you wouldn't keep *me* up here for long. Then again, I used to work for the Met, so I'm used to a little more going on in my day-to-day job,' Rob said. 'I'd be bored to tears up here.'

Morgan stared out of the window as a light rain began to fall. Droplets of water dribbled down the glass.

'I hope you don't mind me saying,' Olivia began, 'but I think DS Hart could do with stronger leadership. She really went off track during our interview with Vishal. I had no idea she was going to say what she did.'

Morgan turned his head away from the window and met her gaze. 'DS Hart is an excellent officer.'

'Oh, I'm sure she is,' Olivia said with a smirk, glancing at Rob. 'I'm just saying a little more guidance might help.'

Morgan was tempted to point out that Olivia was a detective constable, whereas Karen had passed her sergeant's exams and outranked her.

'Well, Scott's an understanding boss, aren't you, Scotty?' Rob glanced in the rear-view mirror, looking at Morgan. 'He understands what it's like to screw up on a case. I suppose it helps you empathise, doesn't it?'

Morgan said nothing, leaving an awkward silence.

Rob was trying to wind him up, hinting about their past case where he'd passed on the wrong address, which had ended in the death of a young joyrider and his brother.

Rob thought it gave him power over Morgan. But it only worked if you gave away your control. Morgan had owned his mistake, and though he still deeply regretted not writing down the address in his logbook, he refused to let Rob hold it over him any more.

Though it did make him think that he should talk to Rick and Sophie about the incident that had led to his move from the Thames Valley to Lincolnshire Police. There had been an internal investigation, and Morgan had been cleared of wrongdoing. It was simply an accident, not negligence, though Morgan still thought about the two boys' deaths on a daily basis. Knowing Rob as well as he did, he was sure he'd enjoy breaking the news to Rick and Sophie. Morgan had already filled Karen in, so when he got back to Nettleham he'd tell Rick and Sophie the whole story, and prevent Rob getting any pleasure from the revelation.

A moment or two later, Olivia put on the radio loud enough to prevent further conversation.

◆ ◆ ◆

Back in the office, Karen arranged for a SOCO team to visit Grace Baker's property as soon as possible and called Grace's neighbour to arrange collection of the front door key. Then she set about filling in the paperwork and risk assessment for the surveillance operation on the haulage yard for tomorrow at three o'clock.

Only she and Rick knew about the address she'd seen on Meghan Cook's phone. She hadn't told anyone else yet. She stared down at the half-completed form, trying to make sense of the situation.

She was worried her past experience was clouding her judgement. At the time of the accident that killed her husband and daughter, Karen had been desperate to believe there was a reason behind their deaths. She'd even gone so far as to suggest there was a police cover-up after the incident. Inevitably, that hadn't won her many friends among the officers investigating the accident.

DI Frank Freeman had been supportive during that sad time and was one of only a few officers who hadn't looked at Karen as though she was crazy. She could tell him about her concerns, but he had enough on his plate at the moment.

If Morgan was there, perhaps she could talk to him, but he wasn't. He was off on a collaborative effort with Rob and Olivia.

She wished she hadn't got rid of the folder she'd kept for years after the accident. She'd meticulously researched every piece of evidence she could get her hands on – accident reports, photographs, names of witnesses – but it hadn't done her any good.

Karen sighed and rubbed her eyes. Since Patricia Perry's nasty taunt she hadn't slept well, and maybe the lack of rest was making her paranoid. She tried to piece together the puzzle, but no matter how hard she tried, she couldn't find the final piece. What had happened the day of the accident? Had the Perrys somehow been responsible? Had another car forced Josh off the road? Or had the car been tampered with? He'd been driving *her* car because Tilly's car seat had been in the back. Had she been the intended victim?

She took a deep breath and stood up, pacing the small area in front of her desk. No, she couldn't think that way, because if she'd been the target, it meant it was her fault. The idea was too painful to contemplate.

It was a mad theory, and distancing herself from the situation, even Karen could see there was unlikely to have been a police cover-up after the accident. But then her mind returned to the notebook, with the codenames listed under the heading *999*. That had to suggest police officers were being paid off in this case . . .

Karen sat back down and opened up another copy of the surveillance request form.

She couldn't ignore the address she'd seen on Meghan's phone. It had to mean something. She was sure Charlie's wife had been trying to tell her something indirectly. It would stretch manpower, but she could organise two surveillance units. She would keep things quiet, on a need-to-know basis.

She filled in the second form, typing the address for the nail bar in Lincoln.

All she needed to do now was get it approved. Karen felt that the fewer people who knew about the surveillance at the nail bar, the better. There was a chance Meghan would tell Charlie or Eric the police were aware of their plans, but Karen got the sense Meghan had wanted to help.

She pushed her chair away from her desk and scooped up both forms from the printer, heading to the superintendent's office. She'd ask her if they could keep the surveillance on the nail bar between them for now, but when she got to the reception area outside the office, Pamela informed her Michelle Murray was in a meeting and couldn't be disturbed.

'Do you want me to give her a message?' Pamela asked, smiling from behind her desk.

'No, that's all right. I'll handle it myself.'

An officer didn't need the rank of the superintendent to authorise the surveillance, and so rather than go back downstairs, she stayed on the same floor and walked across to the office of DCI Moorland.

She'd only worked with him on one or two occasions, and though he wasn't involved in this operation he was DI Freeman's direct boss, which meant he could be asked to sign the surveillance permission forms.

DCI Moorland was in his fifties, with a shock of white hair and bright blue eyes.

'Hello, Karen,' he said cheerfully after she knocked on his office door. 'What can I do for you?'

'I hope you don't mind me bothering you, sir,' she said. 'The superintendent's incredibly busy with meetings right now, and I need the surveillance forms signed. I'm sure DI Freeman's briefed you on what's happening.'

Karen put the forms on his desk.

He glanced at them briefly. 'Ah, yes, Cook's haulage yard.' He flicked through the sheets of paper. 'Oh, a nail bar in Lincoln? We think there's a connection there too?'

'Yes,' Karen said. 'It's owned by Eric Cook, one of his many businesses. We're going to be splitting surveillance between the two locations at three p.m. tomorrow.'

The DCI picked up a pen. 'Let's hope we get something from it then.' He scrawled his signature on both forms, then handed them back to Karen. 'Best of luck,' he said.

195

'Thank you, sir.'

Karen took the forms and headed back downstairs to the large communal office. She felt a little guilty bypassing the superintendent, but Rob and Olivia had no knowledge or relationship with DCI Moorland, so they wouldn't hear about the new surveillance from him. Karen was glad. She didn't trust them at all.

CHAPTER TWENTY-SEVEN

It was just after seven p.m. when they finally checked into the Holiday Inn in Reading. Morgan hung up his clothes for the next day and had a quick shower before heading to the bar for a drink. He planned to have a swift half and then go back to his room to review his notes.

Unfortunately, Rob was already standing by the bar. 'I'll get the first round, Scotty. What will it be?'

Morgan scanned the row of draft beers. 'Half an IPA, thanks.'

'Half?' Rob looked at him as though he was mad. 'Nonsense. It's not like you're driving.'

He ordered a pint of IPA for Morgan and another for himself, even though he still had half a pint remaining in the glass in front of him.

'Where's Olivia?' Morgan asked.

'She doesn't live far from here, so she's staying at home. So it's just you and me. They do food at the bar.'

They took their drinks over to a table.

'How long have you worked with Olivia?' Morgan asked.

'Just under a year. She's a hard worker, determined to climb the career ladder at any cost.'

Morgan sipped his drink and studied Rob.

Rob shifted awkwardly under his gaze. 'Look, it's just as well Olivia didn't hang around tonight. I thought it would be good to clear the air between us.'

'How so?'

'I can tell you're still annoyed because I made you keep an eye on Louise for me.'

'No, you asked me to keep up surveillance on your ex-girl-friend, and I refused.'

'And you warned her.'

'Of course.'

Rob nodded amiably. 'You did the right thing. I know that now.' He gave a boyish grin. 'I was being an idiot.'

'You won't get any argument from me.'

Rob laughed. 'Honest to a fault, that's you, isn't it, Scotty?'

'There's nothing wrong with being honest.'

'I'm not sure that's true,' Rob mused, and took several long swallows of his beer. 'So what are you having to eat? I'll go to the bar and order.'

Morgan quickly scanned the menu and then said he'd have the lasagne. He watched Rob walk back to the bar. What game was he playing? Rob was being friendly – overly so – and that made Morgan's guard come up. He didn't trust him.

When Rob strolled back to the table, he picked up his new pint and took a sip and began chatting away as though they were the best of friends.

When he finally paused for breath, Morgan said, 'While we're having this nice little chat and clearing the air, I've got a question for you.'

'Go on.'

'What does Rameses1979 mean to you?'

Rob's face remained perfectly neutral. 'Doesn't ring a bell.'

He was either telling the truth or an exceptionally good liar. Morgan wasn't sure which.

'It reminded me of an old forum name of yours. Do you remember the forum? It was on an internal server and was used to organise social events and sports between divisions within the Thames Valley?'

A grin spread across Rob's face. 'Now that you mention it, yes, I do remember. I was Rameses something or other. It was a nickname some of the lads on the five-a-side football team gave me. You didn't play with us, though, did you?'

'No, but it was a recreational forum and open to everyone. I remembered you using Rameses1979 when I saw the same name in the notebook.'

Rob grew very still. Then, after a moment, he put his pint glass back on the table. 'So you thought one of those names on the list was me? That's incredibly suspicious of you, Scotty.'

'I'm a police officer. It's my job to be suspicious.'

'Well, I can tell you it's not me. I have no idea what the codes in that book mean any more than you do.'

'It is likely they're police contacts, though. Wouldn't you agree?' Morgan pushed the point. 'After all, they're under the heading *999*.'

'It's possible, yes. But it's nothing to do with me.' Rob's tone had grown cold.

'All right. I'll take your word for it, but I had to ask.'

They paused their conversation as food was brought to the table.

'Just so you know, I'm not annoyed by your questions. I'm actually a little impressed.'

Morgan wasn't trying to impress anyone, let alone Rob. He picked up his knife and fork.

Rob drained the dregs of his second pint. 'It's good to uncover people's secrets. I taught you that, Scotty. Knowledge is power.'

CHAPTER TWENTY-EIGHT

Karen checked her watch. She'd been waiting outside Eric Cook's home in Ruskington for over an hour. There was no one home. She was starting to think the Cook family were trying to avoid her.

Eric's house wasn't as fancy as his son's. It was older, but a beautiful house in its own way. Made of local stone with small traditional windows, it suited its surroundings. Bright green wisteria, heavy with purple blossom, tangled along the exterior stone.

Ruskington was a pleasant village. Karen had visited the garden centre regularly over the past few years, though she hadn't yet made a trip there this year. She was late planning the bedding plants. Who was she kidding? There would be no bedding plants this year. Maybe she'd buy a few ready-planted hanging baskets next weekend. She enjoyed gardening and found it relaxing, but never seemed to get enough time these days. Simply mowing the lawn was about all she could manage in her time off.

With a sigh, Karen leaned forward, ready to start the engine. She'd tried Eric Cook's mobile three times and he hadn't picked up. The haulage yard in Canwick had been shut up, and she was starting to suspect that the Cooks may have deserted their sinking ship.

She'd just glanced in the rear-view mirror before pulling away when she saw a silver Mercedes cruising along the road behind her.

It was Eric Cook on his way home at last.

'Finally,' Karen muttered under her breath, turning off the engine.

She waited until Eric parked on the drive and then got out of her car and called out.

Eric turned in surprise, blinking at her. 'Is everything all right, Detective?'

'I'm looking for your son,' she said, walking across the drive towards him.

'I'm sorry.' Eric spread his arms, palms upward. 'I've no idea where he is.'

'Don't give me that, Eric. You must have some idea. This is a serious situation, and we need to talk to Charlie.'

'I'd help if I could. Look, he's lost his way a bit over the last year or so. He doesn't listen to me. But he's not a bad lad. If he's got himself into any kind of trouble, I'm sure we can sort it out – if you get my meaning.' Eric leaned forward and winked, then tugged his wallet out of his pocket.

She could smell the beer on his breath.

'Have you been drinking and driving, Mr Cook?'

Eric recoiled, taking a step back and shaking his head. 'I just had one on the way home. I had a bad day. I swear, it was just one. I won't be over the limit.'

'Your day is about to get worse if you're suggesting a bribe to keep your son out of trouble.' Karen eyed his wallet.

Eric's body stiffened. 'I resent that implication. I only meant we could sort things out with a conversation like adults. I'm sure whatever trouble he's in can't be that serious.' He shoved his wallet back in his pocket.

'We need to question Charlie about the unlawful killing of a man on Canwick Hill.'

Eric leaned heavily against his Mercedes. 'In that case, I don't know where my son is, and I won't be speaking to you again without my lawyer present.'

'Things will be a lot simpler if you cooperate, Mr Cook. If Charlie isn't involved, he doesn't have anything to worry about.'

'I'll refer you to my previous statement, Detective.'

He turned and walked towards the house. Did he really believe his son was innocent or did he know better? Was Eric involved? He could have ordered Aleksy's murder. As much as she would have liked to arrest Eric there and then, Karen knew nothing would stick at this stage, and they'd be showing their hand too soon.

Though DI Rob Miller was confident Charlie had been removed from the situation, Karen still thought that was unlikely. He'd stopped for a drink on the way home, but Eric didn't look like a man who'd recently lost his only son.

Karen turned and crunched her way over the gravel, deep in thought. Which of the Cooks was in charge? Was Harry running things as Rob claimed? And had Eric really been fishing for a way to cover up his son's ill deeds with a bribe?

She got into her car and checked the time on the dashboard clock. It was seven thirty.

She turned the car around in the narrow lane and headed out of Ruskington via Manor Street, past the discount shop and All Saints Church. As the car flew by the prickly hedgerows and green fields, she cracked the window open a bit, breathing in the soft spring air.

She'd done everything she could tonight. She *should* go home and get a good night's sleep before tackling the case afresh tomorrow, but she was reluctant to spend the night alone with her thoughts.

Every time she closed her eyes, Patricia Perry's face would appear, cackling with laughter as she reminded Karen she should have learned her lesson last time.

On the spur of the moment, instead of turning into her own driveway, she continued on the B1188 out of Branston. She slowed for the temporary traffic lights set up in the section of the road where they were bringing in the new bypass. It didn't look like it was anywhere near ready. When the lights turned green, she pressed the accelerator and drove along to Canwick.

Instead of taking the turn for Hectare Lane and the Cook's Haulage yard, she turned right earlier, driving along Hall Drive, heading towards the centre of the village. It was an interesting development, with a mixture of old buildings and newer residences. Though Canwick House was now a care home, and some time ago Canwick Hall had been converted into flats, they retained their imposing sense of history.

Mature trees and high walls that had once belonged to the Sibthorp estate cut the village off from the outside world. Turning into Montagu Road, she drove slowly past the long limestone wall with a pantile top.

She hadn't visited Canwick village for a long time, but tonight she needed to touch base with someone from the past, someone who'd understand what she was going through.

She slowed outside a large, red-brick bungalow and pulled on to the drive. The frontage was neat and tidy, the dark green lawn free of moss and the daisies that invaded Karen's garden. Karen noticed the grass was mowed in stripes to an exacting standard and smiled as she walked up to the door and knocked.

Anthony Shaw answered. He was wearing reading glasses, a white shirt, grey trousers and a long, beige, baggy cardigan. His round face creased with a smile. 'Karen! What a lovely surprise. Come in.'

She followed him into the living room. 'Am I disturbing you?'

'Not at all. Can I get you a drink?'

'No, I'm fine, thanks. Sorry for turning up unannounced. I hoped you'd let me pick your brain for a case I'm working on.'

Anthony grabbed the crossword puzzle from his chair and tossed it on the coffee table. He settled into his armchair and looked eagerly at Karen, who sat on the sofa opposite. 'I'll be glad to help if I can. I miss it, mad as that sounds.'

It didn't sound mad to Karen at all. She didn't know what she would do without the job to stop her going stir-crazy. 'Actually, it's a local crime. Very local.'

'Ah, the case you were called away to on Sunday? I heard about the body found up near Bomber Command, and then there was the fire in The Red Lion. Are they related?'

Karen smiled at his quick summation. 'Most likely. Obviously everything I say here has to be completely confidential.'

'Of course, it goes without saying.'

'We've been looking into Cook's Haulage. As you've lived here for years, I wondered if you'd heard anything. Any rumours or whispers about the Cooks.'

'There's always grumbles about the lorries making a racket at odd times of night, but other than that, they don't seem to bother people.'

'We're looking into the possibility they could be trafficking people around the UK and possibly even over from Europe.'

Anthony raised his bushy eyebrows. 'I wasn't aware of anything like that.'

'And what about the Perrys?'

'They ran The Red Lion?'

'That's right.'

'Well, I remember having dealings with them shortly before I left the force. We believed they were employing people off the books.'

Karen nodded. 'I'm working on the assumption that the Cooks and Perrys were working together. The Cooks have access to an easy way of moving an illegal workforce around the UK. Not just immigrants, but people who are vulnerable, making them work for a pittance and keeping them in bad conditions.'

'Modern-day slavery,' Anthony murmured. 'It's incredibly sad how some people can treat fellow human beings.'

They saw the worst of human nature in their job, but she liked to believe that the majority of people were good.

She asked her ex-boss other questions about the Cooks and the history of the haulage yard. Then she shifted on to a more sensitive matter, the real reason behind her impromptu visit.

'You remember . . . the accident. When Josh and . . .'

'Of course,' Anthony said quickly, trying to spare her the pain of verbalising it.

'It happened shortly after we were dealing with the Perrys. You'd retired a couple of months prior to that if I remember correctly.'

'That's right. Five years ago now.'

'Well, I visited the Perrys just before The Red Lion was burned down, and Patricia Perry said something that disturbed me.'

Anthony leaned forward, resting his elbows on his knees. 'What did she say?'

'She said I should have learned my lesson last time.'

Anthony adjusted his glasses. 'What did she mean by that?'

'I'm not entirely sure, but it's been worrying me. She wasn't a pleasant woman. During the original investigation she swore at me, even spat at me on one occasion. You know what it's like dealing with people like that. It's hardly unusual to get screamed at and threatened. It's all part of the job. I didn't think it was anything other than an idle threat at the time, but . . .'

She could see from the concern etched on his face that he had put two and two together. He knew how her mind worked.

'You think the Perrys may have been behind the car accident that killed Josh and Tilly?'

Karen found it hard to look him in the eye. Instead she stared down at her hands. 'Yes, it crossed my mind. I don't know how they would have done it, but maybe there was another car involved and Josh was forced off the road.'

'But it happened in daylight hours, on a busy stretch of road,' Anthony said, choosing his words carefully. 'Surely someone would have seen something if that was the case. And the accident report—'

'I'm well aware of what the accident report said,' Karen said, unnecessarily sharply. She took a deep breath. 'I'm sorry. I didn't mean to snap.'

'It's perfectly understandable. Just after it happened you believed there was a cover-up. And I see the passage of time hasn't changed your mind.'

'It did . . . At least, I tried to accept the report. But my mind keeps circling back. I can't ignore it. They said there were no witnesses. No other cars involved. But the tyre marks on the road suggested otherwise.'

'The tyre marks?'

'They said they were old but . . .' She shook her head. 'I thought maybe there had been another car involved. An accident. At the time I thought someone high up used their influence to cover the whole thing up. Maybe a local politician or a senior officer. I looked into it, but there was no proof, and no one else believed it was anything other than an accident.'

Anthony watched her closely.

'But now I'm wondering if the Perrys were involved. What do you think? Honestly, could the incident have been covered up?'

'Anything is possible, Karen, but be careful.'

'Be careful? Why?'

'There was an officer, this would be a few years before your time, but she was convinced there was corruption in the Lincolnshire force. She believed there were bribes occurring in the city. A group of officers and councillors turning a blind eye to imported booze and prostitution and taking bribes.'

'Was she right?'

Anthony cocked his head to one side. 'She had a convincing argument, but she didn't go about it the right way.'

'What do you mean?'

He was quiet for a moment, and then said, 'You should see for yourself. Her name is Alice Price. She lives with her husband in Washingborough. I don't think she'd mind if you paid her a visit.'

Anthony tore a corner from his crossword-puzzle book and scrawled down a road name and house number. He handed it to Karen. 'Maybe talking to her will help you. Maybe it won't. But you can only try.'

Karen studied the address, not quite sure how to react. Was he telling her he believed there *was* corruption within the force?

She stood up. 'Thanks for this, boss.'

He smiled. 'I'm not your boss anymore, Karen.'

She reached out and put a hand on his shoulder. 'You'll always be boss to me, sir.' She smiled. 'I'll see myself out.'

As she left the living room, he called out to her. 'Karen?'

'Yes?'

'Prepare yourself. Alice's story might not have the ending you're looking for.'

CHAPTER TWENTY-NINE

Alice Price lived in one of the recent housing developments not far from Washingborough Hall. The house was a nice size, three storeys, with two small windows in the roof. Karen had noticed this style of property was popular. Probably because it utilised every bit of space possible from a tiny plot of land. The neighbouring houses were a little too close – the property was detached but only a narrow gap separated it from the houses either side. All the new building developments were doing the same, cramming as many houses as they could into the land allocated for development. Which meant parking was a problem, too, because most families had more than one car these days. Despite the fact all the properties had driveways, there were cars parked up on the kerbs.

Karen parked beside the kerb rather than on top of it. Wheelchair users, and families using pushchairs, would have trouble travelling along the pavement the way some of these cars were parked.

The Prices' security light turned on as she walked in front of the house.

The door was opened by a man with dark brown hair that was greying at the temples. He had a friendly face and greeted her with a smile.

'Mr Price?'

'That's me.'

'Sorry to trouble you. My name's Karen Hart.' She reached for her ID and held it out for him. 'I'm with the Lincolnshire Police and—'

The smile slipped from the man's face. 'Oh no. Has something happened?'

'I'm not here on official business,' Karen said hastily. 'Sorry, I just wanted to have a chat with your wife if that's possible.'

He licked his lips and hesitated, his hand still gripping the front door.

'Who is it?' a female voice called from inside the house.

'It's someone you used to work with, a colleague from the police,' Mr Price said, stepping back and gesturing for her to come in. 'Karen Hart.'

Karen didn't correct him. Though their time working for Lincolnshire Police had overlapped, Karen had never spoken to Alice before.

'I'm Declan, by the way,' he said, closing the door. 'I'm sorry I wasn't very hospitable at first.'

'That's all right. It's always a shock to have a police officer turn up at your door. You expect them to deliver bad news.' Karen knew exactly how that felt. Stomach dropping, mouth turning dry, anticipating the worst.

'Oh, yes, and since Alice left the police service I'm a bit protective I suppose. I haven't heard her mention your name before.'

They entered the living room. Alice was sitting in an armchair and slipped a mobile phone into a pocket of her oversized cardigan as she got up with a tentative smile on her face. She was a petite woman and appeared fragile. Her skin was pale, and her eyes seemed too large for her small face. Wispy brown hair surrounded her elfin features.

'Karen?' she asked and bit her lip, her eyes searching Karen's face.

'Yes, DS Karen Hart. I hope you don't mind me dropping in like this.'

Alice's dark eyes were intense, unnervingly so. 'How can I help you?'

'I'll go and make some tea,' Declan said. 'Make yourself at home, Karen.' He gestured to the sofa.

She sat down, and Alice sank back into her armchair, curling her legs under her and watching Karen closely.

'It's a complicated story,' Karen said. 'I've just been to see my old boss, DCI Anthony Shaw.'

'He just called to tell me to expect a visit. I didn't realise he meant tonight. I was on his team for a while,' Alice said with a smile. 'I liked him.'

'The thing is, I'm working on a case at the moment that's very sensitive, and I'm looking at the possibility of police corruption. Anthony suggested I have a chat with you.'

Alice nodded. She got up from the armchair and came to sit beside Karen on the sofa, leaning so close into her personal space that Karen shifted back uncomfortably.

'What have you found out?' she asked, her dark gaze darting around the room as though she thought someone else might be listening in.

'Nothing concrete, and I don't want to go around making accusations when I have no proof.'

Alice's face hardened. 'They're clever. They cover their tracks. And just when you think you've gathered enough evidence, they find a way to cover it up. They turn the tables and make you look like the bad guy.' She turned away from Karen, flopped back against the sofa cushions and looked up at the ceiling. 'I thought you were here to tell me you'd finally got to the bottom of it. Found out who they all were.'

'No,' Karen said slowly. 'I haven't. I hoped you could tell me a bit more about the corruption you believed was going on.'

Alice gripped Karen's arm. 'It's everywhere.' Her cheeks were flushed, and her eyes had a wild look about them.

Karen shifted away, trying to free her arm, but Alice's grip tightened.

'You can't give up. No matter how much they pressure you.' She glanced down, realised how tightly she was holding Karen's arm and dropped it abruptly. 'Sorry. I suppose I still get a bit carried away.'

'It's fine,' Karen said, rubbing the red mark on her skin. 'Was action taken after your allegations?'

'Nobody took it seriously. Actually, that's not really true. I think they did take it seriously, but the fallout would have been too embarrassing for the force to deal with.'

'Who did you suspect was involved?'

'I didn't just suspect it. I knew it. He was taking bribes. He admitted it to my face, but *I* was the one who got in trouble and thrown off the force. I'm the one who's not allowed to say anything about it.' She rolled her eyes. 'Heaven forbid I ruin a dead man's reputation.'

'He's dead?'

'He died two years after I lost my job.'

Declan returned to the room, concern in his eyes when he looked at his wife. 'I don't think this conversation should continue.'

'I'm sorry,' Karen said. 'I didn't mean to cause any trouble. I've run into an issue with a case I'm working on and thought Alice might be able to help.'

Declan put the tea tray on the coffee table so hard the cups clattered together. 'I'm sorry. But Alice can't talk to you about that particular subject.'

'Why not?'

'Because she went through an absolutely terrible time over this. She lost her job and had a breakdown. It's not something we talk about, is it?' He ran a hand through his hair and looked at his wife. Though his words sounded controlling, his tone was almost begging her to agree.

Alice lowered her eyes, staring down at her lap. 'You're right. I shouldn't have said anything. I went too far.'

'And he threatened to sue,' Declan said. 'You can't throw accusations around without evidence.'

'It was true. I know it was true. He told me,' Alice mumbled as she clenched her fists.

Her husband gave her a pitying look. He sat on the arm of the sofa and rubbed her back. 'I know. But he's gone now, and there's nothing we can do to change things. We just have to move on.' He looked at Karen. 'I'm sorry we can't help you, but I can't have Alice getting involved again. It nearly broke her last time.'

'I'm sorry, I didn't realise.'

Why hadn't Anthony warned her? She hadn't known Alice had been driven to a breakdown. The woman was still suffering. She'd had a manic gleam in her eyes when she'd started talking about the corruption. Was that how people saw Karen? When she suggested police involvement in this modern slavery ring, police officers taking bribes to stay quiet, did she look so feverish and obsessed?

Was this Anthony's way of telling her she was losing control? He wouldn't say so directly because he didn't want to hurt her. He was a kind man and he knew her well. He knew she was stubborn and wouldn't listen to platitudes.

This visit had hit Karen hard. Instead of getting information on police corruption as she'd hoped, she'd looked at Alice Price and seen herself reflected there. Apologising for disturbing them,

Karen thanked the Prices and left. She couldn't get out of there fast enough.

Outside, she took a deep breath of cooling air. She didn't want to be another Alice Price.

◆ ◆ ◆

On her way home, Karen was intending to call in to the Co-op in Branston to pick up a few groceries and something for dinner. Perhaps a veggie stir-fry, or a chicken breast and salad, but as she approached the crossroads she caught the hot vinegary smell from the fish and chip shop, and saw a tall man coming out of Mark's Plaice with a white-paper parcel tucked under his arm.

Her plan for a healthy dinner went out the window.

She only had ten minutes before Mark's Plaice closed. She parked in the small car park outside the Co-op, rushed inside to get some milk and bread for the morning, and then headed to the fish and chip shop, walking inside with five minutes to spare and ordered haddock and chips. Despite the late hour, the food smelled fresh and delicious.

At home, she plated up the food and smothered the chips with salt and vinegar before settling in front of the TV with her dinner on a tray on her lap. She didn't sit at the dining table much these days.

She turned on Netflix and selected the series she'd been watching last week. A comedy, light-hearted – nothing serious and no murders – was what she needed tonight.

Meeting Alice Price had really shaken her.

Old Anthony was a wily so-and-so. He would have known the effect the meeting would have had on Karen. She dug into her food, trying to put it out of her mind once and for all, but it wasn't easy. As an outsider looking in, Karen could see Alice sounded desperate and unhinged. Perhaps that was the way her colleagues saw her when she mentioned corruption. She believed her theories were logical, but that's probably what Alice had thought, too.

She wished Morgan was around, but he'd gone to Shinfield to talk to Harry Cook with Olivia and Rob. Though Olivia and Rob weren't part of Lincolnshire Police, and hadn't been around at the time of Josh and Tilly's accident, she still didn't trust them as far as she could throw them.

Maybe that meant she *was* losing it? She had no perspective when it came to this case.

But she kept coming back to those codenames under the *999* heading in the notebook. Surely they had to refer to police officers?

She must have been starving because she polished off the whole plate of food in no time. Yawning, she carried the plate through to the kitchen and loaded the dishwasher before heading upstairs to get changed. It was late, and she wasn't expecting company, so instead of putting on her usual casual clothes, she pulled on a pair of pyjamas and then went back downstairs to continue watching TV.

She'd sit there until she fell asleep and would probably wake up with a stiff neck at three o'clock in the morning, but it was better than lying in bed unable to sleep. She needed the distraction of the television because she couldn't afford insomnia tonight. Tomorrow was a big day.

It was possible that nothing would happen at three p.m. because the Cooks had been tipped off, but Karen needed to be prepared for whatever tomorrow might bring.

CHAPTER THIRTY

DI Morgan had been up since dawn going over his notes. At seven, he went downstairs for breakfast and ordered scrambled eggs and coffee. He'd already packed and checked out, but he had some time to kill before he was due to meet Rob and Olivia for their trip to Harry Cook's haulage yard at eight a.m., so he headed outside for some fresh air.

It was a cool, clear morning. A red kite flew above the hotel, a dramatic sight against the bright blue sky. Morgan put his overnight bag on the ground and watched the bird's circular flight path for a moment, before pulling his mobile from his pocket and calling Karen to check in.

'Any luck tracking down Charlie?' he asked.

'No, it's like he's disappeared off the face of the earth.'

'Rob's theory that he was a liability so they got rid of him doesn't feel right to me.'

'I agree,' Karen said. 'What time are you speaking to Harry Cook?'

'We're heading to the yard in Shinfield at eight,' Morgan said.

'I hope you manage to get more out of him than we did Eric.'

'So do I.'

After a brief pause, Karen said, 'They would have had to get rid of his car too.'

Morgan was confused. Then he realised she was talking about Charlie again. 'No sign of his vehicle?'

'No. No reports of a dumped black Range Rover. No burnt-out vehicles in any nearby fields. Nothing.'

'Well, we've had no alerts from the airports or ports, so it's unlikely he left the country.'

'Unless he did so using a different name.'

'Possible, I suppose,' Morgan said. 'We should be back in Lincoln by three. Is everything ready for the surveillance this afternoon?'

Karen hesitated briefly, before saying, 'Yes, it's all arranged.'

'Good. Thames Valley are going to have a team monitor the yard down here, too. So hopefully by this evening we'll have *something*.'

'Unless they've been tipped off.'

Morgan believed the very fact they were visiting Harry Cook would be enough to tip him off. He did not like the way the investigation had been directed. In his view, they would have been better off delaying visiting Harry until after three.

'It's a possibility, but let's hope luck is on our side.' Morgan heard footsteps behind him and turned to see Rob and Olivia approaching. 'I'd better go. We're just about to head off. Keep me updated.'

'Will do.'

Morgan hung up and put his phone in his pocket.

Rob looked relaxed and confident. 'Ready to go?'

Morgan nodded, and all three of them walked over to the car.

'When we get there, let me handle things,' Rob said. 'I'll lead the questions.'

Morgan didn't want to agree to anything that might compromise the investigation. But one of them needed to lead the questioning, otherwise the interview would have no direction. 'Fair enough. Have you spoken to Harry Cook before?'

Rob shook his head as he got behind the wheel. 'Not personally, but he's had dealings with the police in the past. His company was fined when one of his vehicles was found to have clandestine entrants.'

'That didn't come up when we did a search on prior records for Eric Cook's haulage yard.'

Rob shrugged.

It only took ten minutes to get there. The yard was larger than Eric Cook's in Canwick by a considerable margin. Twenty empty trailers sat in the lot, and a network of oddly shaped, temporary buildings had been set up on the far-right side of the yard. The ground was covered with hardcore rather than tarmac.

They'd parked, got out and were halfway across the yard when a huge man in blue overalls spotted them.

He looked all three of them up and down as he stomped towards them. 'Police, are you?'

'Is it that obvious?' Rob asked.

He chuckled, a sound that echoed around his cavernous chest. 'Just a bit, mate. What do you want?'

'We're looking for Harry Cook,' Olivia said with a smile.

'You'll find him in the main building. I'll show you the way.'

He led them into one of the temporary buildings and through to an office, the floor squeaking beneath his bulky frame. He rapped on the door, then ushered them inside.

Physically, Harry Cook was the opposite of his brother, Eric. Tall, thin, with pale blond hair, neatly styled. His wire-framed glasses perched low on his nose. He looked up as they came closer, tilting his head back and narrowing his eyes.

He focused on Rob, and his eyebrows bunched together briefly before he looked away. Had he recognised him? Had Rob lied when he told Morgan he hadn't met Harry Cook before?

Harry pushed his glasses back into position. 'To what do I owe the honour?' He had a low voice and spoke barely above a whisper. He looked more like an accountant than haulage operator.

Quite a contrast to the employee who'd escorted them into the room.

'We'd like to have a word about some of your recent operations,' Rob said, taking another step forward, making it clear he was the one in charge.

Harry Cook inclined his head and then turned to his employee. 'Thank you, Tom. That will be all.'

Tom grunted and left the room.

Harry got up, pulled out the chair in front of his desk for Olivia and then sat back down himself, waving a hand in the direction of the other chairs in the room. There was one beside a filing cabinet, which Rob claimed, and Morgan grabbed the chair that had been set back against the wall.

Only when Harry was finally settled behind the desk, with his hands resting on the polished surface, fingers interlinked, did he respond to Rob. Morgan read him easily. An outward show of calm, determined to exert his authority. He wanted to respond to Rob on his own terms, when he was ready. The delay was a deliberate tactic to take control of the situation.

'Why would you be interested in my recent operations?' Harry asked pleasantly.

'Eighteen months ago you were fined two thousand pounds after clandestine entrants were discovered in one of your vehicles.'

Harry's expression didn't change. 'Regrettable, but that's the cost of doing business. Of course, the driver had no idea the truck had been boarded. We do our best to minimise the risk, but there's only so much we can do.'

'I see. Would you mind running over the procedures you have in place to minimise your risk?'

As Harry and Rob amiably spoke about security systems and checks, Morgan grew increasingly irritated.

'Is that the only time you've had issues with people getting on board your trucks?' Morgan asked, interrupting their friendly chat, earning him an irritated look from Rob.

'Luckily for us, yes.'

'I imagine finding people stowed on board is a difficult situation for your drivers. If you stop and report them, Border Force might think you're complicit and the company would be fined. If one of your drivers found migrants hiding in their lorry, they might be tempted to drop them off somewhere else and not report it.'

Harry looked amused. 'My drivers are very clear on their instructions. You don't have to worry about that, Detective.'

'Could you tell us how many trucks you have operating over a typical week, and run over some of your regular routes?' Olivia asked with a charming smile.

As Harry humoured her, Morgan sensed Rob sending daggers his way.

What did he expect? He wasn't going to let Harry Cook get away with an easy questioning.

Morgan hadn't wanted to visit Harry yet. He believed turning up now might make the Cooks jumpy and cancel whatever they had planned for three p.m., but Rob had pushed to interview Harry today, and Morgan had to ask himself why. Was he purposefully tipping Harry off? Or did he really believe the scrawled message on the beer mat was irrelevant?

Morgan stayed quiet while Rob directed the rest of the interview. The queries weren't exactly taxing and were hardly likely to make Harry sweat. After a further five minutes of inane questioning, Morgan couldn't bear it any longer.

'Do you know where your nephew is, Mr Cook?' Morgan asked.

'My nephew?' For the first time, a shadow of annoyance passed over Harry's features.

'Yes, Charlie Cook. He is your nephew, isn't he? He lives in Lincolnshire.'

Harry nodded stiffly. 'Yes, I haven't seen him for a while.'

'Neither has anyone else, it seems.'

'How unfortunate. He's always been a little hot-headed. I'm sure he'll turn up sooner or later.'

'Are you and your brother close?'

'We meet up from time to time.'

'Work together?'

'No, Detective, as I'm sure you know, the businesses are two separate entities.'

'When was the last time you visited Lincolnshire?'

'About three years ago. Christmas, I think. Shortly before Eric's wife died.' He let out an impatient huff. 'Look, I'm not really sure where all these questions are going. Yes, we got our wrists slapped eighteen months ago, but we weren't doing anything untoward. It was an unfortunate mishap. One of our drivers took his eye off the ball, and we paid the fine. Now it's over.'

It's not over, Morgan thought, *not by a long stretch*.

'If that's everything, I really do have work to be getting on with,' Harry said, pushing himself back from the desk.

Rob got to his feet first and held out his hand for Harry to shake. 'Thank you for your time and cooperation.'

Morgan was fuming as they left the temporary building. They'd got nothing useful from Harry Cook. Nothing at all.

He'd been suspicious of Rob before they went to the meeting with Cook, and the interview had done nothing to lessen his distrust.

CHAPTER THIRTY-ONE

At ten a.m., bleary-eyed, Karen knocked on Mrs Rowland's door. The woman answered wearing a white fluffy dressing gown and a disapproving look. Karen hadn't expected it to be easy, but she had to try to persuade Joe Rowland's mother to let her talk to Joe.

'No,' Linda Rowland said firmly, keeping a firm grip on the door, as though she suspected Karen might try to rush past her into the house.

'I'll be honest with you, Linda, I'm running out of options. I really need Joe's help.'

'He's not in any position to help anyone. He can't even help himself.'

The worst of it was that Karen knew she was right. Joe *was* vulnerable. Was it really ethical to question him when he was so mentally fragile? But if she didn't, more people like Joe were at risk of being exploited, possibly even murdered.

'Maybe you could ask him to write a statement?' Karen said, running out of options.

'No, he's upset. He doesn't want to think about it anymore. I'm his mum. It's my job to protect him, isn't it?'

Karen knew she was losing the battle. 'I know you care about Joe and want what's best for him, but there are others like Joe who haven't found their way home yet.'

Linda shook her head. 'I'm protecting him. If I don't, who will?' And with that, she closed the door.

Karen stood there for a moment, trying to think of a way around the problem. But until Joe was declared medically fit for interview, he was out of bounds. Now they would only have Vishal's evidence, and that was only if Border Force allowed them access to him.

Despondent, Karen headed back to her car. She tried to focus on the case strategy, but her thoughts kept drifting back to the nightmare she'd had the night before. A different one this time, but filled with the same sense of panic. She'd dreamt of the fire, but instead of the Perrys being trapped inside, it had been Tilly and Josh. Karen had tried desperately to get to them, but her fingers were scorched and her lungs had filled with acrid smoke as she tried in vain to open the door.

Then Patricia Perry had leaned out of one of the upstairs windows, cackling with laughter.

Rather than drive straight back to Nettleham HQ, she headed to the crematorium. She parked and then walked along the main path, past the older graves.

In the distance she saw an old chap wearing a flat cap, a checked shirt with rolled-up sleeves and dark green trousers. She'd seen him here many times before, tending to the graves.

He raised his hand in greeting, and she nodded back but carried on walking to the middle of the cemetery, turning left when the path forked, towards the newer graves.

They weren't technically graves, but stones of remembrance. There were no coffins beneath them, only cremated remains. She paused in front of the two stones she'd laid for her husband and daughter and stared down at them, her eyes swimming with unshed tears.

She would have given anything for just one more conversation with Josh. What happened that day? Had he been forced off the road? Had it been a cover-up? She reached down to wipe away a few pink petals that had fallen on to the stones.

There was movement at the other end of the lot. Mourners in dark colours; ornate flower arrangements and a long, black hearse. Another funeral. As a cloud drifted in front of the sun, Karen shivered.

She stood there silently for ten minutes before finally turning away.

It didn't matter how long she stood there, it didn't help. She wouldn't get the answers she needed here. She had to trust herself. The thought of turning into someone like Alice Price was frankly terrifying, but the thought of doing nothing was worse.

She walked back towards her car, but paused when she spotted the chap she'd seen earlier. He was crouching beside one of the older graves, using a soft brush to clean it.

Karen's eyes skimmed the inscription.

Elizabeth York 1846–1861. The beloved daughter of Michael and Sarah York.

The man sensed Karen and paused, looking up. 'Weather's not quite so nice today, is it?' he said, glancing at the gathering clouds.

'No, it's turned chilly. I've seen you here before, haven't I?'

He turned to face her. 'Yes, I'm here quite a bit.'

It was then she recognised something in his expression, the look in his eyes, the pain – something broken. He didn't work here as she'd first assumed.

'You've got someone here too?'

'Yes,' he said. He got to his feet, brushing down the legs of his trousers.

'Sorry,' Karen said, regretting being overly familiar. She hated talking to people in places like this. When she came here, she wanted to be alone with her grief.

'No need to be,' he said. 'I've seen you visiting from time to time.'

Grief gripped her like she'd been plunged into an icy pool. Coldness crept around her heart, and she took a moment to compose herself before speaking. 'Yes. My husband and daughter are here.'

He watched her with sad eyes that mirrored her own.

'I don't come here that much,' she continued. 'I feel closer to them at home if I'm honest. That's where the memories are.'

'Makes sense,' he said.

'I take it this isn't your relative?' Karen said, gesturing at the gravestone for Elizabeth York.

'No. It's my son who's buried here.'

'I'm sorry.'

'It's not natural to have your child go before you.'

Karen didn't trust herself to speak.

'They have a company that's paid to maintain the grounds, and they come here with a strimmer and one of those petrol leaf blowers, but it's not quite the same as tending things by hand, is it?'

'No, it isn't.'

'I look after my son's plot, but if I see anything that needs tidying up, like Elizabeth here, then I do that. I'm retired, I've got time on my hands, so why not?' He smiled. 'After all, they're all someone's son or daughter, aren't they?'

◆ ◆ ◆

When Karen hung her jacket over the back of her chair, Rick looked up from his paperwork. 'Sarge, the superintendent has been looking for you.'

'Did she say why?'

'No. She asked where you were, but I couldn't tell her because I didn't know.' Rick raised an eyebrow.

But Karen wasn't about to tell him where she'd been. There were some things she needed to keep private.

She stashed her handbag in the bottom drawer of her desk. 'How are you getting on?'

'We're all set for three p.m.,' Rick said confidently. 'I'm just going through the risk assessment. I'll have it ready for you in half an hour.'

'Great. I'd like Sophie to take part in the surveillance on the nail bar. Can you bring her up to speed?'

Rick frowned. 'Wouldn't it be better for her to stay here? We'll need someone at the station to run queries and checks. Besides, she's never taken part in a surveillance operation before.'

'That's exactly *why* she needs to take part. The experience will be good for her. We can use DI Frank Freeman's team too, so DC Shah will be on hand here in case we need support.'

'Okay, I'll let Sophie know.'

'Where is she?'

'She went to talk to Harinder. Again.' Rick rolled his eyes.

◆　◆　◆

'She's been waiting for you.' Pamela, Superintendent Murray's assistant, was busy loading paper into the printer on her desk.

'Sounds ominous,' Karen said with a grimace.

'You can go straight in.'

Karen knocked on the superintendent's door and entered the office. 'Ma'am, you wanted to see me?'

The superintendent looked calm and unruffled as usual, but Karen detected irritation beneath her polished appearance.

'When I went through the paperwork filed yesterday, I was very surprised to see an operation authorised by DCI Moorland. Is there a reason you didn't go through the correct channels and get authorisation from me, DS Hart?'

Karen had been right. If the superintendent was calling her by her title rather than her first name, then she was definitely not happy.

Murray hadn't invited her to sit down, so she remained standing. 'You were in a meeting yesterday, ma'am. I wanted to get the preliminaries underway quickly so we could make a start on risk assessments.'

The superintendent steepled her fingers beneath her chin and looked at Karen through narrowed eyes. 'I see.'

'I knew you were busy, and DCI Moorland was free.'

'So you weren't deliberately trying to bypass me in case I decided not to authorise surveillance on the nail bar?'

'Of course not, ma'am. I can't see a reason why you wouldn't authorise the surveillance.'

Unless you're pulling strings behind the scenes and deliberately diverting attention away from criminal activity.

As soon as the thought crossed her mind, Karen knew it was ridiculous. The superintendent had proven herself time and again to be a good officer with strong morals. The idea Superintendent Murray was involved in any criminal activity, let alone people trafficking and slavery, was ludicrous.

'It is a long shot, Karen. A whole surveillance operation based on an address you saw on Meghan Cook's phone . . .' the superintendent said after Karen described her theory.

'I really believe she was trying to tell me something, ma'am. Allowing me to see that address was Meghan's way of helping.'

'If she was trying to help, why didn't she simply come out and give you the address directly?'

'Maybe she's afraid.'

'And there's still no sign of her husband?'

Karen shook her head. 'No. There have been no reported sightings of Charlie Cook since he left the centre. I'm starting to think DI Miller may have been right and somebody higher up in the network decided Charlie was too much of a liability.'

'But he's Eric Cook's son, Harry Cook's nephew . . .' the superintendent mused. She sat back in her chair and shook her head. 'Surely Eric wouldn't be involved in the murder of his own son.'

'It does seem unlikely, but Eric might not be the one in charge of the operation. Maybe he's simply a middleman.'

Murray sighed. 'All right. So long as the risk assessments are completed, and you can manage both safely within your staff allowance, both surveillance operations can go ahead at three p.m.'

Karen tried to keep her smile inside. 'Thank you, ma'am.'

'But . . .' The superintendent wagged a finger at Karen. 'I want you on the team watching Eric Cook's haulage yard, not at the nail bar.'

Karen considered trying to convince her that the nail bar was the critical spot, but decided against it when she saw the determined look on the superintendent's face. It wasn't a problem. She could trust Rick to handle the surveillance on the nail bar.

She nodded. 'Absolutely, ma'am.'

CHAPTER THIRTY-TWO

When three p.m. rolled around, Karen sat in the back of a white transit van parked on Hectare Lane with DI Freeman. The vehicle was decked out to look like a window cleaner's van, complete with ladders on the roof and a blue sign on the side panel.

They had a camera hidden on the dashboard, trained on the entrance of the haulage yard so they could view the live images from the back of the van.

As the minutes ticked by, cramped and uncomfortable, Karen grew impatient.

She rolled her shoulders. 'Still nothing.'

'It doesn't look like we're going to have any luck here today.' Freeman sounded grumpy.

The rain had been coming down steadily for the past half an hour and was drumming on the roof.

Karen stared at the viewing screen. Nothing but raindrops splashing in muddy puddles and on empty trailers. If there was anyone inside the building, they hadn't seen them. She looked at her watch for the umpteenth time.

'Either whatever was planned for three o'clock was never going to happen at this haulage yard or they were tipped off,' she said.

'What a waste of time.' Freeman shrugged his shoulders, then stretched awkwardly in the cramped space. 'Shall we call it a day?'

'Let's give it another few minutes.'

Karen suspected Frank was right. Nothing was going to happen here today. She only hoped Rick and Sophie were having more luck at the nail bar.

They would certainly find it a bit easier to blend in there. The streets around the nail bar were busy and shoppers would provide good camouflage. Here on Hectare Lane, even a window cleaner's van might be noticed because there were only a few houses along the lane. They'd parked close to one near the yard.

Karen tapped her foot on the metal floor of the van. She hoped *something* had happened at the nail bar and that Meghan really had been trying to tip her off. If not, it meant her judgement was way off. The superintendent would not be happy if resources were being wasted.

Rick sipped his Americano. Sophie was sitting next to him on the bench by the café window practically buzzing with excitement. It was her first time on an official surveillance operation. Technically, they were only there to keep watch and give the go-ahead if an arrest needed to be made. There were two officers in an unmarked car around the back of the salon, two on the street pretending to window-shop, and a marked vehicle was parked up around the corner in case backup was needed.

Rick wore a hands-free earpiece. There were no police radios to give the game away. The rain was falling heavily now, and he was glad they were inside. They could see the front of the salon and the narrow alleyway beside it from their window seat. The awning outside even protected the glass from the rain so they had a great view, considering the weather.

The salon took up the bottom floor of a four-storey building. Above it was a solicitors' office and a recruitment agency, both nothing to do with the Cooks as far as Rick could ascertain. The sign over the large window at the front was printed in graffiti style in neon colours. *Lincoln Nailz.* It looked hideous. He had no idea why they'd used a 'z' in the name. Did they think it sounded modern or funky? Maybe it did, but Rick couldn't see the appeal.

Sophie's gaze remained trained on the salon. She hadn't quite got the hang of surveillance. The whole idea was to blend in and not draw attention to yourself. Rick had been on a training course, but most of the things he'd learned had been common sense. Staying a safe distance away and blending in were the top priorities.

He glanced at the time on his mobile phone just as three o'clock rolled around.

'Nothing yet,' Sophie muttered, tapping her fingers on the edge of her coffee cup.

There wasn't much room to park up around the back. Rick hoped whatever event was due to occur would happen at the front.

He was in luck. Less than a minute later, a dark grey Nissan van pulled up outside the salon, obscuring the entrance.

'That's it,' Sophie said, urgently tugging on his arm. 'That has to be it. Let's go.'

Rick hushed her. 'Not yet,' he murmured.

He wanted to see them get out of the van. If he moved now, he could spook them into driving off. The last thing they wanted was a police chase through this busy part of Lincoln with pedestrians around.

Sophie bit her lower lip and kept staring at the man.

After a moment, the driver got out. A tall, slim, IC1 male. Thinning hair, moustache. Jeans, grey hooded jacket, blue trainers. Rick filed away the details. The man didn't seem especially nervous or on edge, and Rick wondered if this could be a false alarm. He watched him walk to the sliding doors on the side of the van. Perhaps all that was inside was a delivery of nail varnish and some bottles of polish remover.

But after the driver opened the door, he leaned in then yanked someone out. A woman. She was slight and looked fragile next to the tall van driver. She stumbled and cowered as he reached past her. Another woman left the van, then another.

'Now?' Sophie whispered, sounding tense.

Rick gave a subtle shake of his head. He wanted them to go *inside* the salon. Then the salon manager couldn't deny involvement. He needed them all on the premises.

As soon as the group entered the salon, Rick blew out a relieved breath and smiled at Sophie. 'That's it. We've got them.'

He contacted all units, then slid out of his seat to help the other officers with the arrests.

◆ ◆ ◆

Karen's mobile rang.

It was Rick. He sounded upbeat. 'Any luck, Sarge?'

'Nothing. No arrivals, and no one has left the main building here. How about you?'

'A great result.' She could hear the excitement in Rick's voice. 'Three Vietnamese women were dropped off. None of them have documents. We've made two arrests – the man who transported them here and the manager of the salon. We're bringing the women back to be interviewed as well.'

'That is fantastic,' Karen said, grinning. She suspected those women would have been expected to work for a pittance. There would be no minimum wage for them.

If they could get the driver and the manager of the salon to talk, they might be able to accelerate this investigation and move closer to nailing the Cooks.

As Karen finished up the call, she noticed Freeman was watching her closely, a frown on his face.

'What happened?' he asked when she hung up.

'There was an event at three o'clock after all. Women were dropped off at a nail salon in Lincoln, owned by Eric Cook. It looks like they entered the UK illegally. Rick is bringing them in.'

'I see.' Freeman crunched up his face and scratched his short red hair. 'I didn't realise we were running another surveillance operation.'

Karen shoved her mobile in her pocket. 'It was a last-minute thing.'

'Based on what?'

'Based on something I saw when I visited Meghan Cook. It was a long shot. But it paid off.'

'No one mentioned it to me.'

The superintendent had asked Karen to update the rest of the team, and she should have done so. But she'd held back due to a niggling suspicion that wouldn't leave her. She was sure somebody on the force was working against them.

'That's my fault,' she admitted. 'I should have told you directly. But with DI Morgan travelling to Berkshire, everything was a bit of a rush. I cleared it with DCI Moorland. Did he not mention it?'

Freeman frowned. 'No, he didn't.'

CHAPTER THIRTY-THREE

When Karen and Freeman got back to the station, they found Rick and Sophie had beaten them to it. Two men were in custody, and the three Vietnamese women were being processed. Everything was in hand.

'Excellent job,' Freeman said, beaming at Rick and Sophie. 'It appears you had more luck with your operation than we did.'

DC Farzana Shah entered the main office area, carrying a stack of blue files. 'Do you have a minute, sir?' she asked. Her dark eyes shifted to Karen and then back to her boss.

Freeman nodded and left them, walking over to DC Shah's desk.

Sophie was bubbling with excitement after her first successful surveillance operation.

'It was nerve-wracking,' she said, spinning around in her chair to face Karen and grinning from ear to ear.

'You did a good job, both of you.' Karen turned to Rick. 'Any sign of DI Morgan yet?'

'Yes, he's back. He's interviewing the suspects with DI Miller.'

Karen tried to hide her surprise. It was only sensible they interviewed the suspects as soon as possible, but the surveillance on the nail bar had been her idea, and she couldn't help feeling pushed out. But it was unprofessional to feel that way when there was so much work to be getting on with. They couldn't all focus on the exciting bits of an investigation.

'Have the men you arrested volunteered any information?'

'No such luck,' Rick said. 'The only time they spoke was to ask for their solicitor.'

'Let me guess, their solicitor is Andrew Norris?'

'Bingo.' Rick shook his head. 'It's not too clever of them to all use the same solicitor, is it? It makes it obvious they're all working together.'

'It's one thing knowing they're working together, but quite another proving it.' Karen sat on the edge of Sophie's desk. 'Has anyone updated the superintendent on the results from the surveillance operations?'

'DI Miller did that as soon as we got back. He said he was happy to do it while we were busy booking everyone in.'

Karen wasn't surprised to hear that. It seemed it was typical of Rob Miller to take credit for the successful result, even though he hadn't been part of the surveillance teams.

She moved to her own desk and made a start on the paperwork, detailing the results of the surveillance operation at the haulage yard.

An hour or so later, Rob Miller, Olivia Webster and Morgan walked into the open-plan office. Olivia and Rob looked very pleased with themselves, smiling and joking. Morgan was not smiling.

'Right, you lot, get your coats, I'm taking you for dinner,' Rob said, clapping his hands together.

Karen raised an eyebrow. 'I thought you were questioning the two suspects.'

'We were, but the solicitor wants a chance to talk privately with his clients. It's probably going to be a long evening, so I thought we should get dinner while we have the chance.' He grinned at Rick and Sophie. 'Come on, my treat.'

Sophie reached for her jacket, and Rick shrugged and did the same. Freeman and DC Shah declined the dinner invitation, saying they had to talk to the head of the fire investigation team who were looking into the arson attack on The Red Lion.

As Morgan disappeared into his office and Rob resumed his chat with Olivia, Rick asked, 'Are you not coming, Sarge?'

'No, I've got something I need to do.'

'Do you want us to stay here?' Sophie asked.

'No, you go and grab something to eat while you can.'

A few minutes later they left, and Karen was surprised to see Morgan leave with them. He clearly wasn't happy working with Rob Miller again, so why was he choosing to go and have dinner with him?

◆ ◆ ◆

They went to The White Hart in Nettleham. It was a nice old pub, and Rick had been there before on numerous occasions. Today, though, the company could have been better. He couldn't quite put his finger on it, but something about DI Rob Miller just didn't sit right with him.

On the surface, he was charming, always ready with a smile, but there were barbs beneath his comments. Rick had come across his sort before.

The meal had been good, as usual. He'd had the fish and chips and the others had all opted for the special: pan-fried paprika chicken.

Although the conversation had been innocuous enough, mainly focusing on the times Morgan and Rob had worked together, the camaraderie Rob was trying to generate seemed forced.

The boss was never exactly a bundle of laughs, but today he was even more reserved than usual. Even Sophie had picked up on it.

'Is everything all right?' she asked, looking at Morgan when he didn't respond to one of Olivia's questions.

He was distracted. Rick didn't know why, but the boss's mind was elsewhere.

'Fine,' Morgan said shortly, glancing at his watch. 'I think we should make a move back to the station, though.'

'Always the stickler for timekeeping, eh, Scotty?' Rob chuckled and drained his glass.

Morgan gave him a tight smile and left to use the men's room.

Rob had paid the bill, so Rick just left a few pound coins on the table for the tip. He picked up his jacket and looped it over his arm rather than putting it on, as it was a warm evening, despite the rain earlier.

'I suppose you're wondering why DI Morgan ended up in Lincolnshire,' Olivia said, sidling up to Rick.

He stared at her. That had come out of the blue.

'Not really, he probably just fancied a change,' Rick said.

Both Olivia and Rob smirked and exchanged knowing glances.

Rick was prepared to leave it there. He knew when he was being played. They were trying to get a rise out of him, and it wasn't going to work.

But Sophie interrupted, 'Why *did* he come up here? I thought it might have something to do with the property prices.'

Rob chuckled. 'Less to do with property, more to do with screwing up a case.'

Rick looked at Rob with distaste. He really was an unlikable character.

'What happened?' Sophie put in, oblivious to Rick's glare.

'It doesn't matter,' Rick said.

Sophie turned to face Rick. 'But haven't you ever wondered why he came up here? He doesn't talk about his past much.'

'That's his business.'

'He made a mistake,' Olivia announced with a gleeful look on her face. 'He recorded the wrong address, which led to the loss of two lives.'

Sophie paled, clutching her bag. 'I had no idea. No wonder he didn't want to talk about it.'

'No. As you can imagine, he was very shaken afterwards,' Rob said. 'Not that you have anything to worry about. It was a wake-up call for him. Now he pays attention to every detail.'

'We're not worried,' Rick said. 'DI Morgan is one of the best officers I've worked with.'

'Of course, he's a great officer.' Rob backtracked but kept the annoying smirk. 'I'd never imply otherwise.'

'You just did,' Rick snapped, and nodded at the approaching figure of DI Morgan.

'Is everything all right?' Morgan asked when he reached the table.

They all looked guilty. They couldn't have made it more obvious that they'd been talking about him.

Sophie flushed. 'Everything is fine. We were just waiting for you. Let's go.'

She hurried out of the pub and the others followed.

Morgan fell into step beside Rick.

'What's up with Sophie?'

Rick was fuming. Rob and Olivia were the type of people who appeared considerate and well meaning on the outside, when in reality they were dropping poison at every opportunity. 'You really don't want to know.'

Morgan's eyes narrowed. 'I think I can guess.'

◆ ◆ ◆

An hour later, Karen huffed with frustration, put her computer to sleep and pushed away from her desk.

She couldn't get hold of Eric or Meghan Cook.

The fact that Eric Cook was lying low didn't come as a surprise. He would have heard about the raid on his premises and known the police would be wanting to talk to him very soon.

The fact she couldn't get in touch with Meghan, though, concerned Karen.

Meghan had been the reason they'd known to watch the nail bar. If they hadn't had the heads-up, their options would have been limited. Eric owned or was an investor in a number of businesses around Lincoln, from storage facilities to newsagents to a sandwich shop. They simply didn't have the number of officers required to put surveillance on all his businesses.

Even if she hadn't been convinced Eric Cook was involved in criminal activity, the sheer number of small businesses he owned would have made her suspicious. They were the perfect front, and a way to funnel dirty money and make it appear legitimate.

She unlocked her mobile and debated whether to give Meghan's number another try.

Had Eric Cook found out the information had come from his daughter-in-law? Karen shuddered. She didn't want to consider what he would do. If Rob Miller was right and Charlie had been taken out, what else was Eric capable of? If a man was prepared to dispose of his own son, then Karen didn't know where he'd draw the line.

She tried Meghan's number again then hung up when the call went unanswered.

The others had come back from their meal subdued, but she hadn't asked them why.

Both Sophie and Rick were working away at their desks, following the money trail and trying to track down as many of Eric Cook's businesses as they could. So far they'd linked most of them back to a shell company based in a British Overseas Territory, which meant it would be hard to get financial information on them.

The Cook family had woven a tangled web and it was up to the team to try to make sense of it.

Her stomach growled. She'd missed dinner and the canteen was shut, so she made her way to the vending machine on the ground floor and bought a packet of salt and vinegar crisps and a Kit Kat.

She walked back towards the office, eating the crisps. As she entered the stairwell, she heard voices above her.

The conversation stopped abruptly as the door behind Karen clicked shut.

She'd recognised one of the voices – DI Freeman.

When Karen got to the second floor, she saw Freeman and Olivia Webster standing together looking very furtive. The tops of Freeman's ears were pink. He took a step away from Olivia.

'Everything all right?' Karen asked, pausing before she reached the door.

Olivia snapped, 'Fine', then left abruptly, yanking open the door and stalking off.

'What was that all about?' Karen asked, staring after her for a moment before turning back to Freeman. 'You look like you got caught with your hand in the biscuit tin.'

He gave an easy laugh. 'You've got a suspicious mind, Karen. Nothing very exciting, I'm afraid. We were talking about Peter James's latest book. It's very good. Have you read it?'

Karen felt a prickle on the back of her neck. She shook her head. 'Not yet. Has Olivia?'

Freeman nodded. 'Yes, she really enjoyed it too.'

He opened the door and gestured for Karen to walk ahead of him. As she stepped into the corridor, she saw a flash of long, dark hair as DC Farzana Shah disappeared into the supplies cupboard. Had she been watching them? Watching Karen?

Karen craned her neck as they walked past, but Farzana appeared oblivious to their presence, her head hidden behind a stack of printer paper.

When they walked into the main office, Freeman smiled and said, 'Better get on. No rest for the wicked.'

Karen paused before heading to her own desk, the bag of crisps clutched tightly in her hand.

Now that was interesting.

Olivia had told Karen she didn't read fiction. That meant Olivia was lying to Freeman or lying to Karen. Or . . .

The vinegary tang of the crisps suddenly tasted too sharp.

Was Freeman the one who was lying? Had he not wanted to tell Karen what he was discussing with Olivia?

If he'd lied, he was good at it. Very good. It made Karen wonder what else he'd lied about.

CHAPTER THIRTY-FOUR

It was seven p.m. when Karen drove home. It had been a long day and not a particularly successful one. Despite the good result from the surveillance operation, things hadn't progressed fast enough for her liking.

They'd eventually tracked down Eric Cook, but the superintendent wanted them to hold off on questioning him for now and see what they could learn from the three Vietnamese women, the man transporting them and the manager of the nail salon. Only then would she allow them to interview Eric Cook under caution.

That made sense, of course, but it made Karen feel like they were dragging their feet. To make matters worse, Meghan still wasn't answering her phone.

Karen had stopped by the house in Blankney, but no one had answered when she rang the bell. No sign of Meghan, and still no sign of Charlie.

Rick and Sophie had left for home at the same time as Karen. But Morgan, Rob and Olivia had remained at the station. They were planning the interview strategy together, something Karen didn't feel was fair. It was *her* result, but she hadn't been given a look-in. She'd had no opportunity to even talk to the trafficked victims or the man transporting them.

She was being pushed out of the investigation. Was it personal? Was the superintendent worried about her ability to cope? Or had Morgan said something about Karen's hunch that police corruption played a role in this case?

She didn't know. All she knew was that she was out, and Olivia and Rob were in. They were flavour of the month and could do no wrong.

She smothered a yawn as she turned the wheel, following the curve in the A15 past Pottergate Arch. As the traffic slowed, she glanced in her rear-view mirror and her pulse jumped.

Three cars behind her was a black Range Rover.

She kept her eyes fixed on the rear-view mirror. There were plenty of black Range Rovers around, but it looked like the same model as Charlie Cook's vehicle. But if he was driving around the centre of Lincoln, his vehicle would have been picked up on the traffic cameras.

As the traffic started moving again, Karen edged forward, glancing in the mirror every few seconds. As the cars on Lindum Road picked up speed, gaps between vehicles extended, and Karen got a better look at the Range Rover. She was certain it was the same model, but she could only make out the first two digits of the number plate. The rest was smeared with thick mud.

It was hard to get a clear view of the person behind the wheel from her position, but she was sure the driver was male. Keeping her speed steady, she stayed in the line of traffic snaking down the hill. When she passed The Jolly Brewer, she indicated and pulled over to the left, allowing the cars to overtake.

She held her breath as the Range Rover passed. She got a clear view of the driver. Unfortunately, the driver also got a good look at her.

A chill sped down her spine. Karen cursed.

It was him. Charlie Cook. She was sure of it.

She indicated and pulled out sharply in front of a Ford Focus, earning her an angry blast from the driver's horn.

That only drew more attention to Karen's pursuit. The Range Rover accelerated away hard. But he couldn't get too far in this traffic.

Karen didn't have a radio. She turned on the hands free and used the voice-activated control to call the station.

She reeled off the description of the car and asked for backup. It was no coincidence the number plate on the back of the Range Rover was also obscured by mud. She put her foot down, trying to keep up with the vehicle. They were nearing the crossing. It was not a good area for a police chase, and Karen wasn't authorised to pursue a vehicle at high speeds.

She hoped there was a patrol car nearby that was able to take up the pursuit.

The Range Rover slammed on his brakes, almost hitting the car in front. Karen swore. She didn't want him to get away, but she didn't want him to crash into an innocent bystander either.

The lights at the pedestrian crossing ahead of them turned red, but the Range Rover didn't remain idling for long. Instead, it accelerated and weaved around the stationary car in front before roaring across the crossing.

Karen held her breath, heart in her mouth, when she saw the Range Rover hurtling towards a young woman and a little boy who'd just stepped on to the road.

No. No. No.

The words faded in Karen's mouth. She couldn't do anything but watch.

Her hands gripped the wheel, mouth dry.

Someone screamed.

The boy was yanked back by his arm like a rag doll as the Range Rover missed him by inches.

The lights turned green. She pulled over as the rest of the traffic drove on.

Karen had seen the horror on the mother's face when the car had raced towards them. Her quick reactions had saved her child. Had Josh known that terror? Had he instinctively tried to protect their daughter? What had gone through his mind in those last few seconds?

The mask of fear on the mother's face had been disturbing enough, but it was the child's reaction that would really haunt Karen. He'd been oblivious to the danger. Innocently trusting his mother to save him. The same way Tilly had trusted Karen and Josh to keep her safe. Had she sensed danger when Josh lost control of the car? When the brakes squealed and the car skidded she must have been afraid. Had she called out for Karen?

Karen bit the side of her cheek to stop the tears that threatened.

People shuffled forward and then the scene changed. It wasn't the little boy and his mother surrounded by the crowd at the edge of the crossing, it was Tilly and Josh.

No, it wasn't possible. Her mind was playing tricks.

Karen grasped the door handle and jerked forward, staring, but as the group at the crossing moved again, the scene changed back. No Josh. No Tilly. Everything was as it had been.

The driver in the car behind sounded their horn. A cyclist swerved around Karen's car, slowing as it reached the crossing. The crowd was growing around the woman and the young boy.

Karen screwed her eyes shut. *Keep it together*.

She got out of the car and walked briskly towards the group of pedestrians surrounding the shocked and terrified young woman and the sobbing little boy. After making sure no one was physically injured, she called it in and returned to her car.

There were cameras here, so they would have a record of the incident, at least. Maybe they'd be able to track Charlie's progress from camera to camera until they finally caught up with him.

Karen slid back into the driver's seat and sat there for a moment. Her hands were trembling. Closing her eyes, she tried to push away the memory of the car accident that haunted her. The accident she hadn't seen but which had ruined her life.

She rested her head on the wheel.

That had been a close call. Too close.

She ran a hand through her short hair and took a deep, calming breath. It had definitely been Charlie Cook behind the wheel of the Range Rover.

Rob's source had told them he'd been eliminated, but then Karen had always suspected Rob was full of hot air. Either his sources were as reliable as he was or he was covering for the Cooks, taking the heat off so Charlie could lie low.

It took five minutes for Karen's hands to stop shaking enough for her to start the engine and head home.

◆ ◆ ◆

After Morgan had carried out a little more research, he picked up the phone and called the superintendent's mobile number. He didn't want to wait until morning, but when she answered she sounded preoccupied and irritable. He heard voices in the background, muffled laughter and the chink of glasses, and wondered if she was at an official function.

'Yes.' Her tone was curt.

'I'm sorry to disturb you, ma'am. But I need a warrant. I want your permission to access DI Rob Miller and DC Olivia Webster's financial dealings, including bank statements, investments and holdings.'

There was a pause while the superintendent digested the information. He tried to picture her expression. Frowning, lips pursed, was his guess. But he hadn't expected her to be happy about this.

'What's your reason for this, DI Morgan?'

'I have reason to believe they are corrupt and taking bribes, ma'am.'

He heard her sharp intake of breath, followed by a curse. Then she was quiet again, muttering apologies as though she was moving through a crowded room.

'That's a hefty allegation, DI Morgan. I take it you have evidence to back up your claims?'

'I have some evidence, ma'am, but not enough to press charges. That's why I need the warrants.'

The superintendent was quiet again. Morgan could hear her breathing on the other end of the line. Finally she said, 'Right, I'm alone now. Tell me everything.'

Morgan quickly outlined the bare bones of his suspicions.

'The evidence isn't overwhelming. Are you sure this isn't personal?' Murray asked. 'I know you have history with DI Miller.'

That hurt. 'I'm not denying I don't like the man, ma'am, but no, this isn't personal. I'd have hoped you'd know me better than that.'

Superintendent Murray gave a non-committal 'Hmm'.

'I think they're both corrupt, taking payments from the Cooks and others,' Morgan said, driving his point home.

'If you're accusing a fellow officer, it's not enough to *think*, DI Morgan. You have to *know*.'

Morgan was silent.

'Tell me more about the name in the notebook.'

'There was a name in the list I recognised from a long time ago. Rameses1979. It was an old forum handle used by DI Miller.

I suspect they all provided codenames and used some kind of forum or app for communication. The notebook contained the master list.'

'Why would he use his old forum ID when that could lead us to him?'

Morgan smiled. That he could answer. He knew Rob. 'It's his way of showing off. He doesn't believe we'll catch him.'

'Why didn't you come to me straightaway?'

Morgan thought the answer to that question would have been obvious. 'Because it's no secret I don't get on with Rob Miller, and I thought my suspicions might be viewed as sour grapes.'

The superintendent huffed. 'I'll be the one to determine whether it's sour grapes or not, DI Morgan. You should have come to me.'

He resisted the urge to remind the superintendent she'd suggested just that at the start of their conversation. 'Yes, ma'am. You're right. I'm sorry.'

'So the only evidence you have is the name in the notebook and Harry Cook's reaction to Rob when you met him?'

That and Rob's exploitative nature. But Morgan didn't say that. He knew the superintendent wanted proof, not a character assessment. 'That's right, ma'am. I believe I could persuade other officers willing to go on record to provide more evidence. Rob Miller has made many enemies within the Thames Valley police service over the years.'

At least, he hoped he could persuade them to make it official. It was one thing grumbling to Morgan in private, and quite another for them to go on the record.

Superintendent Murray didn't reply, so Morgan pushed on. 'We need to act quickly, ma'am, because there's a chance DI Miller and DC Webster will run if they know we're on to them.'

The superintendent cursed.

Morgan took that as a good sign. She had to accept the evidence was enough to warrant further investigation.

'I really hope you're right about this,' she said softly, before taking a deep breath. 'Because this is going to open up a large can of worms, not to mention create bad feeling with our colleagues in the Thames Valley Police.'

'Yes, ma'am. I realise that, but it can't be helped. Shall I start the paperwork?'

'No.'

'No?' Morgan frowned.

'Professional standards would have a field day if they thought your history with Rob Miller influenced this in any way. The Lincolnshire Anti-Corruption Unit will need to handle this, DI Morgan. Not you. Is that understood?'

'That will take too long. We don't have the time to wait—'

'It's procedure. We need to be above reproach. Surely you see that?'

'I do, but in this case—'

'ACU will handle this, DI Morgan. That's my last word on the matter, understood?'

Morgan squeezed his eyes shut. It wasn't enough. By the time they'd gathered enough evidence for a prosecution, Rob would be long gone.

'I said, *is that understood*, DI Morgan?'

Morgan sighed. It wasn't as though he had much choice. 'Yes, ma'am.'

CHAPTER THIRTY-FIVE

As soon as he'd heard about the incident, Morgan called Karen. Phone clamped to his ear, he listened to the ringing tone and gazed out of the large bay windows towards the horizon. Fast-moving clouds whipped across the dark sky above the village. More rain was on the way.

As lightning flashed, illuminating the angry clouds, Karen finally answered the call.

'Are you all right?' he asked.

'I would be if they'd found him.' She exhaled an impatient breath. 'How can somebody jump traffic lights in Lincoln and get away? The area is full of cameras.'

'They'll find him if . . . Well, are you *sure* it was him?'

'Of course I'm sure.' Karen's voice had a definite edge. 'I *saw* him.'

'I just wanted to make sure because the report said the number plate was obscured.'

'It was,' Karen said. He could hear the strain in her voice. She was making an effort to keep calm, but she was angry. 'I saw him, Scott. It was him.'

'I believe you.'

He could almost feel the tension transmitting through the phone and wished there was something he could do to help. Karen was even more frustrated with their lack of progress on this case than him. He'd been intending to confide his suspicions about Rob taking bribes, but now he thought better of it. She'd had quite a shock and it would keep until tomorrow.

'Well, I'm glad you're okay.'

'He saw me. He knows we're on to him.'

'Let's hope he doesn't do anything reckless.'

'I was the one tempted to do something reckless. Believe me. I didn't want him to get away. But he accelerated towards people crossing the road . . .' Karen trailed off, and after a moment added, 'He just didn't care.'

'You did the right thing.'

'Did I?' He heard her heavy sigh. 'He got away. Maybe I should have tried to follow.'

'No, you acted appropriately in the circumstances. We'll catch him.'

'We'd better. How did the interviews go this evening?'

'Not great. We've got a translator, but the women are too scared to talk, and the driver and manager of the salon are saying nothing. They've employed the services of Andrew Norris, who is as slippery as ever and is using his considerable skills to stop them talking to us.'

'Great. So a pretty unsuccessful day all round then.'

'We've had better.'

Rain began to patter against the glass as a low rumble of thunder sounded in the distance.

'How are you doing anyway?' Karen asked. 'I meant to ask you earlier. It can't be easy working with Rob Miller again.'

'That's an understatement. The last few days have reminded me why I dislike the man so much.'

'He doesn't top my list of favourite people either.'

'I think he "accidentally" spilled the beans to Rick and Sophie as well.'

'About the investigation and the reason you left the Thames Valley?'

'Yes. It's my fault. I should have told them already. I've been meaning to . . .'

Karen swore. 'He really is a despicable character.'

Morgan stared at the rain streaming down the window, obscuring his view. The truth was, he'd had many opportunities to tell Rick and Sophie the reason he'd left the Thames Valley police service, but he hadn't because he was ashamed. He didn't want them to think less of him.

Yes, the investigation had cleared him, but he wasn't without fault.

The news would already be spreading. His colleagues would look at him differently, talk behind his back.

'It'll be all over the station tomorrow, but there's not much I can do about it.'

'It was an accident. No one can hold that against you. We've all been there.'

Morgan was silent.

'Look,' Karen said, 'you made a mistake, and you owned it. You're one of the best investigators I've ever worked with. I wouldn't trust DI Miller as far as I could throw him.'

Again Morgan said nothing.

'I'm paying you a compliment here.'

Morgan managed a laugh. 'I appreciate your confidence in me.'

He'd called to make sure Karen was okay, that she was coping after her run-in with Charlie Cook, but somehow she'd turned the conversation around to give *him* the pep talk.

He'd been feeling sorry for himself, worrying about how he'd face the team tomorrow, now they knew the truth behind his transfer. He needed to stop thinking about himself. This case was difficult for him, with Rob Miller turning up and taking charge, but it was even harder for Karen.

There were constant echoes back to the case she'd been investigating just before the death of her husband and daughter. That had to be hard enough on its own, but then she'd witnessed a near miss, a car bearing down on a young child. That must have left her very shaken.

After he hung up, he eyed the half-empty bottle of Glenfiddich on the kitchen counter, but decided against it and switched on the coffee machine instead.

He wanted to be alert tonight, in case there was a development. Although it felt like they were treading water, a turning point in this case could be just around the corner.

He made the coffee and took it through to his small living room.

Something Karen had said on the phone had given Morgan an idea. He was sure Miller was on the take, but proving it was another matter. Gathering evidence took time, and Rob would have an escape plan. When he sensed the net was closing in on him, he would run.

Morgan settled into an armchair and stretched his long legs out in front of him. ACU investigations took time. Procedures needed to be followed, warrants executed, interviews arranged. It all took too long. If Rob was going to be brought down before he managed to worm his way out of trouble again, it was down to Morgan.

He needed a plan. He had to outsmart Rob. That might mean taking some risks.

Morgan sipped his coffee, mulling things over until he came up with a germ of an idea. It was sneaky, relying on some of Rob's own tactics, but if it worked . . .

No one could behave like Rob Miller and not make enemies. Morgan just needed to find those enemies and discover what they knew. Like Rob himself was fond of saying: *Knowledge is power.*

Miller was many things – corrupt, greedy, narcissistic, to name a few – but he wasn't stupid. He'd know by now that he'd aroused suspicion. He'd probably guess Morgan was watching him closely. Looking at his financial records would take time. Time they didn't have. If he wanted Rob neutralised, Morgan had to act now.

Before he could talk himself out of it, he picked up his mobile and scrolled through his contacts. He stopped at Jeff Michaels, one of the officers who'd backed up Rob's account the night they'd been tracking the joyrider. Jeff had known Rob for a long time. He might have some dirt on him.

'Morgan? How are you doing? I haven't heard from you in donkey's years.'

It hadn't been long really, less than a year since they'd last spoken, but Morgan didn't correct him. 'Not bad, Jeff. How are things with you?'

Jeff gave a grunt. 'Not the best, but mustn't grumble. You still with that solicitor lady?'

'No.'

'That's a shame. Still in Lincolnshire?'

'Yes, I'm enjoying it up here.'

'Quieter pace of life?'

'Not as quiet as you might think,' Morgan said.

'I envy you. I considered moving away from the south-east. It's getting more and more expensive down here, and the salaries aren't going up to compensate. Still, I've only got a few more years before I retire.'

'Are you still playing five-a-side?' Morgan asked.

'Nah. More of a golf man these days – five-a-side football is a bit too energetic for me now.' He chuckled.

'A mutual acquaintance of ours turned up at my station this week.'

'Oh, who?'

'DI Rob Miller.'

There was silence on the other end of the phone while Jeff digested the news. 'What's he doing up there?'

'Our investigations overlapped, apparently.'

Jeff gave a non-committal grunt.

'His arrival made me remember something.'

'Oh yes, what's that?' Jeff's tone was guarded.

'Do you recall the old forum we had at the Thames Valley to organise sports events? It turned into more of a social thing.'

'That's going back a few years, but yes, I remember it. Why?'

'Do you remember Rob's forum ID?'

'Oh, yes, Rameses something or other, wasn't it?' Jeff snorted a laugh. 'He fancied himself as some kind of Egyptian king. He always did think a lot of himself, didn't he?'

'Rameses1979?'

'Yes, I think that was it. Why are you interested in that now?'

'I just wanted to make sure I hadn't misremembered.'

'Right,' Jeff said. An awkward silence followed and then he blurted out, 'Look, I owe you an apology. That's why you're phoning really, isn't it? You've spoken to Rob.'

He sounded flat and defeated.

Morgan played along. 'Yes, I spoke to him.'

'The double-crossing sod. I should have known.'

'He's not trustworthy.'

'You can say that again. And you'd know better than most.'

'Yes.'

'I'm sorry, mate.' Jeff blew out a sigh. 'You know what Miller is like. He had one over on me. I had to back up his story. He said he'd tell the wife about my affair with Annette. We'd just got back together. I couldn't risk it.'

Morgan's grip tightened on the coffee cup handle, so tight it tilted, spilling lukewarm coffee on to his trouser leg. He muttered a curse.

'I know, you're right,' Jeff said. 'But he made me back up his statement, forced me to say you'd reported the wrong address. I didn't want to do it, but I had to stick to the story. He said he'd tell my wife my dirty little secret. He would've done it too. Vindictive weasel.'

'So you lied?'

'I had no choice.'

'I gave the right address that night.' Morgan's voice cracked.

'Yes, but . . . but Rob made me lie.'

Morgan rubbed a hand over his face. 'It wasn't my fault the joyrider and his brother died.'

'No, but listen, I would have come clean earlier, but the investigation cleared you. So I figured no harm, no foul, right?'

Morgan couldn't reply straightaway. He was still reeling from the news. He'd known that Rob was sly and deceptive, but this?

Morgan had truly believed he'd messed up. He'd doubted himself, lived with the horror of believing he was responsible for the death of two people, one of whom was only ten years old.

'You still there?'

'Yes.'

'It was all for nothing anyway. My wife left me six months later. I really am sorry, mate.'

After a pause, Morgan said, 'So am I.'

Jeff babbled for a bit, ranting about DI Miller's behaviour over the years. Morgan was only half listening.

'That's not the worst of it. He's a bent cop. Properly corrupt. He's on the payroll of at least two of the big organised crime gangs down here. Everyone knows.'

That got Morgan's attention. Alert, he asked, 'Why hasn't anyone done anything about it?'

'It's an open secret, you know how things are. Whistle-blowers don't exactly get the red carpet, do they? And afterwards they can kiss goodbye to any chance of promotion. Prospects go down the drain. Reporting a fellow officer messes up your whole career.'

'Well, Jeff, I hope it doesn't in this case, because you're about to become a whistle-blower.'

'What? No, I can't. I've nothing left except my job. If I lose that, then I lose everything. I'm only a few years away from retirement.'

'I need you to go on record to say Rob pressured you into lying in your statement and you believe Rob was taking bribes.'

'I won't.'

'You don't have a choice.' Morgan's tone was no longer friendly. 'Either you go on record, talk to my superintendent and tell her what you know, or I'll report you for lying in your statement and make sure you get chucked off the force.'

'I'll deny it.' Jeff's voice trembled.

'You can deny all you like, but I've recorded this conversation,' Morgan lied.

'That's illegal . . . It's inadmissible . . .' Jeff stammered.

'I'll make sure everyone hears it at my station. Word will spread. The brass will go over your career with a fine-tooth comb until they find something. It's not just you, Jeff. There were others who backed up Rob's story. I'm going to go after them and get them to speak out against Rob too.'

Jeff's voice sounded broken. 'You can't really mean for me to—'

'Yes, I can.'

He felt a pang of sympathy for Jeff. He was right about the treatment whistle-blowers often got from the police service, but right now that wasn't his main concern. His priority was taking down a dirty officer. By the sound of things, Rob had been on the take for quite some time. And it was likely he was on the Cooks' payroll too, which meant working on the modern slavery investigation gave him plenty of information to feed the Cooks.

When he realised that begging wasn't going to get Morgan to change his mind, Jeff reluctantly said he'd tell Superintendent Murray everything he knew. Morgan did not envy the position Jeff found himself in, but he had to reserve his pity for those who needed it most. The men and women who'd been tricked into working for a pittance and treated like commodities.

After Morgan hung up, he went to the kitchen and tried to clean the coffee stain on his trousers, dabbing it with a damp sponge. The trousers were dry-clean only. Typical. He frowned at the stain he'd only managed to make worse. He'd try to find ten minutes to take them into the cleaners tomorrow.

He eyed the whisky on the counter again and then turned away. Tonight wasn't the time to give in to temptation.

The shock was slowly sinking in. The belief his negligence had resulted in the deaths of two youngsters had changed him. The guilt had eaten away at his confidence, made him paranoid – meticulous to the point of obsession – and now, after all this time, he'd discovered he hadn't given the wrong address after all.

It was a relief, but he wasn't entirely innocent. If he'd recorded the address in his logbook as he should have done, and all his paperwork had been up to date, he wouldn't have been vulnerable to Rob Miller's lies and manipulation.

He made a fresh coffee and sipped it, enjoying the bitter heat, and smiled. Things hadn't gone according to plan, but his scheme to bring Rob down was underway. Step one was complete.

CHAPTER THIRTY-SIX

After her conversation with Morgan, Karen had taken a quick shower and changed into a faded pair of jeans and one of Josh's old rugby shirts. Running her hand through her damp hair, she headed downstairs.

She felt oddly out of place at home, like she was running on autopilot until she got back to the investigation. So maybe she *did* use work as a crutch. That wasn't so terrible, was it? It helped to have a routine, a purpose.

Christine had caught her returning from work earlier and had wanted to know if Karen was all right. It took her a second or two to realise Christine was concerned because she hadn't turned up for their prearranged dinner. With everything going on at work, she'd completely forgotten. After apologising profusely, they rescheduled for next week.

Christine had waved off her apologies. 'Don't be silly. These things happen when you're in the middle of a stressful case. By the way, I've heard Grace Baker intends to remain in Louth with her sister.'

Karen wasn't surprised. The incident must have left Grace terribly shaken. Karen was disappointed there wasn't more she could do to help.

She'd followed up with the SOCOs but nothing had come of it. No useful fingerprints. Nothing left behind by the intruder. Just another break-in that would probably remain unsolved, leaving a devastated woman afraid in her own home. It was scandalous how many burglaries went unsolved. Even if, against all odds, the police managed to find the culprit, sentencing would probably be lenient. The after-effects of the crime would stay with the victim far longer than for the criminal.

Grace Baker had been robbed of her sense of security.

Karen settled down on the sofa and tried to switch off by watching mindless television. But it wasn't working. The links between the previous case to do with the Perrys and this current one with the Cooks were getting closer and closer in Karen's mind. Was that because she wanted the cases to be linked? Because she wanted answers, and justice for Josh and Tilly's deaths? Was there really a connection? At times, she thought she'd never have any answers.

Christine had been the perfect sounding board as usual. Karen had told her as much as she could, without giving away the key details of the investigation, focusing on her doubts over her abilities as a police officer.

'I should think your reaction is perfectly understandable,' Christine had said, glancing up at the stormy sky as they stood on Karen's drive.

'But there was an investigation after the accident. The verdict was clear. No other vehicles were involved. Josh lost control of the car,' Karen said, rubbing the back of her aching neck. 'Sometimes I think I'm losing my mind.'

Christine had pursed her lips as she shook her head emphatically. 'Now, I don't know anything about your current case, other than the fact it involves a fire at The Red Lion and the Perrys, but I do know you. And you are *very* good at your job.'

Karen had smiled and hugged the older woman. Though Christine didn't understand the intricacies and politics involved in the police service, sometimes it was nice to talk to someone outside it all. Someone who, no matter what, was always on your side.

Karen had considered telling her about the accident but thought better of it. Christine didn't need to know the details.

Sometimes Karen envied the general public. Going about her day-to-day life without witnessing the monstrosities people inflicted on one another would make a pleasant change.

No one could avoid the news, though. These days, people were bombarded with reports on dictators, hatred, wars, racism and genocide. But seeing it on a television screen or printed page created distance. It was quite different to seeing the direct aftermath of attacks, burglaries and violent assaults in person.

Perhaps it was inevitable that officers were vulnerable to mental health issues after witnessing what they did, day in, day out. And the trauma was one thing, but doubting her own instincts was quite another. Karen found that the hardest thing to deal with. She'd always been confident and sure of herself before the accident. It was as though her life was divided into two stages: before the accident and after.

She had a good life. Better than most. With a roof over her head, a steady job and a family who loved her. Compared to the Vietnamese women shipped into the country and farmed out for slave labour, Karen had an easy life. She wondered how Vishal was getting on at the Immigrant Removal Centre. She'd referred his case to a charity and hoped they'd work on his legal application. After everything he'd been through, he deserved a break. But he was only one of many on the charity's list, and Karen had no sway in getting him bumped up the queue.

She thought back over the previous few days, her mind flitting from incident to incident. Patricia Perry laughing in her face, telling her she should have learned her lesson last time. Charlie Cook pretending to be Aleksy Iskow. DC Farzana Shah's dark, vigilant eyes, seemingly watching Karen's every move. Freeman lying about Olivia Webster reading a book for no discernible reason. Rob Miller's easy claim that Charlie Cook was dead and they shouldn't waste their time looking for him, when he was very much alive. The names in the notebook. Olivia Webster's condescending looks.

But, try as she might, she couldn't make sense of it at all. She'd try to contact Meghan Cook again tomorrow. She was the Cook family's weak link. She was the way in.

Karen gave a jolt when her mobile pinged with an alert.

She blinked. She must have drifted off. The TV was still on. She picked up the phone, rubbing her eyes.

Blearily she peered at the screen and saw it wasn't a message, but an alert. Her security camera had been activated.

Karen yawned and stretched. No doubt it was one of the neighbourhood cats. Probably the big ginger tom Christina had taken to shooing out of her garden because it had been using the gravelled area as a giant litter tray. She swiped the app on her iPhone and opened up the camera footage.

She leaned forward with a jerk when she saw it wasn't a cat but a car parked on her driveway.

It was supposed to be real-time, but the recorded video was delayed just a fraction.

Karen tried to zoom in without success. She then headed to the front door and peered through the glass.

The car was still there. Whoever it was wasn't in a hurry to knock or announce their arrival.

It wasn't late, but the heavy rain clouds made the sky dark. Karen looked around for the keys, her hand on the door handle, then paused. She had a bad feeling. Her gut was telling her to be cautious. She quickly tapped out a text to Morgan.

Not urgent. Someone's parked on my driveway. I'm just
about to go and check it out.

She took a photo of the car through the glass and sent that too.
Better safe than sorry.

She grabbed the keys from the kitchen table and carried them
back to the front door before unlocking it slowly. She stepped out
on to the porch.

Rain was falling steadily. The car was a small, dark Hyundai. A
shadowy figure got out of the car.

Karen breathed a sigh of relief. 'Oh, it's you. What are you
doing here? Is something wrong?'

The slight figure shut the car door and walked towards the
house.

'What are you doing lurking out here? Why didn't you knock?'
Karen asked.

Farzana Shah ran a hand through her hair. Her eyes were intent
on Karen's. 'I wanted to talk to you.'

'Couldn't it wait until tomorrow?'

'No.'

'All right, you'd better come in. You're getting soaked,' Karen
said.

Farzana didn't return her smile or seem bothered by the rain.

Karen's relief was ebbing away.

It was only DC Shah. She'd worked with the younger officer for
years, and although they didn't socialise out of work, they'd always
been friendly. Recently she'd noticed DC Shah's watchful stare, but
as soon as Karen met her gaze, she'd bury her head in paperwork.

Was she really watching her, or was it simply Karen's overactive
imagination? Had this case made her paranoid?

She shut the door behind them. 'Cup of tea?'

'Thanks,' Farzana said, her face stony as she followed Karen into the kitchen.

Karen had just flicked the switch on the kettle when the security alert on her phone went off again. This time it really had to be a neighbour's cat.

She ignored it, not wanting to take her eyes off DC Shah.

'So, what is it you wanted to talk to me about?' Karen asked, getting two mugs from the cupboard above the kettle.

Farzana clasped her hands together. A muscle twitched at her jaw. Before she said anything, they were interrupted by the chime of the doorbell.

Karen jumped, dropping a teaspoon so it clattered on the tiled floor. She was more on edge than she'd realised.

She put the spoon in the sink and headed to the front door. Farzana followed closely.

Peering through the glass panel in the door, Karen felt a chill run through her body.

She turned and waved a hand at DC Shah to make her move back. 'Get out. Go through the garage door off the kitchen. Call for backup.'

Farzana frowned. She craned her neck, trying to look past Karen to the door. 'Why?'

'It's Charlie Cook.'

CHAPTER THIRTY-SEVEN

Why was Charlie Cook at Karen's house? Did he want to hand himself in? If so, why hadn't he gone to the nearest police station? Why come to her?

As soon as she was certain Farzana was out of sight, Karen took a deep breath and opened the door.

Sheltering under the porch as the rain teemed down behind him was Charlie, tall and intimidating. Karen's grip on the door handle tightened. It was hard to believe she'd ever believed this man was Aleksy Iskow. She'd pitied him, believing he'd been mistreated at the hands of the Perrys.

He hunched his large shoulders, bunching up his leather jacket. He'd turned the collar up to protect him from the rain, but his fair hair was soaked, plastered against his scalp. He wiped away the water trickling down his forehead.

'DS Hart,' he slurred, and nodded at her.

He'd been drinking.

'Charlie, what are you doing here?' She made sure to use his real name so he realised she was on to his deception.

He smirked.

Karen really hoped Farzana had called for backup already.

'Can I come in?'

After a brief hesitation, she opened the door wide. 'We've been looking for you, Charlie.'

'I know.' He gave a ridiculous grin as he tripped up the front step.

She adjusted her initial assessment. He wasn't just drunk. He'd had a shedload.

He put a hand on the wall to steady himself.

She looked over his shoulder and saw his black Range Rover parked on her drive beside Farzana's Hyundai and behind her own car. She shivered at the thought of him careering along the roads in that state.

'How much have you had to drink?' Karen asked.

His gaze slipped down to meet hers. Towering over her, his piercing blue eyes cold and calculating, he no longer looked like a helpless drunk. 'That's the least of my concerns right now.'

She pointed to the kitchen and let Charlie walk ahead of her along the hallway, keeping a close eye on him. He wasn't carrying any weapons as far as she could tell, but he could have a concealed knife on him.

He shrugged off his wet leather jacket, throwing it on top of the table.

Karen handed him a clean tea towel so he could dab the water from his face.

'I'm going to arrest you for the murder of Aleksy Iskow, Charlie.'

He held up a hand. 'Wait. I know you've got a job to do, but I came here for a reason. I want to talk.'

Charlie Cook standing in the middle of her kitchen was a ludicrous sight, one that made Karen uncomfortable. He'd found out where she lived. That wouldn't have been difficult. She was well known in the villages as the local police officer. Residents had no hesitation contacting her about parking infractions, suspicious characters and difficult neighbours. It was irritating at times, but nothing like this. It wasn't in the same league as having a killer in her kitchen.

Karen pulled out a chair for him at the table. She drew the line at making him a cup of tea, but if he wanted to talk, she was prepared to listen. Besides, talking would keep him busy until backup arrived.

Karen sat down too, but took the chair furthest from him. 'All right, what did you want to talk about?'

He raked his fingers through his wet hair and looked miserably down at the table. 'I never meant for any of this to happen this way.'

You mean you never meant to be caught.

'Did you kill Aleksy Iskow?' Karen asked.

Charlie's face creased as though he was in pain. 'I didn't mean to do it. I just meant to rough him up a bit. Scare him a little. He told my father he was going to go to the police.'

'Aleksy was bludgeoned to death, Charlie. I think that's a bit more than roughing him up, wouldn't you say?'

Karen's voice was sharp. She was wary of him. He didn't look like he was about to go on a violent rampage, but she shouldn't have snapped. She didn't want to push his buttons and trigger his anger.

He leaned heavily on the table. 'You're right. I got carried away and things got out of hand. But I need your help.'

'My help?'

'Yes. I need you to cut me a deal.'

'I can't do that, Charlie.'

'I've got information. I know a lot of stuff. About all the operations going back years as well as future plans. I can tell you it all, but I need protection.'

Karen watched him carefully. His face was flushed and animated, but it was almost as though he were an actor playing a role. She'd been fooled by him once. Never again.

When she didn't respond, he went on. 'You can do that, can't you? Witness protection and all that? I don't want to go to jail.'

He looked like a frightened schoolboy as he clasped his big hands together. It was hard to believe the scared man in front of her had repeatedly battered Aleksy over the head with a blunt instrument.

'It's something you can discuss with my boss. I can't authorise anything.'

His gaze flicked up to meet hers. 'You know, I was planning to go turn myself in this afternoon. I picked up my car and then I drove around Lincoln, trying to build up the courage.' He gave her what he must have thought was a disarming smile. 'Then I saw you and panicked.'

'You nearly collided with pedestrians on the crossing. Were you drunk then?'

'No, I just panicked. I just had to get out of there. I . . . wasn't ready.'

'And you're ready now?'

Charlie nodded.

'Why did you impersonate Aleksy?'

'It was a spur-of-the-moment thing. You'd caught me red-handed. Pretending to be Aleksy was a gamble, but I thought I'd be safe with the police for a little while at least. My uncle . . . He's a bad man.'

'Harry Cook?'

'Yes, he wasn't happy with me. It was my fault Aleksy got hold of some information that was very problematic for my uncle.'

'The notebook?'

Charlie blinked. 'You found it? Where did he put it? I searched for ages.'

'Canwick Hill, on the common. Not too far from where you killed him.'

Charlie winced at her words and then blew out a breath. 'That notebook caused me so many problems. I *knew* Aleksy had taken it. I gave him a deadline to give it back. I *warned* him. But he didn't listen. Then he went to my father and told him he was going to the police. Dad told Uncle Harry, and the next thing I knew there were whispers of a contract on my head. I freaked out. But I figured if I could find the notebook or destroy it along with any other evidence, he might let me off.' His face turned hard. 'Should have known better.'

'So you were looking for the notebook, going through Aleksy's things when we turned up at The Red Lion?'

'Right. I thought he might have left it in the garage. When you turned up, I thought my luck had run out, but then I decided pretending to be Aleksy could be my way out.'

'And Vishal and Joe went along with it?'

He shrugged. 'I was their boss. They knew better than to contradict me.'

Boss. Karen thought that was an interesting word choice.

'So why turn yourself in now?'

'Because he won't forgive me no matter what I do. I can't hide forever. Not on my own. Not from my uncle. He knows too many people. I *need* witness protection.'

'And you're prepared to tell us everything you know about the organisation?'

Charlie nodded eagerly. 'Yes, everything.'

'What about your wife and father? Will Harry use them against you?'

Charlie shook his head. 'Meghan will be fine. She always is. She only married me for the money. My father couldn't care less about me, so I don't see why I should be bothered about him. If he'd stood up to Harry in the first place, none of this would have happened.'

Karen was taken aback by the lack of concern Charlie showed for his family, especially his wife. But why was she surprised? This was a man who'd battered someone to death and had no qualms about treating people like slaves.

Bargaining with him was like doing a deal with the devil. They needed his information to get solid convictions and a shot at bringing down the entire network, but it would mean handing Charlie his freedom, a whole fresh start. And he really didn't deserve that in Karen's opinion.

'What do you want?'

'No jail time.'

'I don't know if that's possible, Charlie. You're not an innocent victim in all this.'

'I never said I was innocent.' Charlie raised his voice. He put his balled fist on the table. 'But it's in your interest to give me a deal.'

Karen said nothing while she thought it through. He was right. They did need his help and that was galling. She glanced at the clock hanging on the wall behind him. Had Farzana called Morgan as well as uniform?

'I just want you to guarantee my safety,' Charlie said, his tone wheedling. 'Maybe I'll have to serve a little bit of time, but it has to be minimal, and you have to keep me away from other prisoners.'

When Karen didn't reply immediately, he snarled, 'Am I just wasting my time here?'

Karen didn't want him to leave and she didn't want him agitated either. 'No, I'm just trying to work things out. If we're going to do a deal, you need to be honest with me. Tell me everything.'

Charlie was quiet for a moment, then nodded. 'All right.'

Karen put her hands flat on the table. 'The fire at The Red Lion. Who started that?'

His eyes went sly then cleared again quickly. He was considering lying to her.

He puffed out his cheeks as he blew out a long breath. 'Okay. If we're being honest . . . That was me. Tying up loose ends. I knew it was what Harry wanted. The Perrys were a weak link. We had to get rid of them, and I thought if Aleksy had hidden the notebook somewhere on the premises, it would be destroyed. I'd already searched the garage, so I knew it wasn't there.'

'Rod and Patricia Perry died in the fire, along with their fourteen-year-old son.'

Not a flicker of remorse showed on Charlie's face as he said, 'Yes, I'm sorry about that but it had to be done.'

Karen swallowed her distaste and tried to keep her expression neutral. 'So you killed the Perrys because they might talk?'

Charlie grunted. 'Don't look at me like that. They weren't nice people. It's hardly a big loss to the world.'

Fourteen-year-old Barry Perry had died alongside his parents, murdered by Charlie Cook. But the boy's death meant nothing to him.

The man had no morals. No qualms about killing. He'd kill again given the chance. Aleksy's injuries, his smashed face and skull, had made it clear his killer was a man out of control. The cool, conceited way he delivered his lines told her this was rehearsed. Charlie Cook was a monster. He wasn't a victim, forced to commit murder on the say-so of his uncle. He enjoyed it.

Karen pushed back from the table. She needed a minute to think things through. She walked over to the sink, looking out through the rain-splattered window. She closed her eyes and took a breath, counting to ten.

Stay calm. Screaming at him won't help.

A flash of lightning illuminated the garden as she opened her eyes. Where was backup? Had something happened to Farzana? Had she not been able to call for help?

Behind her, Charlie growled, angry now. 'I knew this was a mistake. I shouldn't have come here.'

Karen turned to face him. 'It's not a mistake, Charlie. It's just a lot to take in. I had dealings with the Perrys in the past. Were they working with your father and uncle five years ago?'

Charlie's eyes narrowed. 'Yes.'

Karen's mouth grew dry. She pressed a hand against her chest. It hurt. It was supposed to be over. She was past this now, wasn't she? Moving on? She'd finally accepted the verdict. Josh and Tilly had died in an accident. There was no proof of a cover-up, and she'd looked for evidence, she'd searched for anything that could make sense of their deaths, but in the end she'd listened to those she trusted, the officers she'd worked with so closely over the years that she'd come to view them as extended family.

It wasn't the time to ask these questions. It was better to wait until he was under caution at the station, but she couldn't hold back. 'There was an accident five years ago. My husband and daughter died when their car veered out of control on Canwick Hill.'

Her gaze met Charlie's ice-like eyes. She was showing vulnerability. Madness when dealing with a man like Charlie Cook. She shouldn't be asking him about the accident. She should stick to procedural questions, but she couldn't stop herself.

'When I spoke to her on Sunday, Patricia Perry said I should have learned my lesson. Do you know anything about the accident?'

Charlie's eyes were guarded. The sly look was back. 'Yes,' he said slowly, lowering his voice. 'The Perrys were responsible for the crash.'

Karen's stomach churned. The silence in the kitchen seemed deafening. She stared at Charlie, but his face was impassive and blank.

She wanted answers so badly. Needed them. But had it really come to this? Relying on this man for answers? He was a psychopath. There was no remorse for what he'd done, no empathy for his victims.

Now he was watching her reactions carefully before responding, giving her what she wanted. He was trying to appear normal.

'What happened?' Karen asked.

Charlie leaned back in the chair and looked up at the ceiling, as though trying to think back. 'You'd been digging around, investigating the Perrys. They weren't happy about it. They thought you were getting a bit too close for comfort and wanted to give you a warning.' He tilted his head and looked at Karen. 'They thought you were driving. They wanted to give you a little scare, that's all. But your husband overreacted and lost control of the car.'

Karen swallowed the lump in her throat. 'Why did he veer off the road?'

'They went up alongside him, only planning to give the car a little nudge. They even pulled back when they realised it wasn't you driving. But it was too late, your husband swerved, put the steering on full lock and the car rolled.' Charlie shrugged. 'Couldn't have predicted the outcome.'

'The report said there were no cars around.' Karen's voice was barely a whisper.

Again that sneaky look flitted across his features. 'Reports don't mean much when you've got cash to wave around. If you think about it, I did you a favour. After what the Perrys did, you should be grateful.'

A favour? Karen's mouth grew dry. 'But how did the Perrys have access to that sort of money? It must have come from your father or uncle, but why would they protect the *Perrys* . . .'

'Business,' Charlie said. 'Covering their own backs.' He was oblivious to her reaction. He kept talking about what happened that day, describing the timeline of the accident exactly.

He didn't just know a few details. He knew everything.

Karen gripped the kitchen counter, forced herself to breathe. The Perrys hadn't been the ones who'd forced Josh to crash. It had been Charlie Cook.

CHAPTER THIRTY-EIGHT

Charlie continued describing the incident in a monotone voice as Karen watched him, blood rushing in her ears, her skin slick with sweat.

She was standing in her kitchen with the man responsible for the death of her husband and daughter.

Karen started to pace. Her throat burned, her eyes stung. She balled her fists, trying to keep control.

'So you can help me, though, right? Get me protection?' Charlie asked.

His arrogance was unbelievable. He thought she'd eat up his lies, believe his manipulative tale that the Perrys had caused the accident. More than that, though, was his attempt at coercing her into helping him. As though him killing the Perrys was some kind of favour. That she should be *grateful* to him.

Karen nodded distractedly. 'I think we should be able to do that. There'll be procedures we'll need to follow, and it will have to be authorised.'

'But my information is valuable. You won't be able to bring charges without me. At least, none that will stick.' Charlie looked smug.

Karen stopped pacing and stood by the kitchen sink, gripping the edge of the counter. She eyed the wooden block of knives beside the microwave.

Would she kill him if she could get away with it?

She pictured her fingers closing around the handle of a knife, hiding the blade under her sleeve and slowly walking over to Charlie Cook before sliding it deep into his flesh.

She could take the law into her own hands. Take her own vengeance. Say it was self-defence. DC Shah was here, but she was outside. She wouldn't be a witness. No one would know.

As Charlie continued to boast about his knowledge, she moved closer to the knife block. He was drunk. His defences would be lowered, and she knew exactly where to plunge the knife to cause the most damage.

'Are you listening?' Charlie said, turning in his chair.

Karen turned her head and stared back at him, hating him more than she'd ever hated anyone in her life. She didn't think it was possible to despise someone this much.

She squeezed her eyes shut and stepped away from the knives. He'd taken her husband and daughter, but she wouldn't let him take her humanity, too. She sucked in a breath.

Karen wouldn't kill him, but she was going to make sure he paid for what he'd done.

'Let me call my boss,' she said, pulling her mobile from the back pocket of her jeans. 'She'll be able to give me the go-ahead and then we can move on to the first step.'

Charlie screwed up his face, scrutinising her. 'I don't know. How do I know I can trust you? You lot might decide to fit me up for everything and let my uncle and father walk away.'

'I suppose that's just a chance you'll have to take, Charlie,' Karen said, accessing her contacts.

Stupid. She'd taken her eyes off him. Let her guard down.

Charlie moved fast, darting towards her and slapping the phone from her hand. It clattered to the floor. 'No, I'm not ready yet. Don't call anyone.'

A fierce surge of anger had her gritting her teeth. 'Back off. Or you'll get nothing!'

He flinched and took a step back, not sure how to react.

Why hadn't the police arrived yet? Had Farzana called them? Or was she one of the corrupt officers working for the Cooks? Had she known Charlie was coming here? She could be working as a spy for Harry and Eric.

'You broke the screen,' Karen snapped, picking up the phone and inspecting the long, thin crack running along the length of her phone. 'I thought you wanted a deal.'

'I do, but I've not finished talking.' He pouted like a child. 'I want to know you're serious about this.'

I bet you do, thought Karen, putting the phone on the counter behind her.

'What do you know about police corruption?' Karen asked, her gaze magnetically drawn back towards the knife block.

A broad grin spread across Charlie's face. 'That's more like it. Now you're using your brain. I know quite a bit actually. I can give you several names.'

'There was a list in the notebook under the heading *999*. That's police officers on the Cook payroll, right?'

Charlie laughed. 'Yes, and there's quite a lot of them.'

'All from Lincolnshire?'

'No, not just Lincolnshire. Harry's got feelers everywhere. He calls them his little pets.'

Karen couldn't stop the shudder that gripped her body. She folded her arms, hugging herself tightly. 'Give me some names.'

'Not yet,' Charlie said, grinning as he wagged a finger at her. 'Can I have a drink? It's been a hell of a night.'

Karen thought he'd had enough already. 'Tea? Coffee?'

'I was thinking something stronger.'

'Whisky?'

'That'll do.' Charlie sniffed and ruffled his hair, which was now nearly dry.

Karen made to walk past him.

'Where do you think you're going?' He reached out a long arm and snared Karen's wrist.

She glared at him. 'To get your whisky. The drinks cabinet is in the living room. Let go of my arm.'

As she made her way to the living room, she paused near the front door, gazing out. Was Farzana still there? She thought she saw a movement as the security light came on.

'What's going on out there?' Charlie hissed.

Karen turned quickly to see him right behind her.

His face contorted with rage. 'You tricked me. This was a trap.'

Karen put her hands against his chest, pushing him back. 'No, it's just the security light. It's nothing.'

'Don't lie to me,' he yelled, grabbing her shoulders and then shoving her aside.

Her head cracked against the wall.

His eyes searched the driveway. 'There's someone out there.'

He reached for the door handle. Karen grabbed his arm to stop him. She couldn't let him leave now.

But Charlie flung his arm back, his elbow connecting with Karen's stomach, winding her.

Breathless, she gripped his arm again, yanking it, trying to get it behind his back so he couldn't use his size advantage against her.

But despite the amount of drink he'd obviously consumed, he was too strong and too quick.

With a shout of fury, he turned, ripped her hands from his arm and kicked out. His foot connected with the side of her knee.

The pain was a fiery arrow shooting up her leg. She sank to the floor, clutching her knee. As Charlie made his way outside she tried to stand, but her leg gave way under her, the pain causing her to cry out.

Refusing to give up, she pushed herself to her hands and knees. Dots and flashes of light swam in front of her eyes.

'You're gonna pay for double-crossing me,' he snarled, and aimed a kick at her head.

The thick sole of his boot connected with Karen's jaw with a thud that reverberated around her skull. She tasted blood and her vision blurred.

Haven't I already paid? Karen wanted to scream as he turned away from her. He'd taken two people she'd loved. He'd destroyed her life.

Charlie ran to his Range Rover as thunder boomed overhead.

Where was Farzana's car? Had she left to let Karen handle things alone? She should have asked Charlie if DC Shah was one of the corrupt officers on the list.

Karen tenderly touched the side of her knee and then snatched her hand away in agony. It was already swollen.

Clutching her head, she limped back into the kitchen for her phone. Despite the long crack running along the centre of it, the touchscreen was still working.

Muttering a curse, she dialled the direct line to Nettleham. If Charlie was trying to run, she needed every traffic unit in the vicinity on the lookout for his vehicle. The phone clamped to her ear, she made her way back to the front door as he got back into his Range Rover and started the engine.

The security light was on, but the heavy rain and trees made it hard to see.

In the distance she could hear sirens.

Karen willed them to get here faster.

The Range Rover's engine roared and Charlie reversed towards the road. The crunch of metal against metal made Karen start. The Range Rover came to an abrupt halt.

Her face creased in confusion as she frowned and stepped out on to the drive. Rain hit her like needles. She put a hand up to shield her face.

Farzana's car was parked parallel to the drive's exit, blocking Charlie's escape.

Despite the throbbing pain in her knee, Karen managed a smile as she spotted DC Shah standing at the edge of the driveway, close to the hawthorn hedge, watching anxiously as the Range Rover rammed her car again.

'You stopped him escaping,' Karen said.

Farzana came closer. She had a smudge of grease on her right cheek. Her hair fell in wet strands around her face. 'I hope so. It's a powerful vehicle though. He might be able to push my car out of the way.' Her eyes widened as she got a better look at Karen. 'He hit you?'

'Kicked,' Karen said grimly, wiping away the blood from her lower lip. 'I'm all right though,' she added quickly, pulling away as Farzana reached out.

They both watched as the Range Rover reversed into the car again. This time the Hyundai moved at an angle. The drive wasn't long enough for him to pick up any speed, which worked to their advantage, but he was making headway. A few more seconds and the car would no longer hold him back.

Karen looked at Farzana and attempted a smile, though her jaw ached with the effort. 'That was quick thinking. It might slow him down just long enough.'

The sirens were getting closer.

Farzana grinned. 'I found a jack in your garage, and thought I'd try something to immobilise the car in case he tried to get away before backup arrived. I wanted to remove a couple of the wheels, but in the end I figured blocking the driveway entrance was a better option.'

Charlie thumped the steering wheel in frustration as the sirens grew louder. Karen got a glimpse of the blue flashing lights through the trees. They had him.

When the first patrol car pulled up, Karen felt relief knowing Charlie couldn't escape now, but it didn't ease the burning anger bubbling through her system.

Wet, cold and shivering, Karen wouldn't go inside out of the rain until she'd seen Charlie Cook hauled out of the Range Rover and handcuffed.

'We got him,' Farzana said, and punched the air.

'We did,' Karen agreed.

She appreciated DC Shah's enthusiasm, but the hard part still lay ahead. If Charlie got his deal, would she be able to live with it? Knowing he'd initiated the accident that had led to her husband and daughter's deaths, would she be able to watch him walk away unpunished?

CHAPTER THIRTY-NINE

Karen sat at her kitchen table with PC Mackintosh taking her pulse. He was a first-aider and a member of St John Ambulance, so he'd volunteered to check her injuries. He'd felt all around her scalp and neck for trauma and seemed concerned by the small lump on the back of her head.

It must have happened when Charlie Cook had pushed her against the wall. Karen was more concerned with her knee. It was hot to the touch and throbbing.

'What's the date today?' PC Mackintosh asked.

'Twenty-second of May,' Karen said. She wasn't likely to forget that date for a long time.

'How are you feeling?' He checked her pupils.

'Not too bad considering, but my knee hurts.'

'Hmm. I think you'll need to rest it for a few days and keep it elevated. If it gets worse, you should go to A&E. In fact, because you've had a bump to the head you might be better off going to the hospital now to get checked out.'

'I don't think that's necessary. My head feels fine now.'

'Did you lose consciousness?'

'No.'

'Have you been sick?'

Karen shook her head. 'No.'

Morgan appeared in the kitchen doorway. His coat was dripping wet.

'Are you okay?' he asked, his face a mask of worry.

'I'm fine apart from a few bruises and a sore knee. Charlie Cook has been arrested and taken to Nettleham station.'

'Looks like you won't be interviewing Charlie then?' He nodded at her elevated leg with a sympathetic look.

But that wasn't the only reason Karen wouldn't be doing the interview. Now she knew what Charlie had done, it wouldn't be ethical, and she didn't want to do anything that might ruin the chance of a conviction.

Karen gave a regretful smile. 'I'm sure you'll do a good job.'

Morgan put a hand on her shoulder and gave it a gentle squeeze. 'Farzana told me what happened.'

As they'd stood in the rain, watching Charlie being carted off, Karen had told Farzana she knew Charlie Cook was responsible for the death of her husband and daughter. It hadn't taken DC Shah long to spread the word.

Karen frowned and shifted in her seat to fully face Morgan. 'I'm not imagining things. I *know* he was behind the accident. I'm also certain it was covered up.'

PC Mackintosh raised his eyebrows and held up his hands. 'Don't mind me.' He reminded Karen to go straight to A&E if she felt worse and then left the kitchen.

'Don't tell me I'm overreacting,' Karen warned.

Pain made her tetchy, and she was in no mood to pander to police politics. She *knew* Charlie was responsible.

Karen was expecting Morgan to shrug off the idea and try to convince her she was wrong, but he didn't. He nodded slowly.

'I believe you,' he said, taking the wind from Karen's sails.

'Oh . . . I thought it would be harder to convince you than that.'

'I'm on your side.'

'So you're not going to tell me that I'm being overemotional?' Karen asked coolly, remembering the comments made by some of her colleagues in the months following the crash.

'I've never said that.'

'Sorry, that was uncalled for.' Karen rubbed her hands over her face, suddenly feeling very tired.

Morgan sat down beside her.

'He's going to get away with this, isn't he?' Karen said. 'He'll get a deal and get away with everything.'

'No. We won't let that happen.'

Karen looked into Morgan's eyes and wished she could believe him. But he knew as well as she did that some convictions required a high price.

She swallowed the bitterness and looked at the floor. 'I was so tempted to forget the case and punish him myself.'

Her gaze flickered back up to Morgan's, and she knew he understood.

His jaw set in a firm line. 'We need to handle this the right way.'

Karen exhaled a long breath. 'I know, but it's not easy.'

'Will he be able to tell us which police officers were involved in the cover-up after the accident?'

'I think so.'

'That's a good start.'

Karen wasn't sure a good start was sufficient to bring this network of lies and corruption down. She wanted to believe they could root out the bribery and deception that had allowed the Cooks to carry on operating and exploiting people for so long. And she desperately wanted Charlie Cook to be punished, but was a good start enough?

◆ ◆ ◆

Morgan's phone rang. He apologised to Karen and moved away, expecting it to be the superintendent wanting an update.

It wasn't.

It was DI Rob Miller's name on the screen.

The warrant had been approved, but Rob's accounts hadn't yet been scrutinised. Morgan was confident they would see a number of unidentified payments coming into Rob's account over the past few years. He was sure Rob was on the Cooks' payroll.

It would take time for officers specialising in financial fraud to plough through accounts and statements, trying to find links between Rob and the Cooks. So far they'd determined the Cooks used a shell company set up in a British protectorate. That would make it hard to trace.

They'd already discovered Olivia Webster had two accounts at the same bank, one in her maiden name, though she'd married seven years ago and divorced two years later. Innocent, or was she using that account for her payments from the Cooks?

He answered the call. 'DI Miller, where are you?'

'Missing me already, Scotty?'

'Something like that.'

'I just wanted a word with you.'

'It's a bit late to call for a chat.'

'You're hurting my feelings.'

'Are you at the hotel? Something big is going down with the Cook case. We could do with your help.'

Rob laughed. 'I wasn't born yesterday. You'll have to do better than that, Scotty.'

He knew. Someone had tipped him off. So why the phone call? Was he calling to gloat?

'You're not going to hand yourself in then?'

'That's not my style. But you've got what you wanted,' Rob said. 'I'm out of your hair for good now.'

He *had* been tipped off. By who? Morgan gritted his teeth and stared down at his shoes.

The police force was like a leaky pipe – information managed to dribble out no matter how many times you tried to patch it up.

'Where are you?' Morgan repeated.

'You don't need to know that. Just know that I'm leaving. No hard feelings, eh?' Rob chuckled.

He was so confident he was going to get away with it. It made Morgan's blood boil. Rob wasn't calling to apologise for almost ruining Morgan's career; he was calling to boast they couldn't catch him. Once again, he wanted to prove he had the upper hand.

'I never said the wrong address that night,' Morgan said. 'You let me believe I'd messed up for so long.'

Rob laughed again. 'Don't tell me you're expecting an apology? Honestly, Scotty, it's far too easy to play you.'

'Not any more. We're on to you. You're not getting away with this.'

'We'll see,' Rob said, sounding smug.

Always wanting to be the one to get the last word in, he hung up, but before the call disconnected Morgan heard a tannoy announcement. Last call for a flight leaving for Edinburgh.

DI Rob Miller was about to discover things didn't always go his way.

Morgan put his phone back in his pocket. Step two of his plan was already in play.

CHAPTER FORTY

DI Rob Miller hung up, grinning. Winding Morgan up always put him in a good mood. He was so serious, so boring, so annoyingly righteous. After this, maybe he'd finally learn to lighten up a bit and be less of a goody two shoes.

Morgan had irritated him since the day they met. He was clever – book-clever, not street-smart like Rob. The first time Morgan had corrected him during a training session, Rob had wanted to rip him apart for embarrassing him in front of the rest of the team.

Who did that sort of thing to their *boss*? DI Scott Morgan had needed to be taught a lesson. And Rob had happily stepped up to be the one to do so.

But when Rob tried to put him in his place, Morgan had argued his point, oblivious to Rob's growing anger. The fool had no idea he was creating an enemy for life.

Morgan thought he was better than Rob, more intelligent, more successful.

But who was top of the pile now? Morgan was stuck in that miserable job until the day he retired, not him. Rob was off to live a life of luxury and enjoy his spoils. He gave a satisfied smile. Who was the winner now?

Things hadn't quite worked out the way he'd anticipated. But he was adaptable. You needed to think on your feet in this game. It had always been his plan to leave the force as soon as possible, but he'd wanted to wait until he was eligible for a nice payout on retirement.

Not that he had to worry about money for the foreseeable future. He had a fancy new pad in Cambodia, all set up and ready to go.

A couple of flights and everything would be sorted. The chances of extradition from Cambodia to the UK were pretty low, so he wouldn't have to worry about that.

He wouldn't be able to return to the UK to see family or friends, not that that was much of a hardship. He couldn't wait to get away from the grey gloomy weather, and his family had never really understood him anyway. So he'd miss a few Christmas get-togethers – it would be worth the sacrifice. With the money he'd stashed away over the years, he was going to live like a prince.

He'd had the house in Cambodia specially designed by an American expat who'd set up a business out there. It was built in the modern style, with huge windows looking out on to lush green vegetation and landscaped grounds. He'd employed a full-time housekeeper as well as a gardener, and had a top-of-the-range Jeep sitting in his new garage.

He hadn't had time to take extra insurances and would be leaving the country on his own passport, but his flight was only five minutes away. He doubted the Lincolnshire police force would get their act together in time to stop him. In fact, he was confident they wouldn't. Soon he'd be sunning himself on his rooftop garden.

There hadn't been time to pack. Not that he was too bothered. Clothes were cheap out there, and he could buy everything he needed. He grinned. Yes, life would be good. The sooner he left England, the better.

'Are you all right?'

Rob blinked. Olivia Webster was nursing a gin and tonic and looking at him intently.

Rob lifted his pint. 'Never better.'

Olivia was already starting to annoy him. Her constant prattling on the drive to the airport had eroded his patience. She was panicking because they'd had to make a *minor* change to their schedule. He'd tried to tune her out, but it wasn't easy.

She started up again with her whining. *What about this? What about that?*

Would she ever shut up? He wondered how long he had to put up with her before they could go their separate ways.

'This is all your fault,' she moaned. 'If you hadn't riled them up, we wouldn't be in this mess.'

'We're not in a mess,' Rob said. 'We're going to be fine. And I don't remember you being particularly nice to them. Correct me if I'm wrong, but I didn't notice you making an effort to get in their good books.'

Olivia huffed and muttered something under her breath.

'Don't look now.' Rob widened his eyes for emphasis. 'I think they're on to us.'

Alarmed, Olivia whirled around in her seat, and Rob laughed heartily at his own joke as two pensioners – one wearing a large straw hat, the other with a walking stick – took the table beside theirs.

She jabbed a finger at Rob. 'Not funny!'

He enjoyed watching her panic. If Olivia wasn't going to settle down, he may as well have some fun with her.

'They'll probably wait until we're at the boarding gate to nab us.'

She tensed, her gin and tonic halfway to her mouth.

'I'm having you on. Relax. Everything is going to be fine.'

Her usually attractive face scrunched up in a scowl.

'It's all working out as planned. They'll never get their act together in time to catch us. Not while Scotty is blundering around in charge of the operation.' He took another sip of his pint and started to tell her about his new pad in Cambodia.

◆ ◆ ◆

He went on and on about his plans. Did he realise how boring he was?

It's not all about you, she thought. *The world doesn't revolve around Rob Miller.*

Rob was just a means to an end, a way out. As soon as she was back on firm ground, she wouldn't need him any more. She planned to dump him and find work. She had Harry Cook's number as well as some of her other contacts. Once the heat was off, she was sure one of them would give her a role overseas. She'd proven herself invaluable, hadn't she?

Besides, this was probably the best ending. She was ambitious. Power and money went hand in hand, and she wanted more than the police service could ever give her. It was time to move on to the next stage in her career.

She sipped her gin and tonic and tried to relax. She envied Rob his ability to ignore the pressure and let stress wash over him.

She ran a hand over the leather handle of her new Louis Vuitton bag. It had been a gift she'd bought herself, a marker of how far she'd come. A smile curved her lips as she reached inside and pulled out her silver compact.

Opening it, she checked her appearance in the small mirror, patting her hair. Then she froze. In the reflection, she saw two burly men making their way over.

'Rob,' she hissed. 'We've got company.'

◆ ◆ ◆

'You're not going to catch me out like that,' Rob said, rolling his eyes, but he felt a tingle run along his neck.

Olivia's eyes had bugged out of her head. Her mouth was slack with panic.

Why hadn't he paired up with a professional? She was useless. Still, at least he'd have no qualms laying all the blame at her door if it came to it.

Cautiously, he looked up.

Two airport policemen clothed in dark blue uniforms, complete with stab vests, and holding intimidating weapons, approached.

Panic buzzed in his brain, nausea making his gut churn.

He made himself stay calm. It had to be a false alarm. There's no way they could have acted this quickly. No way . . .

'Robert Miller? Olivia Webster?'

Rob licked his dry lips and cleared his throat. 'Yes, that's right. Is there a problem?'

Olivia said nothing. She just stared at them as though in shock.

'You're going to have to come with us, please.'

'I think there must be some mistake.'

'I don't think so, sir. On your feet.'

'Sorry, but we have a flight to catch.'

'Not any more you don't.'

Olivia chose that moment to react. 'You can't do this! We're getting on that plane. We have to leave!'

She threw her glass on the floor, where it shattered by the first officer's feet. A second later, both she and Rob were forced on to the floor and handcuffed.

Rob's Cambodian dream evaporated as he was led away from the bar. People around them stared and spoke in shocked whispers as his plans gurgled down the drain.

How had this happened? He'd only just spoken to Morgan. There was no way he'd been able to get a warrant and authorisation to stop them at the airport in time. So how had he managed it?

There was only one possible answer. Morgan had been on to him for a while.

He'd never suspected Scotty would have the guts to stand up to him. Rob had been sure Morgan wouldn't act until he had concrete evidence. He'd assumed that as long as there was an element of doubt, Morgan wouldn't go out on a limb and risk his career to bring Rob down.

He'd gambled on that fact. But it looked like he'd bet on the wrong horse.

CHAPTER FORTY-ONE

Karen's head was aching.

She rubbed her temples and wondered whether the headache was down to stress or the bang on the head she'd got courtesy of Charlie Cook.

Someone – she wasn't sure who – had made a pot of coffee. Karen poured some into a mug and sat down at the kitchen table to drink it. Officers and SOCOs were still milling about outside, but they'd finished what they needed to do inside.

Christine had knocked on the door in a panic after seeing the flashing blue lights and hearing the sirens. Karen reassured her she was fine, but that wasn't really true. Physically, she'd recover, but mentally she was shaken.

She sipped the coffee, barely tasting it. Now she had some answers. She knew what had happened the day of the accident, but still her mind couldn't settle. Pieces of the puzzle floated around in her brain. Abstract elements. The answer just out of reach.

She lifted her mug again, and suddenly things clicked into place.

She knew.

Farzana tapped on the kitchen door. 'I'm about to head home. I just wanted to check you're all right.'

Karen set the coffee down and walked over to her. 'I know why you came to see me tonight.'

Farzana blinked. 'You do?'

'You wanted to talk.'

'Well, yes, but I think it can wait until tomorrow.'

'Earlier you said it couldn't.'

'I know, but that was before . . .' She trailed off, shaking her head. 'It's nothing.'

She bit her lip and looked down at the floor, unable to meet Karen's gaze. The young officer was upset, but the truth had to be told.

She understood why DC Shah had been acting so strangely. It made sense now.

'You suspect DI Freeman is corrupt, don't you?'

Farzana's eyes grew wide. She looked around, making sure there was nobody else listening in.

'I . . . I had some suspicions. I wanted to confide in you because I didn't know what to do. He's my boss, and he's always been good to me.' She looked down at her hands. 'Maybe I'm wrong.'

But it all fitted together. Freeman claiming he'd chatted to Olivia about books, despite her dislike of reading. His concern for Karen's well-being. His irritation at not being told about the second surveillance operation at the nail bar.

Karen pressed her fingers against her forehead, trying to push away the pain so she could think clearly. 'You need to tell the superintendent.'

'I'm not sure.'

'You don't have a choice.'

Farzana's large eyes were full of worry. She raked a hand through her damp hair.

'It's going to be awful.'

'Do you want me to talk to the superintendent with you?'

Farzana covered her face with her hands, muffling a groan. 'You've been through enough. You don't have to hold my hand. I shouldn't have come to you first. You don't need this on top of everything else.'

'I'm glad you came to me.'

She bit her lip. 'They don't teach you how to handle stuff like this in training.'

'He can't get away with it.'

'You're right. I'll do it first thing tomorrow.'

Karen shook her head slowly and put a hand on Farzana's arm. 'No, you need to do it tonight.'

◆ ◆ ◆

It was after midnight when DC Farzana Shah sat down with Superintendent Murray. She'd been hoping for an informal chat, but even at this early stage the superintendent was doing everything by the book. They were in the superintendent's large office on the top floor, but everything was being recorded.

Tomorrow Farzana would have to go through it all again in the presence of an officer from the Lincolnshire Anti-Corruption Unit, in a small, claustrophobic interview room with no windows. She clasped her hands in her lap. Tomorrow would be worse.

The superintendent put two bottles of water on the desk as Farzana eyed the tape recorder suspiciously. She didn't much like being on the other side of an interview. Her hands were sweaty and her mouth had gone dry. It wasn't supposed to be like this when you were the innocent party. She hadn't done anything wrong, so why did she feel so bad? So scared?

The police didn't have the best reputation for dealing with whistle-blowers, and she couldn't help worrying she was putting her career on the line over this.

But some things were more important. Integrity, honesty, loyalty. They were all things she believed in. Telling the superintendent what she knew was the right thing to do.

The words had stuck in her throat when she'd tried to explain what she'd overheard to Karen. It didn't make sense. How could her boss be involved in this corruption? Her boss, who was always so kind and considerate. Who'd never delivered so much as a harsh word to Farzana, even on those occasions when she'd messed up. Instead, he'd wink and say, 'We'll keep that between us, DC Shah. Just don't do it again, eh?'

She rubbed the back of her neck. At first she'd refused to believe it. After all, whispered phone calls and suddenly shutting down his computer when she walked into his office didn't necessarily mean anything, did it? They were all things that could have a logical explanation. It didn't mean her boss was bent.

It was easy to tell herself she was imagining things, that she was jumping to conclusions, because she *liked* him. He'd always made time for her and encouraged her questions, no matter how trivial they might seem. And he was always ready with a supportive word if she was finding the job difficult.

But 'difficult' didn't come close to describing what she was struggling with today. It had been the most nerve-wracking day of her career.

She'd tried to convince herself she was wrong, that there could be an explanation, but she knew there wasn't. There was too much evidence against him, things that couldn't be explained away.

She'd really been prepared to give him the benefit of the doubt on every occasion, until she'd overheard his conversation with Olivia Webster.

She'd been watching him closely over the past few weeks, more so since Rob and Olivia turned up. Her mother had always said those who eavesdrop never hear good things, but when she'd heard their voices, Farzana hadn't been able to walk away. She'd edged closer, listening intently to the conversation.

Olivia had wanted to know about DI Freeman's friends in traffic and how much they'd been paid to keep quiet about the accident. He had reacted angrily, asking how she'd found out.

Farzana hadn't known what accident they were talking about at first, but things soon made sense when DS Hart's name was mentioned.

It had taken time for Farzana to build up enough courage to approach Karen. She'd been filled with doubts and worries, wondering how on earth her smiling, considerate boss could have covered up for someone whose careless actions on the road had killed Karen's husband and daughter.

She should have approached Karen at the station. That would have been proper protocol, but she was terrified. DI Freeman was covering up the accident for the Cooks, and they'd already shown they weren't afraid of killing people who got in their way. Farzana didn't want to be another statistic. But she couldn't stay quiet either.

The superintendent cleared her throat as she shuffled the papers in front of her. 'DC Shah, let's make a start, shall we?'

Farzana gave a nervous nod.

The superintendent pressed record on the machine, and after stating the date and time, introduced them both for the purpose of the tape.

'Could you begin by describing the conversation you overheard, please, DC Shah?'

Farzana grabbed one of the bottles and swallowed a mouthful of cold water. 'Yes.' Her voice trembled, but she couldn't stop it. 'I overheard a conversation between DC Olivia Webster and DI Frank Freeman in the main stairwell at Nettleham station. They spoke about an accident. I later realised they were talking about the accident that resulted in the death of DS Hart's family, ma'am.'

'How far away were you when you heard their conversation?'

'I was in the corridor, ma'am, so not far.'

'There was a door between you and them?'

Farzana swallowed, her mouth dry again. 'Yes, but it was open.'

The superintendent frowned. 'It's a fire door. They're designed to close.'

'Um.' Farzana twisted her fingers in her lap. 'That's true, but I'd propped it open a little.'

'So you could listen to them, watch them?'

Farzana felt a rush of blood warm her cheeks. The superintendent made her sound like a voyeur. 'Well, yes, but I was watching them because I thought DI Freeman was hiding something.'

'What?'

'I wasn't sure, but DS Hart said she believed someone on the inside could be leaking information to the Cooks.'

'So DS Hart influenced your opinion of your boss?'

'No, I didn't mean that.' Farzana rubbed her eyes. She was so tired.

The superintendent's expression was sombre. It was a heavy accusation to levy against any officer, but this was DI Freeman, someone who'd worked for the Lincolnshire force for over a decade.

They all knew him – or at least, they all *thought* they knew him.

'You're aware DI Freeman is an officer with an unblemished record and over ten years' service in the department?'

Farzana nodded miserably.

'I need you to be absolutely sure about what you heard, DC Shah.'

'I am, ma'am. I wish I wasn't, but I am.'

'You're willing to stand by your statement when questioned by the Anti-Corruption Unit and possibly, if it gets that far, testify in court?'

Farzana reached out a shaking hand for the bottle of water again and gulped it down. 'Yes, ma'am.'

The superintendent continued the questioning, coming at the events Farzana had witnessed from different angles, interrupting, causing her to stumble over her story. She'd given evidence in court before, but this was different. This was *Frank*. The way the super intendent was talking it was as though she believed Farzana was making it up.

It wasn't true, of course. Superintendent Murray was testing her story, looking for holes, for gaps in consistency. It didn't mean she didn't trust her.

Trust. What was it worth anyway?

She'd trusted DI Freeman and look how that had turned out.

Farzana finished the last of her water and tried to focus. She stumbled over her words, used far too many errs and ums for an officer with her experience, but she didn't change her story. She stuck to the facts as she knew them. No speculation, no embellishment.

She simply told the whole truth, as Karen had instructed.

It felt like hours had passed when Murray pressed pause on the machine and walked over to the window. It was still raining. The Nettleham countryside and open fields were dark.

'I know that was hard for you. It was for me too.' The superintendent didn't turn away from the window.

Farzana understood. She wasn't giving her a hard time because she didn't believe her account. She was angry, embarrassed that this had gone on under her nose and she'd had no idea.

She pressed a hand to the glass. 'All those years' service, working side by side with us, and I never suspected a thing.'

'He hid it well, ma'am. I worked with him every day and I . . . well, I still don't *want* to believe it.'

Murray nodded slowly, finally turning around to face Farzana. 'And Karen? She knows about this?'

Farzana grimaced. 'Yes, I went to her first. I thought she should know.' She waited for the reprimand. But the superintendent was preoccupied.

'This is a devastating blow to all of us who worked with him, but Karen will feel this betrayal most of all.'

'Yes, ma'am. I can't imagine what she's going through right now. She'll need our support.'

The superintendent sat down again and leaned forward, forearms resting on the desk. 'She'll need more than that, DC Shah. She'll need justice. And it's our job to make sure she gets it.'

CHAPTER FORTY-TWO

At nine a.m. on Thursday, Karen sat in Superintendent Murray's office, leg stretched out awkwardly in front of her. Her knee felt like it had swollen to at least twice its usual size.

'Thanks for coming in, Karen. How are you feeling?'

Karen frowned. *Thanks for coming in?* Where else would she be? This was her job.

'Not great, but no permanent damage.'

'DI Morgan will be interviewing Charlie Cook today.'

Karen gave a curt nod.

'I think it's best if you sit that one out.'

For once, Karen didn't protest. She wasn't sure she could trust herself alone in a room with Charlie Cook. It scared her how close she'd come to committing a crime herself.

'I agree.'

The superintendent's eyebrows lifted.

'DI Morgan will do a good job.'

'He will. Now, I have to recommend counselling, Karen. After everything—'

Karen held up her hand. 'I agree with that, too. I've made an appointment with my old counsellor, Amethyst. I'm seeing her tonight.'

'Ah, that's good.' The superintendent took a deep breath. 'How did you get here this morning, anyway?' She looked pointedly at Karen's knee.

'Rick picked me up.'

'Is he dropping you off home later, too?'

Karen nodded impatiently. The super was avoiding the elephant in the room, wasting time on small talk, when all Karen wanted to know was what was going on with DI Freeman. He wasn't getting away with this betrayal. Not on her watch.

'With respect, ma'am, I thought you called me up here to discuss DI Freeman.'

'Yes, I wanted to give you an update. ACU will be investigating the allegations against DI Freeman. You'll be kept abreast of progress.'

'Have ACU questioned him yet?'

'They started at eight this morning.'

Karen shifted in her seat. 'He's here? At the station?'

'Yes,' Superintendent Murray said coolly. 'I'm sure I don't need to remind you to keep away from him.'

Karen tried to look innocent. Would it really be her fault if she just happened to run into him here at the station? Though it was hardly likely she'd run into anybody or anything for the foreseeable future, thanks to Charlie Cook. She winced as she shifted her leg.

'Has he lawyered up?' Karen asked.

The superintendent inclined her head. 'Yes, he has legal representation. In fact, his representative has already reached out to us.'

Karen narrowed her eyes. 'Why?'

'She says DI Freeman is prepared to take a reprimand and early retirement in return for us dropping the investigation.'

Anger burned through Karen. 'That's not enough!'

The superintendent raised her hands. 'I know. The request was refused. He won't get away with this. Trust me.'

Karen took a deep breath. She was running low on trust right now. 'Sorry, I shouldn't have snapped. It just kills me to think he'll get away with a slap on the wrist.'

'He won't. I'll do everything in my power to make sure ACU throw the book at him.'

◆ ◆ ◆

Charlie Cook smirked at Morgan as they sat opposite each other in interview room two. They'd been talking for an hour. Morgan was trying very hard to be detached and come at this interview the same way he would for any informant. It wasn't easy though. He kept picturing Karen's pale face and the dark smudges beneath her eyes as she'd limped across the kitchen last night.

Looking at it from an unemotional point of view, the interview was going well. Charlie was talking freely and had already confirmed Rob Miller and Olivia Webster were on the payroll as well as identifying locations around the country the Cooks used for people trafficking and exploitation.

He was helping their enquiry, playing his role as informant perfectly, but when Morgan looked at him all he could see was a man who'd roughed up Karen, bludgeoned a man to death and set fire to The Red Lion. Of course, he changed his story under formal questioning. He now denied killing Aleksy Iskow and starting the fire, probably after advice from his legal team.

As Morgan circled back to one of his original questions, trying to pressure Charlie into making a mistake in his story or contradict himself, Charlie frowned.

'We've already gone over this. Why are you wasting time?'

'I need to make sure I have all the details. Did your uncle ask you to kill Aleksy Iskow?'

'No. Like I said, I was looking for Aleksy, but I didn't find him.'

'Did your uncle ask you to set fire to The Red Lion?'

'No, that wasn't me.'

'You told a different story last night.'

'I was under a great deal of stress. I was confused.' He smiled at his solicitor, who nodded in approval at his answer.

Morgan was glad he didn't have to deal with Andrew Norris again, but this new legal representative was pretty sharp. She was about Morgan's age, with dark hair, bright blue eyes and a ruddy face. Her lips were constantly pursed as though in disapproval.

'So we won't find any incriminating evidence in your vehicle?' Morgan asked.

Charlie tensed. 'My vehicle?'

'We have a team of scene-of-crime officers looking at it now.'

Charlie put his hands flat on the table and pushed himself up, his head whipping towards the solicitor. 'They can't do that!' He turned to Morgan. 'That wasn't part of the deal. I'm immune from prosecution. I signed the paperwork.'

'You did, but the immunity doesn't extend to murder.' Morgan narrowed his eyes. 'I'm sure your solicitor advising you of that fact was the reason you changed your story.'

A flare of colour appeared in the centre of Charlie's cheeks. 'I don't give you permission to look at my Range Rover. You need a court order.'

'Don't worry. We have that covered. A warrant has been issued.'

Beads of sweat dotted Charlie's forehead.

There was a knock at the door.

'Excuse me,' Morgan said, pausing the interview.

Outside the interview room, he walked along the corridor with Rick so Charlie and his solicitor wouldn't overhear them.

'Tell me it's good news.'

Rick grinned. 'Excellent news for us, not so good for Charlie.'

'Go on.'

'SOCOs found a metal pipe from an exhaust in the back of the car. It was covered with dried blood. Initial tests confirm it matches Aleksy's blood type, but we'll need to wait for the DNA match. They also found traces of accelerant in the vehicle. No containers, but I'm thinking a small amount must have spilled—'

'When he transported the accelerant to set fire to The Red Lion?'

'Exactly, sir. It will take a couple of days to confirm the accelerant matches that used in the arson attack on the pub, but I'd be willing to bet it does.'

'That's fantastic news. We'll have him for the murders of Aleksy Iskow and the Perrys and their son.'

'Can I pass on the good news to Karen, boss? It's just she's been really down about the fact Charlie could get away with everything he's done.'

'Absolutely. Keep her updated.'

Rick started to move away and then suddenly stopped and turned back. 'If Charlie gets witness protection, how will he serve time?'

'We still need to iron out the details, but I suspect he could be charged and sent to prison under a different name.'

'Good. I'm glad he won't escape unpunished. I can't believe he didn't even try to get rid of the evidence.'

'Maybe he intended to.' Morgan rolled his shoulders, feeling some of his earlier tension ease. 'Or he assumed his immunity would be against all charges, so he didn't believe the evidence mattered.'

'I'd like to be a fly on the wall when he learns we're opening a fresh investigation into the deaths of Karen's family.'

Morgan smiled. 'I have to admit I'm looking forward to telling him that.'

Rick handed Morgan the initial report on the findings from Charlie Cook's Range Rover.

Back in the interview room, Morgan selected the image of the blood-coated metal pipe and slid it across the table to Charlie. 'Do you recognise it? The pipe was discovered in the back of your Range Rover.'

Satisfied they had this case in the bag, Morgan sat back in his chair as Charlie covered his face with his hands and let out a low groan.

The following Monday evening, Rick and Sophie were sitting side by side at Rick's computer, sipping coffee. The paperwork on this investigation had been a real pain, and it was likely to continue for a long time. They wouldn't be able to put the case to bed until they had iron-clad evidence against all the Cooks.

'Do you think Karen is going to be all right?' Sophie asked Rick in a low voice.

There were still a few people milling about the open-plan office, but Karen had left work just after five to visit her old boss.

He nodded. 'She's tough.'

But Sophie saw the conflict in his eyes. He was worried about her, too.

It had been a tough case. Really gut-wrenching for everyone involved, but especially Karen.

Earlier, Sophie had helped Lucja by liaising with officials and dealing with paperwork so she could take her father's body back to Poland today.

'It's been a horrible case,' Sophie said, putting her coffee mug down beside the keyboard.

'Yeah, it makes it worse when it's one of your own.'

Sophie sighed. 'I never warmed to Rob Miller or Olivia Webster, but DI Freeman . . . He always seemed so *nice*.'

'It came as a shock to me too. I thought he was one of the good guys.'

Sophie went to her own desk and grabbed a packet of ready salted crisps she'd stashed in her bottom drawer. She pulled open the packet and walked back to Rick. They had enough evidence on Rob Miller and Olivia Webster to put them away for a long time. Unidentified payments had been registered to both of their accounts, originating from shell companies. Their assets had been seized, including Rob's palatial, modern villa in Cambodia.

Thames Valley had arranged for a new unit to work on the Cook investigation from their end. Rob Miller and Olivia Webster had been a huge disappointment and embarrassment.

'At least Charlie is singing like a canary,' Rick said as Sophie sank back into the chair beside him and offered him the bag. 'Eric and Harry Cook will be formally charged tomorrow.'

'He'd say anything to save his own skin.' Sophie crunched a crisp.

Rick shrugged. 'It won't work. His deal doesn't include protection from prosecution when murder is involved.'

Charlie had cut a deal which meant he wouldn't be prosecuted for his involvement in the people trafficking and modern slavery ring, in exchange for the information he could give them on his father and uncle.

Sophie strongly felt he should also be doing extra time for causing the accident that killed Karen's family. But so far no charges had been pressed against him for that. The investigation was complicated, not least because it involved police corruption.

She didn't know how Karen was dealing with it. She seemed to be going through the motions at work but looked tired and distracted. Understandable after she'd learned the truth about the accident. Not only had Charlie Cook killed her family, but one of her closest colleagues, DI Freeman, had covered the whole thing up.

DI Freeman wasn't talking. But two of the officers in traffic he'd paid off had confessed. The investigation into Freeman's actions was likely to take some time, but whatever happened, he would never work as a police officer again.

'Did you file the 19 sheet?' Rick asked, pointing at the screen.

'Yes, that's done.' She ticked it off the list.

'I meant to ask, did you book that holiday with your mum you mentioned earlier?' Sophie asked as Rick searched for the next form on his computer.

He smiled. 'Yes. I've booked Friday and Monday off work. Mum's really looking forward to it.'

'Is Priya going with you?'

Rick nodded happily. 'Yes, she said she'd love to go. I thought it would be a nice break for all of us.'

'The weather is supposed to be nice this weekend too.' Sophie scrunched the empty crisp packet into a ball and threw it in the bin.

'That's it, we're up to date on the paperwork,' Rick said, smothering a yawn.

'Finally.' Sophie picked up her mug and walked over to her own workspace, glancing across to Morgan's office.

His head was bowed over his desk. He'd been putting in long hours, determined to do everything he could to make sure the charges stuck. They all had.

Sophie hoped it was enough.

CHAPTER FORTY-THREE

DC Farzana Shah walked hesitantly into the open-plan office. Head bowed, she tucked her glossy black hair behind one ear and shuffled over to her desk. Her discomfort was clear to see. Everyone at Nettleham had been talking about the claims of corruption against DI Freeman, and the entire staff were aware Farzana was the one who'd come forward with the allegation.

A hush fell over the office, heads turning to gawp. It was a human reaction, and Sophie knew her fellow officers weren't trying to be unkind. They were just shocked and interested in the situation.

Sophie set her mug down beside her keyboard and headed over to speak to Farzana. 'Have the interviews finished?'

Farzana had been questioned by the ACU, who were investigating the corruption claims. At first it had been the younger officer's word against her boss. He was adamant he was being falsely accused. But slowly the case against him had started to build, and his web of lies began to unravel. Witnesses came forward. Financial records were unearthed, and Freeman's story started to change. He wanted to cut a deal.

Then the two officers from traffic had added their evidence and admitted to accepting payments from DI Freeman after he pressured them into hiding witness reports and falsifying evidence, making it look as though no other vehicle was involved in the road collision that had ended in the deaths of Karen's husband and daughter.

'Yes,' Farzana said, looking at the floor. 'I mean, it's not *all* over. There's still a long way to go, and if it goes to court I'll have to testify. But the ACU interviews are out of the way for now.'

'So you're back at work, under DI Morgan?'

Farzana glanced up, her brown eyes focused on Sophie. 'Yes. Bit nervous, to be honest.' She leaned closer. 'I know everyone is talking about me.'

'Only because we've all had a shock.'

Farzana gave a half-hearted smile.

'It must have been hard to come forward.'

'It wasn't easy. But I wanted to do the right thing.' Farzana unlocked her desk drawer and grabbed her phone and keys.

'Are you leaving now?'

DC Shah nodded. 'Yeah, it's been a long day.'

'I was planning to leave soon, too. Thought I might go for a drink if you fancy it?'

Farzana's face lit up. 'Sounds good.'

Later that week, Karen drove slowly through Canwick village. The past few days had been a blur of fury mixed with sadness. She'd kept going, one foot in front of the other, feeling like she was treading water.

She had answers now. Answers she'd wanted for so long, but the truth was bitter. She'd expected resolution to make her feel better, to help her move on, but it hadn't. She was drained, and so tired. It didn't help that she wasn't sleeping through the night.

After stopping outside the large bungalow, Karen leaned back in the driver's seat and rubbed her eyes. Perhaps once the Cooks had been sentenced and DI Freeman punished, she'd start to feel better.

Her old boss opened the front door before she'd even got out of the car. Karen smiled. He was eager for an update, and he deserved to hear it from her.

She waved as she walked to the house, trying to smile and look less shattered than she felt so that Anthony didn't worry about her. It didn't work. Concern filled his eyes as he took her hands.

'Oh, Karen, I am so, so sorry.'

Her cut lip had healed, her bruises had faded to yellow and were covered with foundation, and she wasn't limping any more, but he already knew what had happened. She could tell. He must have spoken to the super.

'It's not been the best week, but we'll make sure they'll be held accountable.'

'Of course.' He ushered her inside, and Karen took a seat on the sofa opposite Anthony's easy chair.

'I take it Superintendent Murray filled you in on what's been going on?'

'Ah, yes. Don't be annoyed. It wasn't gossip. She was worried about you, thought I might be able to help.'

'I'm not angry. She's been great. The whole team have. Everyone has been so supportive . . .' Karen's voice cracked.

Anthony moved to her side and squeezed her shoulder. 'Can I get you a drink?'

'No, I'm fine. I won't stay long. I'm not the best company at the moment, but I thought you'd want to hear the latest.'

'DI Freeman?'

Karen gave a grim nod. 'Yes, he's trying to arrange a deal for a lighter charge.'

'So he's really guilty?'

'Without a doubt.'

'I'm stunned. I thought I was a good judge of character, but I never suspected for one moment . . .'

'Neither did I. It seems he pulled the wool over lots of people's eyes.'

Anthony walked away from Karen and sank back into his chair and gazed at the unlit fireplace. 'How are you coping?'

'All right.' She forced a smile. 'I did get some good news. One of the men we found in the Perrys' garage had his case taken on by a legal aid charity.'

When she'd spoken to him earlier, Vishal had sounded confident he'd eventually be able to get out of the Immigration Removal Centre in Swinderby and be permitted to stay in the UK. It was far from a simple matter, though, and the process would take time.

'How did they find out about his case?'

'I made a few calls, figured he could do with a break after all he's been through.'

'What did you make of Alice Price?'

Karen gave him a sharp look. 'I know why you sent me there.'

'You do?'

'Because she's a very troubled woman. You were warning me I could turn out like her.'

'Not exactly.' Anthony leaned forward. 'She *is* troubled. But I believed her. It was easy for the brass to write her off as a hysterical woman, but I always felt there was some truth to her allegations.'

'I've found no links between Alice Price and any of the officers accused of gross misconduct.'

'Yet,' Anthony muttered, raising an eyebrow.

Karen thought for a moment. 'Alice said the man she thought was behind the corruption had died.'

'Yes, that's true.' He waved a hand. 'Anyway, you have enough to contend with at the moment. Now, tell me about the charges against Charlie Cook.'

◆ ◆ ◆

After Karen left Anthony, her mind kept flitting back to Alice Price. Perhaps the corruption was even bigger than they thought. But Alice wasn't exactly a reliable witness. Bringing her evidence into the investigation could risk the entire case tumbling down. She couldn't chance it now, but maybe one day she could follow up on Alice's story.

She remembered Alice's intense gaze, her certainty. Maybe now wasn't the time to unravel her past. But what if the corruption went deeper than Frank Freeman, Rob Miller and Olivia Webster? Could she really ignore that possibility?

Abruptly, Karen turned her car around and took the Heighington Road to Washingborough.

No one answered when Karen knocked on the Prices' front door. Feeling a mixture of relief and frustration, she turned to walk back to her car. She'd only taken a few steps when she heard footsteps, along with scraping and banging.

Alice Price appeared at the corner of the house. She was pulling a brown garden wheelie bin behind her and clutching sharp secateurs in her right hand.

'Alice?'

She looked up, her face blank, hand dropping from the bin. Then, as she recognised Karen, her features took on a guarded wariness. Her gaze flickered to the houses across the street. 'What are you doing here?'

Not the warmest welcome. 'Just wanted a chat – to give you an update, really.'

Alice kept the small garden shears gripped in front of her, almost like a weapon. 'I don't think that's a good idea. My husband . . . Well, he doesn't think it's a good idea.' Before Karen could say anything, Alice pointed at her with the secateurs. 'I'm not one of those women that does everything her husband says, but he's been through a lot. *I* put him through a lot.'

'I don't want to cause any problems between you and Declan. We don't have to talk about the corruption that led to you leaving the force if you don't want to. But I thought you might want to know, three corrupt officers have been arrested and charged.'

Alice brightened. 'Really?' She darted towards Karen and then seemed to realise how she was brandishing the sharp garden tool in front of her. She let her arm fall to her side. 'That's good news. Really good. I guess you succeeded where I failed.'

'I had help, Alice. That's the difference.'

'I did too. Or so I thought at the time. DCI Shaw backed me up, even took it to the chief constable, but it wasn't enough.'

'DCI Shaw?' Karen wondered why her old boss hadn't told her the full extent of his involvement. If Anthony had spoken on Alice's behalf to the chief constable, why hadn't he mentioned it? She'd had no idea DCI Shaw had been so involved. She thought back, picturing the way his bushy eyebrows had come together as he'd frowned in concern when she'd updated him on the investigation.

'Yes, he was one of the few who believed me. Or he said he did. Sometimes I wondered.' Alice glanced at the house opposite and then gestured for Karen to follow her around the side of the house.

Alice led her into the back garden, which was more private, sheltered from prying eyes. She stopped by a rose bush that had been recently deadheaded. Alice spotted a lone rose hip and snipped it from the bush. 'Corruption needs to be cut out of the force. Maybe you're the one to do it.' She smiled at Karen, but the smile held no warmth.

Karen shivered, even though the sun was still warm. 'We've got three of them so far, and can prove they were on the payroll of a local criminal.'

'What are the names of the officers?'

Karen considered telling Alice she couldn't divulge that information and then thought better of it. It didn't matter. If Alice wanted to, she could find out by other means. 'DC Olivia Webster, DI Rob Miller and DI Frank Freeman.'

Alice paled and shook her head. 'Frank Freeman. I never suspected him.'

'No, it surprised me too.'

'You're sure?'

'Positive.'

Alice looked away, nodding, processing the information. Then she whipped her head back around to face Karen. 'I don't recognise the first two names.'

'No, they're Thames Valley, not Lincolnshire.'

Alice's mouth twisted. 'So only one from Lincolnshire. There must be others, you see that, don't you?'

Her eyes burned fiercely, and it was all Karen could do not to take a step back. Were there others? It was possible. Could Alice help her uncover further corruption? Again, it was possible, but the feverish glow of Alice's cheeks, her startling behaviour and her obvious obsession reinforced Karen's concerns that she wasn't a good witness, and that if Karen brought her in to talk to ACU she'd risk the whole case falling apart, which she wasn't prepared to let happen, not until Frank Freeman was serving time and enduring his punishment.

But after that?

Yes, after Freeman was prosecuted, then maybe she could talk to Alice formally and find out what she knew. If there was corruption, Alice was right. It needed to be cut out before it spread.

They both heard a car door slam.

Alice sucked in an anxious breath. 'Declan. He can't find you here. He'll think I'm planning something. Quick, go around the side!'

She turned away, rushing to the sliding glass doors at the back of the house as Karen swiftly moved out of sight. She wasn't doing anything wrong, but she really didn't want to cause trouble between Alice and her husband.

She got into her car, glancing in the rear-view mirror. Would Declan have recognised it? Perhaps. Alice would have to explain her way out of that one. Despite her frailty and obvious psychological wounds, Karen suspected Alice would have no problem coming up with an explanation. Behind her obsession was a sharp mind. After all, she'd detected the corruption others had failed to see, hadn't she?

As Karen turned out of Barn Owl Way, she realised she believed Alice. Reliable witness or not, there was something compelling about the woman's past. Yes, she was damaged, raw, but she was honest.

Karen took a deep breath. Hands gripping the steering wheel, she thought about Frank Freeman's deception. Making sure he got a just punishment was her first priority.

Alice and her secrets would have to wait.

Karen headed along the Washingborough Road, a route she had generally avoided since the accident. As she drove past the cemetery, the traffic slowed to a crawl. Then, as she reached the junction with the B1188, the traffic lights turned red.

She stopped at the lights and swallowed hard. For five years she'd been driving past the section of road where the accident that claimed Josh and Tilly's lives had happened.

Usually she kept her eyes forward, not wanting to look directly at the scene, not wanting to remember, but today was different. She wouldn't look away any more.

Turning her head, she held her breath.

The photographs taken of the scene after the crash had shown twisted metal, shattered glass, black tyre marks and flattened shrubs where the car had left the road.

She exhaled slowly. Today there was nothing left to indicate what had occurred in that spot. The plant life had grown back, the road and pavement were cleared of marks.

It was simply a section of road. It held no power over her. Looking at it didn't cause panic to flutter in her chest or bile to rise in her throat. She felt nothing except sadness.

When the lights turned green, she accelerated away from the junction, feeling that although this was far from over, she was coping with her grief better than she had been.

She continued on to Grace Baker's house and was surprised to see a For Sale sign at the edge of the road.

Karen indicated and turned into the driveway.

Grace's Fiesta was parked in front of the garage. The car doors were open and the boot and backseat were filled with boxes.

Karen pulled on the handbrake and got out of her car just as Grace walked out of the front door holding another cardboard box. Her cat followed close behind.

'Grace, how are you?' Karen asked, leaning down to stroke Dolly.

'Not too bad considering,' she said, shoving the box into the last available space in the boot and dusting off her hands.

'You're moving?'

'Yes, I found a little bungalow in Louth, near my sister.' Grace turned to look at her home. 'I don't want to live here now.'

Karen winced. She understood the fear victims experienced after break-ins, the fact home didn't feel the same any more. It didn't feel safe.

'I'm so sorry.'

'Me too. Did you ever find out who did it?' She shivered, probably remembering returning home to find the pool of red paint on her floor and the threatening graffiti on her table.

'They were careful and left no forensic evidence, but I've a fair idea the person who did it won't be bothering you again.'

Grace folded her arms over her chest and narrowed her eyes. 'It was one of the Cooks, wasn't it?'

'I can't say for sure.'

Grace huffed under her breath. 'I can't believe they'll just get away with it.'

'They'll be punished.'

'Not for my break-in though, or for scaring me half to death!'

'No.' Karen nodded at the house. 'So you're selling up because of what happened?'

'I must admit that was the catalyst, but I need a new beginning. My husband and I loved this house. We were happy. I stayed here because I thought it would make me feel close to him. But it just made me sad.' She gave a soft smile. 'I don't suppose that makes much sense to you, does it?'

Karen smiled. It did make sense – more than Grace knew. She'd stayed in her family home for much the same reason. Because she wanted to stay close to her memories. But, unlike Grace, Karen wasn't ready to leave.

◆ ◆ ◆

Later that evening, Karen sat cross-legged on the floor of her living room, music playing in the background, papers scattered all around her. She paused to take a sip from a large glass of red, and scanned the contents of a file.

It had taken her a few days to regather the evidence relating to the accident. Remembering how kind and considerate Frank Freeman had been after the incident, explaining gently that traffic had found no evidence of foul play or any other vehicles involved in the collision, Karen clenched her teeth.

He'd been so convincing.

Karen gripped the paper in her hand so tightly it crumpled.

DI Freeman was now being held accountable, along with the officers from traffic he'd bribed, but what if it didn't end there? What if other officers were involved?

No matter how long it took, she was determined to root them all out. They'd matched up a few of the codenames in the notebook, thanks to Charlie Cook, but there were still four unidentified names. It didn't mean they were all from the Lincolnshire force, of course, but maybe some of them were – and if they were, Karen was determined to dig them out like weeds.

She felt the familiar tug of her old obsession – the uncertainty, the paranoia – but it was different this time.

Now, she wasn't working alone.

She looked up and handed Morgan one of the forensic reports.

He smiled as he took it from her. 'It might take a while, but we'll get answers.'

Karen returned his smile and raised her glass. 'Yes. This time, we will.'

ACKNOWLEDGMENTS

I am very grateful to all the people who have worked hard to produce the books in the DS Karen Hart series. Many thanks to Jack Butler and the team at APub. It's been a pleasure to work with you all.

A huge thanks to my family and friends, especially my mum who has always been the first person to read my books and give me invaluable feedback.

And a special thanks to all the amazing readers who have shown me so much support. The messages and emails I get from people who have enjoyed the stories mean the world to me – thank you all so very much!

ABOUT THE AUTHOR

 Born in Kent, D. S. Butler grew up as an avid reader with a love for crime fiction and mysteries. She has worked as a scientific officer in a hospital pathology laboratory and as a research scientist. After obtaining a PhD in biochemistry, she worked at the University of Oxford for four years before moving to the Middle East. While living in Bahrain, she wrote her first novel and hasn't stopped writing since. She now lives in Lincolnshire with her husband.

Made in the USA
Middletown, DE
22 August 2022